GIGOLOS
GET LONELY TOO

GIGOLOS
GET LONELY TOO

Dwayne S. Joseph

Roy Glenn

Jihad

www.urbanbooks.net

This is a work of fiction. Any references or similarities to actual events, real people, living, or dead, or to real locals are intended to give the novel a sense of reality. Any similarity in other names, characters, places, and incidents is entirely coincidental.

Urban Books
74 Andrews Avenue
Wheatley Heights, NY 11798

ISBN 1-893196-33-X

First Printing March 2006
Printed in the United States of America

10 9 8 7 6 5 4 3 2 1

Submit Wholesale Orders to:
Kensington Publishing Corp.
C/O Penguin Group (USA) Inc.
Attention: Order Processing
405 Murray Hill Parkway
East Rutherford, NJ 07073-2316
Phone: 1-800-526-0275
Fax: 1-800-227-9604

ONLY WHEN YOU'RE LONELY

Dwayne S. Joseph

Also by Dwayne S. Joseph

Never Say Never
The Womanizers

Anthology:
Around the Way Girls
Gigolos Get Lonely Too

Prologue

"You were exceptional as always, Carter."

I smirked to myself. "Did you expect anything but?"

Resting her D-cup breasts against my back and wrapping her arms around my six pack, my top client nibbled on my right earlobe and said, "Not for the money I pay you."

I unclasped her hands from my midsection and stood up. "Keep the money; right and exceptional is the only thing you'll get."

Deanna purred. "And what if that money gets better? What do I get then?"

My back to her, I clenched my jaws, closed and opened my eyes slowly, and took a deep breath, wanting to tell the bitch to kiss my naked ass that she was now grabbing, and lose my number.

But unfortunately, I couldn't.

Although she was a sexy fifty-something-year-old who was finer than Halle Barry on her best day, she was a deep-pocketed bitch with her head so far up her own ass that she swore her shit smelled like perfumed roses. My number one client, Deanna, paid me ten thousand dollars to tap her ass twice a month. As much as her personality irked the hell out of me, I had big plans that required big money. So far I'd made damn near one hundred and twenty thousand dollars off of her alone. Now she was talking about paying me more.

"How much more?"

"Be mines exclusively whenever I want you, and I'll pay you twenty thousand dollars a month."

As much as I didn't want her to, she had my attention. She'd been my client now for a little over a year. Multiply twenty thousand by twelve months, and she'd have your attention too. But still . . .

"I don't know how your husband doesn't miss the cash now, but I'm sure he'll miss twenty Gs a month."

"I was a math major in college. Being the caring wife that I am, I convinced my husband that he didn't need to pay an accountant a salary to do what I could do for free." She gave my ass another squeeze then reached between my legs and cupped my testicles.

The average man's dick would have been rock hard with Deanna's manicured claws cupping him, but I wasn't average. I knew what her silent actions were implying. I removed her hands, stepped away from her, and grabbed my boxers from the floor.

"I have other clients," I said, stepping into the boxers.

"Drop them."

I slipped into my white linen button-down. "I can't do that."

"Why not?"

My beige linen pants on now, I said, "They're good clients."

"My pussy's better," Deanna said, her voice laced with the arrogance that I couldn't stand.

"They pay me good money too."

"Nowhere close to what I pay you, I'm sure."

I nodded. "No, but combined, it's still damn good

money." I walked into the bathroom of the hotel we were in and turned on the faucet to do my hair. No comb, no brush. Just water. That's all my natural curls needed.

When I finished, I stepped back into the room. Deanna was propped up on the bed, still naked, with her legs spread open. She was touching herself. I watched her for a few seconds, my manhood growing beneath my Calvin Kleins. I might not have liked the bitch, but I'm a man, and that shit was turning me on. Deanna knew it, too, and increased the intensity of her motions.

I licked my lips, throbbed, but didn't give her what she wanted. "Same time next month?" I said, looking away from her finger action and looking her in the eyes instead.

Deanna smiled. "What about my offer?"

"I'll have to think about it."

"Don't think too long, Carter. My pussy can find another maintenance man to satisfy it."

My turn to smile. "Nowhere near as good as I can."

With that said, I grabbed the five thousand she'd laid out on the table and walked out of the room.

Carter

The first thing I did after depositing my money into the bank was jump in the shower. I had to wash off the five Gs I'd worked for. Sex usually wasn't work for me, but unfortunately, any time spent with Deanna was just that. I guess I should be happy that her personality didn't match her looks. As sexy as she was, were she a sweetheart, it would probably have taken me longer to amass all of the money I had, because even though she could afford it, I'd feel bad about taking as much money from her as I did. Now, I know that doesn't sound right, but I'm a gigolo. I'm in this business to make money. Taking my clients for all they have is what I'm supposed to do in order to make a living.

Gigolo = sex = cash = a living.

For a lot of cats in this line of business, that's the equation. But for me, it's different. I had my living long before the rich, neglected, desperate housewives. Before the career change, I used to work in the corporate world as a consultant. Basically, one screwed up company after another paid me big bank to pretend to give a shit and help them straighten out their financial situations. Made over one hundred thousand dollars a year pretending to care whether the companies survived their own self-implosions. I lived the good life. Drove a Benz, lived in a fly-ass three-bedroom condo. My clothes were never out of style. Women were never in short supply.

Gigolo = sex = cash = an accident.

I was in New York on a business trip when my life changed. Chilling at the bar in the hotel restaurant, sipping on a rum and Coke, I was watching the Miami Heat play the Detroit Pistons on the TV hanging in the corner when Cheryl Roberson approached me.

"Is this stool taken?"

"If it were, I'd get rid of whoever was occupying it so that you could sit down." That was my response after looking away from Shaq disrespecting Ben Wallace with a monster dunk, and laying my eyes on quite possibly the finest female I'd ever laid my eyes on.

Tall and slender, with mahogany-colored skin, hypnotic brown eyes, full I-know-you-want-these lips, and a pair of beautiful breasts begging to be released from the black halter top she was wearing, Cheryl flashed a sexy smile and said, "Thank you."

"My pleasure." Once she was seated and had placed her purse to the side, I extended my hand. "Carter Reed."

"Cheryl Roberson," she said, taking it.

"I take it your husband will be joining you soon?" I asked, noticing the diamond on her ring finger.

Cheryl pursed her lips, raised her eyebrows a bit and said, "My husband is upstairs sitting on the bed, making love to his laptop. He could give two shits about joining me for anything."

I nodded. "Didn't mean to upset you."

Cheryl shook her head. "I'm not upset. Just stating the facts."

"Nothing but the facts, huh?"

"Nothing but."

"Can I buy you a drink?"

"Cosmo, please. And thank you."

After ordering her Cosmo and another rum and Coke for myself, I said, "So, is your husband here for business?"

"Yes, he is."

"Do you usually come with him on his trips, or are you here for business as well?" I asked as the bartender brought our drinks.

Cheryl took a sip of hers and said very matter-of-factly, "No, I just came to spend his money. Are you here on business?"

"I am."

"And your companion?"

"Non-existent. I'm happily single."

"Gay?"

"Hell no."

"Had to ask."

I nodded, took a sip of my drink, and after a brief couple of seconds of silence, said what I was thinking. "Your husband's a fool to neglect a woman as beautiful as yourself."

Looking at me over the rim of her glass, Cheryl said, "Would you neglect me, Mr. Reed?"

"Mr. Reed is my father. Call me Carter. And let's just say that the laptop is the last thing I'd be making love to right now."

Cheryl's eyes closed a fraction, and a slight smirk appeared on her lips. "Is that right, Carter?"

"Just stating the facts," I said honestly.

"Nothing but the facts, huh?"

"Nothing but, Mrs. Roberson."

"Call me Cheryl. Mrs. Roberson is sitting upstairs on my husband's lap."

My turn to smirk. I took another sip of my drink and

looked back to the TV. Shaq had just received his fourth foul and was being taken out of the game. The Heat were in trouble.

I wasn't looking at her, but I could feel Cheryl's eyes on me. The sexual tension between us was high. She wanted me—or at least she wanted me to give her what her husband wouldn't. I wanted to oblige in every way, but she was married. The move was hers to make.

As if reading my thoughts, Cheryl said, "Carter?"

Dwyane Wade just split two defenders and made a nasty lay-up to drop the Pistons' lead down to twelve. I turned away from the screen and looked at her. "Yes?"

"Take me upstairs to your room."

"Won't your husband miss you?"

"I told you, his wife is already upstairs. He won't miss shit. Take me to your room and show me how serious your comment was."

I nodded, downed the rest of my rum and Coke, looked up at the game to see Rasheed Wallace hit a three-point buzzer beater, then looked back at Cheryl. Her gaze on me was deadpan. She was as serious as a heart attack. I reached into my pocket, pulled out my wallet and removed a twenty-dollar bill and laid it down beside my glass. Cheryl was already on her way to the elevator.

On the way up, we were silent. An older couple was riding with us. Their stop was the twelfth floor, ours the eleventh. Before we got off, the woman, a sophisticated Ruby Dee look-alike told us we made a beautiful couple. As we stepped out of the elevator, I caught a glimpse of us in the hallway mirror and thought she was right. In another time, another place, maybe she could have been Mrs. Reed instead of a pissed off Mrs. Roberson.

Another time, another place, maybe.

I let those idle thoughts go as we reached my room. The

door was barely closed behind us before Cheryl placed her hand on my crotch. Downstairs, she was calm, controlled. She was different now. "Fuck me, Carter," she said, unzipping my slacks and finding her way to my stiffening manhood. "Fuck me like my husband doesn't. Fuck me like I know he can't." Her breath was ragged, her stroking hungry. She'd been neglected far too long.

I guided one hand beneath her halter top to play with her nipples. I guided the other through the slit in her skirt and past her thong to play with her secret garden.

"Carter . . . oh God . . . Carter. . . ." She paused as I applied pressure on her clitoris and made circular motions. "Car . . . ter . . . oh . . . God. . . . Feels so . . . so . . . shit . . . so good."

Seconds later, I felt the gush.

Cheryl stopped stroking, looked at me and smiled. "You have skills," she said.

I gave a slightly arrogant nod. "I like to think so."

"We just met, so I won't take you in my mouth."

"Fair enough," I said.

"But I want you inside of me."

"Fair enough."

"Do you have condoms?"

"In my bag."

Cheryl slipped out of her clothing, went over to the bed and got on her hands and knees. "Get a couple and come and fuck me, Carter."

I stood still for a few seconds, admiring the damn near perfect ass she possessed, before taking my own clothes off and moving forward to apologize on her husband's behalf. Two hours and four condoms later, Cheryl and I were naked on the bed when she made an offer that would change my life.

"Carter, my husband is a rich man with no sex drive."

"I gathered that," I said.

"Do you have any idea how frustrating that shit is?" she asked, the anger in her tone increasing.

"I can only imagine."

"Not even once in a while would he give it to me," Cheryl continued.

"His loss," I said.

"You fucked me like I deserved to be fucked."

"I try to please."

"Where do you live?"

"Maryland. You?"

"California."

Cheryl took my penis in her hands and stroked it until it hardened. "You said that it was my husband's loss. Do you want it to be your gain?"

I looked at her. "What do you mean?"

"I'll pay for your flight, pay for the hotel, pay for your food and drinks. I'll pay you three thousand dollars to fuck me like that again when I call."

I didn't say anything at first, as her proposition caught me completely off guard. Finally, after a few seconds, I said, "Are you serious?"

"Carter, when it comes to spending my husband's money, I'm always serious."

"You want me to be your trick?"

"My companion on call."

"I have a job. I make a hell of a decent salary."

"Think of this as your bonus."

"I get bonuses already."

"Well, then consider this a paid vacation," Cheryl said, sitting up.

"You're serious?" I asked again as she grabbed another

condom from my half-empty box, opened it and slid it down on me.

"Three thousand dollars to fuck me like this, Carter," she said, mounting me and guiding me into her wet pool. "All . . . expenses . . . paid. A couple of . . . of . . . hours of your time. Three . . . oh God . . . you're so big . . . three thousand dollars . . . to . . . to . . . fuck me like this."

I grabbed her ass and thrust upwards, driving myself deep inside. She wasn't the best I'd ever had, but she was damn good. Cheryl cried out, told me how good I felt, and upped the amount to five thousand as she orgasmed.

"Five thousand to fuck me like that again," Cheryl said, lying down on my chest, breathless.

"How *on call* would you expect me to be?"

"Twice a month."

"Twice? That's a lot of my time."

"Five thousand. I'd say it's worth it."

"Why me? Why not someone else who lives closer?"

"I've had others, Carter. None could compare to you."

I stroked my chin as my head swelled. "You haven't even had it all," I said, my voice filled with bravado.

Cheryl purred. "I know. That's why I want more."

"And what if I wanted more?"

"You can have it as much as you want."

I thought about the proposition, did some quick calculating in my head. If she agreed to what I was about to say, this would be a very nice bonus. "I want five thousand for each trip."

Cheryl lifted her head from my chest and without an ounce of hesitation or thought, looked at me and said, "Do you promise to please each time?"

"I'll make you sing."

"And you'll come when I call?"

"I'd want a call one week in advance. But yeah, I'll come."
Cheryl smiled. "Deal."

After that day, true to her word and desires, Cheryl called
me twice a month, flew me to Cali, put me up in the
Marriott, and paid me to sex her down. I have to admit, before Cheryl, I regarded prostitutes and gigolos as people
who shed all morality and allowed their bodies to be disrespected for cash because of a lack of pride. But my views
changed after my first trip.

Cheryl spent from Thursday to Sunday with me and
treated me like a king, not giving a shit about how much of
her husband's money she spent. Clothes, shoes, some jewelry—she spent it all on me. We ate with movie stars in five-
star restaurants, and partied with them at the hottest clubs at
night. After that, we went back to the suite, showered together to get rid of the sweat we'd worked up on the dance
floor, then created fresh sweat fucking like rabid dogs.

Like I said, before that trip I had a one-sided opinion of
anyone in this profession, but on the plane ride home, with a
five-thousand-dollar check in my pocket, my view was very
different. The last thing I had done was get rid of my morality, and I damn sure hadn't disrespected my body. As a matter of fact, I'd simply done what I would have normally done
after a night out at the club, only instead of just busting a nut
with some random female, I was busting a nut and being
paid handsomely.

Where was the disrespect of self in that?

I was being paid; Cheryl was being satisfied. I scratched
her back; she scratched mine.

Life was sweet. I made cross-coastal trips to be treated like
a king, and then came back home and fattened my bank account. And the best part about the money was that it was all
tax-free. Five thousand was five thousand. Five thousand

twice a month for twelve months was one hundred and twenty thousand. Uncle Sam didn't get shit. All I had to do was continue working my 9-to-5 and he'd never know about the extra income.

So, why did I eventually quit and become a gigolo full-time? Because the money was just too damned easy to make.

Samantha

"**I**s that him again?"

I looked at the display screen on my cell phone and sucked my teeth. "Unfortunately."

"Want me to talk to his ass?"

I shook my head. "No. You said enough to him the other day."

My best friend, Kris, hmph'd. "Believe me, there's plenty more I could say to that asshole."

Kris's declaration made me crack a smile. "I'd love to let you go off on him again, but he's already had more than enough of our time wasted on him."

"Hmph. I still can't believe he cheated on you with his skank-ass secretary."

Although I'd finally come to grips with that fact, my eyes still threatened to well with tears. After a string of one too many bad relationships, Andre Bauer came along like a thief in the night and completely swept me off of my feet.

I was going into my sixth consecutive don't-need-a-man-for-shit month when we met. As I was sitting at the bar in Club H20 in DC, waiting for Kris to join me for our Friday happy hour, Andre approached me with an attention-catching routine I hadn't encountered before.

Tapping me on my shoulder, he said, "Excuse me, but I'm here to inform you that I'm placing you under arrest."

Already coming off of a stress-filled day, I was in no mood to deal with any bullshit, so in a fierce nigga-back-the-hell-up-off-me tone, I looked up at some of the sexiest brown eyes I'd ever seen and barked, "Excuse me? What do you mean you're placing me under arrest?"

His brown eyes serious and unblinking, Andre said, "I'm sorry, but it's the only thing I can do to protect myself."

It usually wasn't in my nature to give a guy at a bar the time of day, but something about Andre's sexy set of brown eyes made me hold back the fire and attitude I would normally have let loose and ask, "Protect yourself?"

"Yes."

"And what would you be protecting yourself from?"

His gaze still intense, his tone still no-nonsense, Andre said, "Well, it's like this: if I don't place you under arrest, then I'll be forced to go against all principle and do something I vowed to never do."

Unable to look away from him, I asked, "And what would that be?"

Andre opened his mouth to speak, then paused and let out an overly dramatic sigh. "If I don't place you under arrest right now," he said, moving several barstools out of his way, "I'll be forced to go down on one knee . . ."

Which he did.

"Grab a hold of your delicate hand . . ."

Which he did.

"And ask for your hand in marriage, because quite frankly, you are the most beautiful woman I've ever laid my eyes on."

Although my skin is the color of dark chocolate, I had no

doubt that anyone who was standing around the bar could see me blushing. I'd heard the you-are-the-most-beautiful-woman-yada-yada line before, but no man had ever been so smooth about it. Needless to say, I was impressed—and thoroughly embarrassed when my girl Kris walked up and yelled out, "Say yes, girl! You ain't never gonna find a man like—" She paused, leaned down toward Andre and said, "What's your name?"

"Andre," he answered, looking at me with a captivating smile.

Kris stood up. "Like Andre again! Say yes! For the love of God. For the love of your momma . . . say yes!"

Unable to do anything else, I covered my face with my free hand, shook my head, and laughed with everyone else at Kris' antics. Seconds later, Andre stood up, gave me back my hand and chuckled.

"Tell you what," he said, grabbing a stool and sitting beside me. "At least say yes to me buying you a drink. We'll work on the proposal later."

Nodding and enjoying the beauty of his smile, I said, "Okay."

"I hope you know you're buying her girl a drink too," Kris blurted out, sitting beside me.

Andre's smile widened. "Of course," he said. "Just one thing. I'd at least like to know the names of the lovely ladies I'm buying drinks for."

"I'm Kristina, but you can call me anytime," Kris said.

I elbowed her as Andre laughed.

"What?" Kris said. "I'm just saying if it don't work out for you two, and you're into sexy Asian females, then give me a holla."

"You need help," I said, laughing.

"No, what I need is his brother's phone number. You do have a brother, don't you?"

Laughing, Andre said, "Unfortunately, I don't."

"Damn. That's all right. Give me your number anyway. Or better yet, you take mine. Sam can be a pain in the ass sometimes, and you might need someone to vent to."

"Girl!" I yelled, slapping Kris playfully on her arm.

We all broke out in laughter.

After a few seconds, Andre looked at me. "So, is Sam short for Samantha?"

"Yes, it is."

"It fits you."

"Thank you. Andre fits you too. Or do you prefer Dre?"

"No. Andre is just fine." He stuck out his hand. "Now that we've been formally introduced, it's nice to meet you, Sam."

"It's nice to meet you too, Andre."

"So, it's not nice to meet me?" Kris said.

I shook my head while Andre took her slender hand. "It's definitely a treat meeting you, Kris."

Fanning herself, Kris put her hand on my shoulder. "Whew. I need to go and set up a booty call now." She stood up. "Andre, honey, I'll have a Long Island Iced Tea." She playfully traced her hand along his cheek, turned and gave me a wink, then walked off to make her call.

Andre passed his hand over his bald head and chuckled. "Now, she's a trip."

"No, she's a journey," I said, watching her switch her narrow behind past a group of brothers in suits.

"Black mother?" Andre asked, watching her sashay.

"Nope."

"Black father?"

"Nope."

"Adopted into a black family?"

"Nope."

"You mean she's straight Asian?"

"Don't tell her that," I said with a chuckle.

"Damn. She's real, huh?"

"Very real. And she likes you."

"And what about her friend?" Andre asked, looking at me.

I smiled. "Her friend gives you an A for effort. Order her an Apple Martini and go from there."

As I knew she would, Kris came back to get her drink then left Andre and me alone to become acquainted. He told me all about his job as a marketing director for Coca Cola, while I told him all about my career as a clothing designer. When we weren't talking, we were on the dance floor in the Latin side of the club, getting our salsa groove on.

Falling for Andre was never my intention. Like I said, I had that whole I-didn't-need-a-man-for-shit-because-they-are-full-of-shit mantra going for me. I was jaded, and falling in love to be played for a fool again was just not going to happen. Now here I was, sitting with tears welling, my heart broken, and a ringless finger that once bore a diamond marquise.

"Sorry-ass son of a bitch," Kris said as my cell phone rang again. "Let me speak to him, girl."

I let out a long sigh and wiped tears away from the corners of my eyes. "No. I'll deal with him, for the umpteenth time, later. Right now, let's just get inside and work off these calories of ice cream we just consumed."

Kris and I gathered our gym bags, got out of my white Mercedes-Benz SL500 Roadster and headed inside the gym. I usually left my phone on for business at all times, but this time, before stepping through the gym entrance, I shut it off.

Carter

"Sometimes, Carter... sometimes you make me think about being straight."

"Is that right?"

"If all men were like you... could do what you do... were thick like you... I wouldn't want pussy. Hell, I wouldn't need it."

"There are other men out there, you know. I'm sure some of them are better than me."

"Perhaps. But Cheryl didn't give me their numbers."

As my ego swelled, I smiled and rose from the bed, where my client was still lying naked. A full-blown lesbian, Tricia called me every couple of months when she needed a dick-fix.

"I don't think Deborah would be too happy if she heard you talking like that right now."

Tricia chuckled. "Deb would have a heart attack if she knew I was taking a real dick inside of me. Either that or kill me."

Gathering the two thousand she'd placed on the hotel's nightstand, I said, "I won't tell if you won't."

Stretching her svelte frame, Tricia said, "Mmm, I wish I

could tell. As a matter of fact, I wish I could get her to join us for my fix."

"Now that," I said, slipping into my shirt, "would be a challenge."

Tricia purred. "I love a challenge."

"My pops always said challenges keep us young."

"Really? How?"

"When we're faced with a challenge, we're in constant motion, constant thought, so our minds and bodies are always sharp. But when we're complacent, everything about us gets dull and slow."

Tricia nodded. "Makes a lot of sense. Your father must be one of those older men who's always doing intense things like skydiving and bungee jumping."

"If he was alive, he probably would be," I said.

"You mean he's dead?"

"Passed away at forty-two."

"But what about challenges and keeping the body and mind young?"

"Unfortunately, he was a drug addict and died of an overdose."

"I'm sorry to hear that."

"He picked the wrong challenge," I said, shrugging.

"Really sorry, Carter," Tricia said again, her voice more somber.

I shrugged again. "It's cool. I grieved a long time ago."

Tricia stood up, walked over to me, and draped her arms around my neck. "Thank you for fixing me up, Carter." She kissed my lips gently and smiled.

I gave her ass a squeeze. It was a shame she only liked pussy. "Until the next call," I said then headed to the door.

Tricia purred again. "Who knows? Maybe I'll have Deb with me."

My hand on the knob, I turned and looked at her. "Just

make sure you have double the amount for double the pleasure."

Tricia smiled. "No breaks, huh?"

"Even for a woman as sexy and sweet as you."

Tricia blew me a kiss. "Until the next call."

After leaving Tricia at the hotel, I headed to the bank to
make my deposit then decided to hit the gym to run the
treadmill, lift some weights, and go a few rounds with the
punching bag. I wasn't hardcore about my workouts, but I
liked to stay lean and ripped. The women liked that too.

It was 12 o'clock when I parked my Escalade, and to my
dismay, the gym was packed. I thought about leaving for a
second, because a packed gym usually meant I would have to
wait to use equipment. If there was one thing I hated doing,
it was waiting. Finally, after a few seconds of heavy delibera-
tions, I groaned, grabbed my bag and opened the door of my
Escalade.

"You cheating son of a bitch! I hate you! We were supposed to be getting married in four months. How could you
do this to me?"

I usually don't listen to other people's conversations, but
the outburst I'd just heard as my door swung open had my
curiosity peaked.

"Don't give me that didn't-mean-for-it-to-happen bullshit,
Andre. If you didn't mean for it to happen, there wouldn't
have been a second, third, fourth, or fifth time!"

Curious to see who the sweet-sounding yet enraged voice
belonged to, I took a discreet look through my tinted windows and laid my eyes on a stunning, dark chocolate sister
with a Fantasia-length hairstyle, piercing eyes slit with con-
tempt, luscious full lips, and a body as fine as Mariah Carey's
but with a healthier behind. Andre was a fool to mess around
on that.

I couldn't help it. As wrong as it was for me to sit there and eavesdrop on her conversation, I continued to stare and did just that.

"No, I don't want to talk to your ass in person, and I don't need any more explanations. I got all the information I needed from that juvenile bitch, remember? I'm being unfair? You know what, Andre? Fuck you. Fuck you, fuck you, fuck you!"

And with that, she slammed her cell phone shut and said, "Asshole!" Five seconds later, her cell began to sing an Alicia Keys song. Instead of answering it, she cursed Andre out loud again, threw her cell, leaned against a white Mercedes-Benz SL500 Roadster, covered her face with one hand, and hugged herself with the other while she cried softly. I watched her, oblivious to the various people walking past her, either going to or leaving the gym.

Andre.

A woman like that.

At that moment, I wanted to kick Andre's ass.

Even before my career change, it had been a long while since I'd been involved in a serious relationship, because I enjoyed being a bachelor. The freedom to make moves when I wanted, do what I wanted, do who I wanted without the obligations and headaches; it was all about me. No brothers, no sisters. It's always been about me.

Relationships meant going to the movies to see drama instead of action. Replacing the black leather sofa for one riddled with flowers and covered with cushions. Relationships meant petty arguments over watching a Lifetime show instead of watching *Fear Factor;* squeezing the toothpaste from the bottom instead of the middle. Relationships meant break-ups, broken hearts, and a lot of name-calling.

Relationships weren't for me.

So why the hell did I step out of my car and walk over to

where her phone lay? Why did I pick it up and walk toward her? Why was it that the closer I got to her, the more I thought that, even though I'd never thought of anyone being The One, she could possibly be The One? Why the hell didn't I turn around instead of opening my mouth and saying, "I think you dropped this?"

And why, after she removed her hand from her face and looked up at me with teary, slightly puffy yet perfectly beautiful eyes, could I only think again that she could definitely be The One?

"Excuse me," she said softly.

"Your phone," I said, offering it to her.

She looked down at it in my palm. "Oh. Thank you." She took it and threw it onto the passenger seat of the car.

"No problem. I just happened to notice it flying across the parking lot. I was going to drop it off at the lost and found inside, but when I looked over and saw that you were upset, I figured you must have lost it somehow."

Cracking a slight smile, she said, "Yeah, I lost it all right."

"Don't sweat it," I replied. "Other than the fifteen or twenty people that walked by, no one seemed to notice."

Cracking a bigger smile, she said, "I was a little loud, huh?"

I squinted my eyes and brought my thumb and index finger close together. "Just a little."

This time her smile was accompanied with laughter. With the mood changed, I put out my hand. "Carter Reed."

"Samantha Jones."

Shaking her soft hand, I smiled and said, "So, do you always come to the gym to work on your cell phone throwing technique?"

Samantha chuckled. "No. That was . . . was . . . Ugh, forget you saw that."

"Kind of hard to forget a beautiful woman shedding tears."

Samantha let go of my hand. "Sorry about that," she said, the corners of her mouth dropping a bit.

"Believe me, if anyone should be apologizing, it should be the jerk that ruined your day." That brought the corners back up a little. Feeling pretty good about the vibes, I continued. "I'm not trying to get in your business, but are you okay?"

Samantha nodded. "I'm fine. Thanks. I normally don't act that way. It's just not a good time for me right now."

"I understand. Well, hopefully your man can get his act together so you two can be back on track again." Of course, after listening to her tirade, I knew there was no chance of that happening.

Samantha curled her lips. "There's absolutely no chance of that happening. He cheated on me with his secretary."

Grimacing, I said, "Ouch. Sorry to hear that."

"That's not the worst part," Samantha said. "We were supposed to be getting married in four months."

With an even bigger grimace, I said again, "Ouch. Let me have your phone so I can throw it, please."

Samantha busted out with laughter.

"I'm really sorry about that," I said. *Damn, Andre,* I thought, admiring Sam's beauty. "At least tell me that his secretary was Toni Braxton fine. Because—now, this is going to sound like a line—but to cheat on you, she would have to be."

Samantha smiled and sighed. "She's young, skinny, cute, but no Toni."

"And since she's his secretary, I take it that means she's not rolling around in a Mercedes-Benz either."

Samantha cocked her head back a bit. "Try a Dodge Neon."

Another grimace. "Ouch. He cheated on you for a young chick with no money? Damn, I feel bad for him now."

Samantha laughed. "You know, when you say it like that, I think I do too."

We both enjoyed a laugh over that then became quiet as we looked at one another. I didn't know what she was thinking at that moment, but I know I was tripping off of the obvious sparks between us. Like I said, relationships weren't for me, but right then, right there, I wanted to look at Samantha and say, "I'll see you when I get home."

Maybe she was reading my thoughts, because at that exact moment, she gave me a smile then opened her mouth to speak.

"Girl, where the hell you been?"

I followed Samantha's eyes as she looked toward the gym's entrance. An Asian female with slender hips and small breasts, lugging two small gym bags, was sauntering in our direction.

"Sorry, girl," Samantha said, flashing an apologetic smile.

Dropping one of the bags at Samantha's feet, her friend gave me a once-over then smirked at Samantha. "So, now I see why you couldn't find your gloves. Are you going to introduce us?"

"Sorry," Samantha said. "Kris Malone, this is Carter Reed."

Kris looked at me, licked her lips and smiled. "Nice to meet you, Carter," she said, holding out her hand.

I took it. "The pleasure's mine," I said easily.

Kris raised her eyebrows. "It could be," she said before looking back to Samantha. "So, Sam, about those gloves. Girl, you know when you're not around I don't push myself in there."

"I know. I'm sorry. I was distracted."

With another look in my direction, Kris said, "I'd say so."

Sam rolled her eyes. "I spoke to Andre."

"You did?"

"Yeah. I don't know why, but I called him to lay into his ass."

"Nothing wrong with that."

Sam groaned. "It was a waste of my time. I should have never called."

Before the friends could continue their discussion, I cleared my throat. "Ladies, before you go any further, I think I'll head on inside."

"Oh, I'm sorry," Sam said. "I didn't mean to keep going on about him."

"No apologies," I said. "I'm just glad you're okay."

"Well, thank you for returning my cell."

"Whenever they decide to allow the cell phone throwing competition into the Olympics, just give me a call. I'll gladly be your coach."

Sam gave me a beautiful smile and a look that prompted my next move.

"As a matter of fact," I said, removing my wallet from my pocket, "Use this when you're ready." I removed a card and handed it to her.

Sam looked at it. "So, you're a financial consultant."

I nodded. "Yeah. I help people with their money."

"And this is your office number?"

"My cell, and it's always on."

Sam cleared her throat. "That's good to know."

I shrugged. "Hey, you never know when the Olympic committee will make that decision."

"True," Sam said, her voice softening a bit. "Guess we'd want to get started right away."

"Exactly," I said with a nod.

Sam smiled.

I smiled.

Electricity.

Hot.

Whether I wanted it or not, there was a definite connection there.

Her friend, Kris, cleared her throat, breaking us from our seconds of silence. I looked at her and smiled. "Kris," I said taking her hand again. "I hope to see you again."

Kris smiled and let out an, "Umph. Don't worry, you will."

"I hope so," I said, casting a glance at Sam. "So, Sam, it was a pleasure talking to you. If I ever meet Andre, I'll have to thank him for being a fool."

Sam nodded. There was no doubt she was thinking the same thing. "Thanks again for being a gentleman."

"My mother always told me to never leave a woman alone in distress. My pops always added to that and said, 'Especially a beautiful one.' "

Sam blushed. Kris let out another "Umph."

I nodded to both of them. "Until next time." With that said, I gave Sam one last smile before leaving the two women alone. As I headed inside, eager to lift some iron, I heard Kris behind me say, "Girrrrl, you better call that number."

Sam

"Please tell me you're going to call that hellafide fine brother from the gym earlier. Please, please, please say that's the first thing you plan on doing when you walk into your house."

I'd just pulled up in front of Kris's four-bedroom town-house. I shrugged my shoulders. "I don't know."

"What do you mean you don't know?" Kris asked, looking at me as though I'd lost my mind. "Do you need to go to the eye doctor and have your vision checked? Did you not see how fine he was?"

"Yes, I saw how fine he was," I said, remembering Carter Reed's sexy, brown bedroom eyes, and pretty boy smile.

"So, what's the problem, Sam? Calling him should be a priority."

I sighed. "Kris . . . I just broke up with Andre four weeks ago."

"Okay?" Kris said, still giving me that look.

"We were supposed to be getting married in four months, remember?"

"Of course I remember. I just finished paying for my

custom-made, non-returnable maid of honor dress, remember?"

I groaned. "I feel really bad about that."

"Nothing for you to feel bad about, girl. . . . It wasn't your fault."

"I know, but still, that was a lot of money. I'll make sure you get it back."

"Don't worry about my money. I'll make sure Andre's ass pays me back. The only thing you have to do is call that number."

"I'm not really looking for a relationship, though," I said, not really sure why I uttered the word.

"Relationship? Who said anything about a relationship?"

"So I'm supposed to call him just to get my freak on?"

"Bingo."

"Come on, Kris. You know I'm not about that."

"You say that like sex with a sexy-ass man is a bad thing."

"I'm not saying that," I said, fiddling with my keys dangling from the ignition before finally turning off the engine. "I'm just saying that in today's day and time, with all of the diseases that are out there, getting your freak on isn't necessarily the best thing to do."

"Girl, please," Kris said, sucking her teeth. "Use a condom, and no sucking the dick unless he's your man, and you'll be all right."

Wrinkling my nose, I said, "You are nasty."

"Yes, I am," Kris confirmed with a nod. "But I'm also disease-free."

"Whatever," I said, chuckling.

"Whatever, nothing. Just make sure you call him before I do.

"I'll think about it," I said, looking out of my lowered window and staring at a squirrel scurrying up a tree.

"Don't think," Kris said. "Just call."

I turned and looked at her. "Maybe."

"Maybe nothing. You better call."

I frowned. "Like I said . . . maybe. Anyway, why are you so pressed about me calling him? You act like you have a stake in this. Is there something you're not telling me? Was my meeting him a coincidence or did you set this all up?"

Kris rolled her eyes. "No, I didn't set this up."

"I don't know," I said, eyeing her skeptically. "You've tried this before. Remember Gary?"

Kris thought for a moment. "You mean Gary with the lisp?"

"Lisp? Please. His lisp was so bad I needed an umbrella to talk to him."

"Whatever, Ms. Picky. Lisp or not, he was fine."

"So, why didn't you go out with him then?"

Kris gave me a sly smile. "I would have," she said, her mouth spreading into a smile, "but I have this thing about other people's saliva."

"See," I said, slapping her on her arm. "That was just wrong. I thought we were girls."

"We are," Kris said, laughing. "I was looking out for you. Besides, how was I supposed to know you had a thing about saliva too?"

"Oooh," I said, giving her the evil eyes. "You know what, Kris? Let me hip you to something."

"What's that?"

"I know you hate to hear the truth, but you're Asian."

Pouting her lips and struggling to hold back a smile, Kris said, "Shut up."

"China doll."

"Whatever," Kris said, holding her palm up to me.

"Mulan."

"You know what . . . kiss my ass."

I puckered my lips and let loose an exaggerated kiss into

the air. Kris gave me the finger. We both fell out into laughter.

"Anyway," Kris said, regaining her composure, "are you going to call him or not?"

Wiping tears away from the corners of my eyes, I said, "I told you I'll think about it. I'm still trying to deal with this whole Andre situation."

"What's there to deal with, Sam? He cheated. You dumped his sorry ass. The situation has been dealt with. It's time to move on now. Live a little. And no, I'm not saying to go and get buck naked with every man you talk to. I'm just saying to have some fun. If fun is a casual date with a handshake good-bye, then fine. At least you won't be up in your house sulking. Live, Sam. Make up for the time that you wasted with that fool."

I fiddled with my keys again, but didn't respond right away as I thought about everything Kris said.

Live. Make up for the time wasted. Have fun. I hadn't thought about it in that way, but she was right. An independent and career-driven woman, my life did a complete stop and U-turn once Andre came into it, while his remained on the straight path, with a side road branching off into his secretary.

"Okay," I said. "I'll call him."

"That's what I'm talking about, girl."

"But. I'm only calling to talk. Really, just to thank him for being a gentleman and returning my phone."

"Sure, sure. Just make sure you say yes when he asks you out."

"What makes you think he'll do that?"

"Please. I saw the way he was looking at you. He was very intrigued."

I made a face and gave a half-shrug like I could have

cared less about Carter's possible interest in me. Kris wasn't buying it.

"Don't even try to act like you don't care, Sam. Andre issues or not, I saw your nostrils opened wide too."

I rolled my eyes and stuck out my tongue. "Get out of my car so I can leave."

Kris gave me a playful scowl. "I need to leave with your funky ass."

"Whatever," I said, laughing. "You were funkin' it up with me too. As a matter of fact, even with your skinny ass, you sweat more than I do."

Kris gave me the finger. I gave it back.

"Trick."

"Wench."

"Ho."

"Mulan."

"See, that's just wrong."

More laughter.

"All right, girl, let me go inside and call Alex."

"You're still talking to him?" I said, surprised.

"For now."

"Uh-oh. Don't tell me that the jump around queen is now sprung."

"Please. Sprung nothing. It's more like he can't get enough of me."

"Ooh, excuse me."

"There is no excuse for you."

"Heifer."

"*Monster's Ball* Halle Barry."

"What?"

Kris smiled. "Just trifling."

I was going to snap a comeback, but I had to laugh. "Good one," I admitted.

"Okay, Samantha dear, I'm out of here. Make sure you call me after you talk to that fine Larenz Tate-looking brother."

"If I call him, I will."

"You better call him."

"Bye, Mommy."

"Bye." Kris stepped out of the car and started to close the door when she paused. "Hey, not to bring up a sore subject, but . . . have you spoken to your father yet?"

At the mention of the man I loved unconditionally with all of my heart, what had been a bright and sunny day quickly changed to a dark and gloomy one, overcast, with rain threatening to downpour.

I cracked the knuckle on my middle finger, as I often did when frustrated. "No," I said, all cheer gone from my voice. "And I don't intend to."

"It's been two months, Sam."

I cracked the knuckle on my empty ring finger this time. "And your point?"

"Don't you think you should try to patch things up again?"

I cracked the knuckle on my thumb now as I thought about the day I stopped by my father's house to somehow try to repair a relationship that months ago had been broken, when I discovered a sold sign posted on a sign in the front yard. Six months prior to that day, my mother, a victim of lung cancer, passed away in the middle of the night. Dealing with the loss of my mother had been an incredible ordeal to endure. Although we were mother and daughter, we were very much like sisters. I'd tried to get her to give up cigarettes for as long as I could remember. I complained about the scent, told her how unattractive she looked with a "cancer stick" in her mouth, complained about the dangers of second-hand smoke, and gave her all the statistics about the chances of her winding up with some type of cancer.

But my mother, a die-hard fitness junky, swore that despite the one vice she couldn't do without, she was not going to die before her time. When she gave me the news of the diagnosis her doctor had given her after what was supposed to be a routine physical, I never had to say a word, because she'd said it all with tears in her eyes.

"You told me so."

Caught too late, my mother was spared the pains of chemotherapy and was instructed by her doctor to relish the three months she'd been given to live. Seeing my mother, who'd always been so physically fit, deteriorate so rapidly had been torturous, and I found myself deteriorating right along with her. Weight loss, sleepless or nightmare-filled nights, unimaginable bouts of depression and public breakdowns; I suffered through it all. Although I couldn't stand his ass now, Andre had really helped me endure, and for weeks before and after her death, his shoulders had been the only pillow I needed. Though it wasn't easy, I finally came to grips with the fact that I wasn't going to see my mother again, and learned how to smile instead of cry whenever I thought about her.

Initially, I marveled at how strong my father had been through everything. Without a shoulder to call his own to lean on, his tears remained at a minimum, and his spirits, though lowered a bit, remained high.

Initially, I marveled—until I discovered that the man I swore could do no wrong had never been without a shoulder at all.

Four months after my mother's death, I walked in on my father practically having sex with the next door neighbor, a woman I never trusted. After a huge fight with Andre, I'd gone over to the house to lean on my father's broad shoulders. The news that in two months my daddy was going to be remarried was something I never expected.

My father and I never really argued until that day. Using the harshest of words and the most acerbic tone, I called my father a traitor, a cheating, lying bastard, and a few other choice words. Apparently, he and my mother had been having issues for a while, and instead of doing whatever it took to work through them, he began to have an affair with the woman my mother once called "the breakup of a marriage waiting to happen." I'd never been disrespectful with my father until that day. I was even worse to the new "love of his life," as I got in a good couple of hits before he pulled me off of her and told me to leave.

Two weeks passed before I answered his millionth phone call and went off about how I didn't want any explanations and how I didn't give a shit about him being happy.

"My mother was dying while you were busy screwing the neighbor. Go to hell!"

Needless to say, two months later, I didn't attend the wedding. Two months after that I came across the sold sign.

"I don't care how long it's been, Kris," I said, starting my car, signaling that I didn't want to talk about my father any longer. "I'm not talking to his ass."

Kris frowned, nodded, and without saying a word, closed the door. She knew that wasn't an issue to be pressed with me. I cracked another knuckle, my mood completely fucked up, and put the car in drive.

"I'll talk to you later," I said.

Kris barely got off an "All right, girl," before I pulled off.

Carter Reed's business card never left my purse.

Carter

God damn! I thought, taking a glance at the group of Stairmasters behind me. Why the hell was I tripping?

Sam. Short for Samantha. I'd only met her once, but I absolutely could not get her off of my mind. Shit.

What the hell was wrong with me? How could this woman be plaguing the hell out of me the way she was? So much so that I'd come to the gym at the same time every damn day for the past two weeks, hoping to run into her again, only to be completely disappointed when I didn't.

Women, love, relationships; these words were never supposed to be mentioned in the same breath. Not unless the words *drama, aggravation,* and *loss of sanity* were mentioned with them.

"This is ridiculous," I said, hitting the end button on the elliptical machine I'd been running on.

"I think the same thing too," a heavyset brotha huffing away on the machine beside me said. "I keep telling my wife that I'm always gonna be a big dude, but she insists that I keep coming here."

I gave him a that's-the-kind-of-headaches-you-get-with-women look and said, "Good luck."

Frustrated at myself for wasting my own time over a woman I didn't really know, I grabbed my towel and walked off. *No more*, I thought. I was done tripping. Five minutes later, I fell flat on my face, because as I was stepping out of the gym, my tormentor was coming up the steps toward me. *Figures,* I thought. Just when I was ready to get a grip, she shows up.

Too late to go back inside, I couldn't do anything but watch the way she moved. Watch the way her lips moved as she told someone she'd talk to them later. Watch the way her slender, well-manicured fingers closed around the banister as she ascended toward me. It was all of five seconds, but I watched.

Unfortunately, I didn't bother to think, because when she approached me and said, "Hi," it took me three all-too-long seconds to say, "Hey" back.

"Carter, right?" she said with a beautiful smile.

My mind working again, I replied, "Yeah." And that was it. See, I didn't know if she'd noticed my temporary moment of mental incapacity or not, but I knew that if she had, calm, cool, and forgetful was the hand I had to play.

She looked at me, her eyes saying, *You don't remember me?*

I looked at her, my eyes saying, *No, I don't.*

Neither one of us spoke, as we were both waiting; she, for me to acknowledge her, and I, for her to play my hand.

"Sam," she finally said, allowing me to yell *Checkmate!* in my mind.

I closed my eyes a bit. "Sam?" I said, pretending to rack my brain as to who she was.

"We met a couple of weeks ago in the parking lot."

I smiled and nodded. "The cell phone," I said.

Sam flashed an embarrassed smile. "Yeah, that would be me."

"I see you got a new one," I said, motioning toward the one attached to her hip.

Another embarrassed grin. "Yeah, I did."

"You don't plan on throwing this one, do you?" I asked with a smile.

"Ha, ha," Sam said. "Very funny."

I shrugged. "Hey, I just took a course on cell phone insurance, and if you did plan on practicing your cell phone toss technique again, I just wanted to make sure and sign you up."

Sam laughed and shook her head. "You're stupid."

"For what? Not wanting to let an opportunity go by?"

Giving me her palm, she rocked her neck from side to side a bit and said, "Anyway."

We both laughed for a few seconds as people walked past us, going in and leaving the gym. "So, where's your friend?"

"She's out of town this weekend."

"Oh, really? Business or pleasure?"

"Pleasure. Her new man, who she emphatically denies is her man, took her to South Beach on Wednesday."

"That's the spot."

"Yeah. I'm overdue for a trip back there. I haven't been there in a couple of years."

Knowing that I should have let it go, I logged that bit of information in the back of my mind. "So, when does she come back?"

"Sunday."

"And until then you . . ."

"Enjoy the silence."

I let out a laugh. "Very funny."

Sam raised her eyebrows. "No, it's very true. Kris is my girl and I love her to death, but that chick can run her mouth."

More laughter. "You know you miss her."

"I know," Sam replied. "But I still like the quiet."

"So, besides enjoying the peace and quiet, what else do you plan on doing this weekend?"

Sam shrugged. "Get some reading done. Maybe redecorate a little. Watch my plants."

"Sounds exciting."

"You have no idea."

"And do you plan to take a break from all of the excitement to eat some food?"

Sam cradled her chin with her thumb and index finger and mocked deep thought before saying, "Possibly."

I smiled. Her personality was infectious. "I tell you what. Because I think you're a nice person, and because I wouldn't want you to starve before Kris gets home, why don't I take you out for a bite to eat? I mean the last thing you'd want is for your best friend to come home after her romantic weekend and find you dead in front of your plants."

"You're such a good person to look out for my friend like that." A second later, she stuck her finger down her throat.

I chuckled. "That's just the way I was raised."

"Mmm-hmm," Sam said, giving me a you-ain't-slick look. "So, dinner to keep me alive, huh?"

"Dinner. Just to keep you alive."

"And do I get any input on the type of cuisine we'll be eating?"

I shrugged. "Sure. Although I'm pretty sure McDonald's has it all."

Sam snapped her head back. "McDonald's?"

I did my best to suppress my laughter. "Yeah. Is that a problem? Or would you prefer Burger King? You can have it your way there."

Sam chuckled. "Very funny. You know, I don't really know you. Backing out of this dinner wouldn't be a problem for me."

"But what about Kris? Don't you want to be alive so she can give you all the steamy details of her trip when she comes home?"

Sam adjusted the Nike bag around her shoulder. "I'll make sure to stop with all of my activities and get a bite to eat."

"Mmm, I don't know that I can trust that," I said. "I tell you what. I'll give in and take you somewhere else besides McDonald's or Burger King. Deal?"

Sam gave me a you're-a-trip look and then said it. "You're a trip."

"I'm just looking out for your friendship."

Sam gave me another look, thought for a moment, and said, "So, dinner?"

"Dinner."

"No fast food."

"Not this time."

Sam smiled. "I don't even really know you. For all I know you could be a serial killer or a rapist."

"Have dinner with me and get to know me. And the serial killing/raping gene skipped my generation."

"Is that right?"

"Want to do a background check?"

"Maybe I should."

"Maybe I should too," I said, enjoying our flirtatious conversation. "I mean other than your name and that you're a champion cell phone tosser, I don't know anything about you either. For all I know, you may try to kill or rape me."

Sam threw her head back and laughed. "I only kill when threatened, and there's no raping on the first date."

"So, this is a date?" I asked.

"Just a dinner date between strangers."

"So, we're strangers now?"

"Until we can prove we're not serial killers or rapists."

Sam gave me a wink as I stroked my faded goatee. It was true. Other than her name, I didn't really know anything about her. But despite this being the longest conversation we'd ever had, you couldn't tell me that I didn't already know all I needed to know. I had a feeling she felt the same way too. Strangers or not, there was a connection.

"Do you still have my card?" I asked.

By the look in her eyes, I could tell she was lying when she answered, "No. Why don't you give it to me again?"

"Why don't you give me your number and I'll call you? I wouldn't want you to lose it again."

"Promise not to call at three in the morning?"

"Only if I'm calling to let you know I've arrived."

Sam blushed and cleared her throat. "Have a pen?"

"I'll put it in my phone."

"So, what time are we eating?" Sam asked as I saved her number.

"Be ready by seven-thirty."

"And no McDonald's, right?"

"And no Burger King. Don't worry, you won't be disappointed."

"I hope not."

"Trust me."

"Not until after the meal."

I nodded. "Right."

"Well, I guess I better get inside and get my workout on if I'm going to be ready on time."

"Yeah," I said. "Punctuality would be a good thing."

With one final, captivatingly sexy smile, Sam said, "Take care, Carter."

"Until tonight, Sam."

We stared at each other for a few seconds before finally going our separate ways. I didn't know what she was thinking, but on my way to my car, I couldn't stop asking myself if I'd lost my mind.

The One.

I kept hearing those words in my head during the whole drive home. I was excited and bothered at the same time.

Sam

O^{*h*} *My.*
God!

I tugged at my hair as I stared into my walk-in closet, trying figure out what I was going to wear. I took another quick glance at my clock. It was 6 o'clock, I was naked beneath the fluffy cotton robe I'd taken from a Marriott hotel, and I couldn't find one decent outfit to wear among the far too many decent outfits I had. "Come on, Sam. Get it together."

I tugged at my hair again and cracked a knuckle. I'd been frantic ever since seeing Carter at the gym again. I didn't know if he could tell, but I was nervous as hell the entire time we spoke. He'd been so damned fine, standing there in his tank top and sweats, that he had me shook. It took everything I had not to let my eyes linger on his sculpted biceps or his all-too-sexy lips too long. Hopefully he hadn't noticed the couple of times I'd been unsuccessful.

I took another glance at the clock: 6:15. I'd just been on the phone with him a half-hour ago, giving him directions, and swearing that I was going to be ready when he arrived.

"Damn it, Kris. Where are you when I need you? On the beach, getting your groove on, that's where."

Getting your freak on.

Those words lingered in the air around me as I thought about Carter's arms again.

"Mmmm. I bet he's good," I thought out loud.

Wait a minute! What was I doing?

"You just broke up with your fiancé, girl," I said to myself. "There'll be no thought about getting your freak on with anybody. Besides, you don't really know him. Don't let those sexy brown eyes fool you. What if he really is a serial killer or rapist?" I cracked another knuckle and thought about backing out at the last minute. Then I reached for the phone. I was desperate and needed help. I grimaced as I dialed Kris's cell number. Hopefully I wasn't interrupting anything.

"Hey, girl," Kris said, answering on the third ring.

"Hey, Kris," I said, feeling immediate regret for calling her. "I'm so sorry to be calling you right now. Please, please, please tell me I didn't interrupt anything."

"Nope. You called right on time. Alex and I just finished getting our freak on ten minutes ago."

"Is Alex there beside you?"

"No, he's in the shower right now. What's up? I know you wouldn't have called unless something happened. And since I don't hear any tears, I know it's not something tragic, which means that you're calling because you're having issues with a man."

I smiled. Our friendship was only four years old, but my girl definitely knew me. "I'm desperate," I said, jumping in head first.

"Whoah. What do you mean desperate? Desperate how?"

"Do you remember the guy from the gym—the one that gave me back my cell phone?"

"You mean the fine brotha that you never called?"

"Yeah. That would be him."

"What about him?"

"I saw him at the gym earlier today."

"Oh, really?"

"Yeah."

"And?"

"And we started talking and flirting a little and . . ."

"And?" Kris said with what I could tell was a smile on her face.

"Long story short, he'll be here at seven-thirty to pick me up for dinner, and I have no idea what the hell I should wear."

I had to wait a few seconds as Kris exploded in a fit of laughter. Finally, she said, "Girl, you are a trip. I can't believe he's got you that shook."

I sighed as Kris exploded with laughter again. I couldn't believe it either. I stole another glance at the alarm clock on my night table. With no outfit picked, my hair not done and my makeup not made up, time was definitely not on my side.

"What should I wear, Kris? You know what's in my closet. Dress, pants, skirt? What?"

Kris chuckled. "Calm down, sweetie. You're making this too hard. It's your first date, so you don't want to give him too much, but at the same time, you want to give him just enough to make him want more."

"So, a skirt then?" I asked, looking at one on a hanger.

"Nope. A skirt is definitely not the move. Not yet. Too much leg too soon gives him the wrong impression of you. Besides, too much leg gives his eyes too much to roam over. Having said that, you can't do anything too low-cut either."

"So, pants and a simple top then?"

"No pants. This isn't a business meeting."

"A dress?"

"Hold on, I'm thinking."

"I'm running out of time, Kris."

"Time, schmime. Relax yourself. You're supposed to make him wait a bit anyway."

"I still have to do my hair and makeup!"

"Okay, okay. Let's see . . . blue? No. Yellow blouse? No. Black spaghetti strap? Oops, that's with me. Too bad. That would have been perfect too."

I groaned.

"I got it. Your sheer black dress with red flowers. The one that dips in the neckline to show just enough cleavage."

"You sure?" I said, pulling it from the closet.

"It's perfect. Short enough, but not too short. And it hugs you just enough to let him see your curves, but not let him see any rolls you want hidden."

"Rolls?" I said in an excuse-me tone.

Kris sucked her teeth. "Don't even try it. We all have a couple here or there whether we want to admit it or not."

I rolled my eyes and smiled. She was right. "Whatever," I still said.

"Whatever, nothing. Now, go and get dressed."

"Okay. Thanks for your help, girl."

"Anytime. I will be calling you for details later tonight, just so you know."

"No you won't. You'll be too busy with your ass in the air."

Kris laughed. "You are right about that. I'll call you tomorrow."

"Okay. See you."

"Bye. Oh . . . before you go."

"Yeah?"

"I think you should try ending the night with your ass in the air too."

"Sorry," I said. "Not all of us do things like that on the first date."

"Hey, just remember what I said before. No sucking the dick, and use a condom."

"Eeew."

"A man that fine shouldn't go to waste, girl."

"Whatever. Just make sure you bring my dress back without any stains."

"Bye, Mother Theresa."

"Bye, skank."

I hung up the phone and smiled. I loved my girl. She'd definitely been born to the wrong parents. It's a wonder, as traditionally Korean as they were, that they hadn't disowned her.

I laid the dress out across my bed and looked at the clock again: 6:45. Damn. With Marion Jones-like quickness, I proceeded to get dressed, do my hair, and apply my makeup. I was just sliding on my platinum bangle bracelet when the doorbell rang.

I took a look at myself in the mirror. I have to admit, I was looking good. My hair was up and on point. My curves were looking just right. I had on just enough makeup and just enough jewelry. I gave my reflection a nod and took a deep breath, held it for a few then let it out slowly to calm myself and my heartrate before moving to the door.

I was nervous. I hadn't gone out on a date since before Andre and I had started dating, and after having been with him for over three years, I was severely out of casual dating practice. Hopefully I wouldn't stumble over my words during dinner.

I gave myself the once-over and then, satisfied, headed to the door.

Carter

"I shouldn't be going out on a date. At least not without being paid. This is ridiculous. I'm a gigolo, for Christ's sake!" I shook my head and looked behind me to my Escalade parked by the sidewalk, and thought about hightailing it out of there. I mean it wasn't like we traveled in the same circles, and other than my stakeouts at the gym, I knew that the chances of seeing her again would be slim to none. And to even keep the coincidental chance of that from happening, I could just cancel my membership and join a different gym. Of course Sam would be pissed about my ditching her, but I had no doubt she'd get over it. Besides, in the end, whether she was pissed or not wouldn't matter, because at least if I left right then and there, life could go back to normal for me.

I tightened my grasp around my car keys and clenched my jaws. All I had to do was put one foot in front of the other and leave, and forget all about Sam and her beautiful eyes and beautiful smile. Leave and forget all about her sharp personality and curvaceous figure. Most of all, I could leave, and from that point on, ignore the crazy feeling churning in the pit of my stomach about her being The One, because for a man like me, that feeling was one I didn't need to feel. I clenched my jaws, looked at my jet black Escalade, and shuffled my right foot forward. Leave and I could go back to being a gigolo with nothing but dead presidents on my mind.

Leave.

And then Sam's door opened behind me. "Hi."

I turned around. "Hey," I said.

Sam smiled, causing goosebumps to rise from my skin. We looked at one another for a few seconds, neither one of us saying a word. I smiled, and as I took in the very essence of beauty that stood before me, I realized and accepted one thing: my life was never going to be the same again. I could turn and walk away. I could switch gyms. I could move to another state, another country. I could do whatever it took to put as much distance between Sam and myself as I could, but no matter what I did or tried, two facts would remain. One, I would never be able to forget about Sam. And two, no matter where I was or what or who I was doing, when I did think about her, it would be with the notion that she was the one I'd let get away.

I barely knew her, and the attraction I had for her was more than just a lustful one. Love at first sight. I'd heard the term before, heard people talk about it happening to them.

Love at first sight.

Sam stood in her doorway, looking finer than two Halle Berrys put together, with a dab of J Lo, a hint of Salma Hayek, a sprinkle of Sallie Richardson, and a touch of Angela Bassett.

Love at first sight.

This was fucked up. I was not supposed to be feeling this.

"You look . . ." I paused as I took in how sexy she was.

"I look what?" Sam asked, her smile dropping.

"Stunning."

Sam blushed. "Thank you."

"No need to thank me. I'm just being honest."

"You look good yourself."

"Just good?" I asked playfully.

Sam's smile broadened. "Very good," she said, her voice lowering a little.

We stared at each other for a few silent seconds. Neither one of us could read minds, but I think we both had pretty good ideas about what the other was thinking.

"So," Sam said, breaking the silence. "I told you I was going to be ready."

I nodded. "That you did."

"So, an *A* for effort so far?"

"B-plus," I said. "An *A* is what you're shooting for by the end of the night."

Sam rolled her eyes and stuck her tongue out at me. "Want to know what your grade is so far?"

I shook my head. "Tell me right before we say goodnight."

Sam gave a nod. "Deal."

"So, are you ready to go?"

"Let me get my keys."

Sam ducked back inside and came out a minute later with her keys in hand. "I'm ready."

"You left a light on inside."

"I always do. It gives the impression of someone being home."

A half-hour later we were in Georgetown enjoying non-stop, easy-flowing felt-like-we'd-always-known-each-other conversation. We'd been that way since I started the ignition in front of her townhouse and the R&B group SHAI, who we both happened to be big fans of, began crooning from my speakers. I had their new CD *Back From the Mystery System* playing, and Sam was in awe that someone else had known about it.

On the way to Georgetown, we talked about our love for the mid-80s to mid-90s R&B, and how the groups of today couldn't hold candles to the likes of the SHAIs, Silks, Jodecis or SWVs of our era. We both agreed that today's so-called R&B had more to do with thug love than it did with true love. And we both agreed that rap was in an even worse state. We still held on to a sliver of hope, though, thanks to artists and groups like Usher, Frankie J, Common, Joss Stone, and Beyoncé.

With our entrees—steak for me, shrimp and pasta for Sam—half-eaten, and our glasses—Mojito for me, Cosmo for her—half-empty, we talked, laughed and obvious to both of us, connected.

"So, do you feel better now?" Sam asked.

"Better?"

"You've succeeded in putting food into my stomach, so I should be alive when Kris comes home."

I shrugged my shoulders. "Mmm . . . not really."

"Not really? Why not?"

"Well, I've been thinking. You've eaten *tonight*. But Kris comes home on Sunday."

"Right. So, you don't feel better?"

"Sunday's a whole day away. What's to say you don't starve tomorrow?" I held back a smile as Sam let go of hers.

"I haven't eaten all of my food. I could just have it boxed up and eat the rest tomorrow."

"You could," I agreed. "But let's be honest. How many of us actually do eat the leftovers from a restaurant? It's not like home-cooked food. It doesn't taste better the next day. Besides, you'll probably be so busy watering your plants and reading that you just may forget to eat, and for your best friend's sake, I can't have that."

Wiping condensation from around the rim of her glass,

Sam said, "I see. So, what do you think I should do about to-morrow?"

My eyes focused on hers, I answered, "Have dinner with me again."

In a very non-sexual way that was all too sexy, Sam licked her lips and cleared her throat. "For Kris' sake, right?"

"All for Kris."

Sam and I looked at each other for a few sexually charged seconds. Although we weren't coming right out and saying it, there was no denying the attraction. It was real and raw. To fight it would have been the smart thing, but it would have been useless, and staring at one another with nothing but the restaurant's activity going on around us, we both knew it.

Pregnant seconds of silence passed before Sam cleared her throat again. "So . . . tell me about yourself. Remember, I need to make sure you're not a rapist. Especially if I decide to have this dinner for Kris again."

I shrugged. "There's not much to tell, really."

"Do you have family here?"

"No brothers, no sisters. My aunts and uncles live in New York, and my parents live on the West Coast."

"Do you see them often?"

"Once a year."

"Wow. That's it?"

"If you knew my parents, you'd probably say that was one time too many." I paused and marveled that I was actually about to tell her the truth—something I'd never done with any other woman. "My father's an alcoholic. My mother's a closet one with a chain-smoking habit from hell. I visit them at Christmastime every year. Every year we argue—my father and I about his penchant for guzzling down the Jack Daniels and then using my mother as a punching bag to relive his glory days as an amateur boxer. My mother and I argue about how I need to stay out of their business. I usually arrive on Christmas Eve, and I'm usually home in my own bed the day after Santa's visit."

Sam looked at me sympathetically. "I'm sorry," she said, her voice soft and genuine.

I shrugged again. "No apologies needed. I was just dealt a lopsided deck. What about you? Have any parental war stories? Although I'd be willing to bet you don't."

Sam sighed. "You'd lose that bet. They may not be as bad as yours, but I have some scars. Actually, they really just came about within the last couple of years. I know all about the chain-smoking parent. My mother died from lung cancer."

"I'm sorry to hear that."

"It's okay. We tried to warn her—my father and me—but she just refused to quit. She was so into health and fitness. I mean she was in better shape than I am. Her only vice were those damn cigarettes. When she died, I was devastated for a long time. My mother was my mother, but she was also like my sister. It took me a while to get over not seeing her anymore, but eventually I did. But once that happened, my world was flipped upside down again when, four months after my mother passed, I walked in on my father tonguing it down with the next door neighbor. The very same neighbor my mother couldn't stand and didn't trust."

I made a pained facial expression. "Damn."

Sam cracked a knuckle. "Don't *damn* yet. There's more."

"More?"

Sam tightened her lips. "A few months after that, he married the bitch, talking about how she was the love of his life."

Another pained expression. "Damn."

"And a couple of months ago, he sold the house my mother died in to move all the way across the coast just because the bitch wanted him to."

"Damn. I'm really sorry about that."

Sam cracked a few of her knuckles and knotted her forehead. "My father was and will always be the first man I've ever loved, and up until this point, I thought he was perfect. I never, ever thought he would have had an affair behind my mother's back, but obviously . . ." Sam paused and cracked another knuckle before continuing. "He's not different. Him, my ex before my ex, they're all the same. Dogs."

Silence fell between us after her brief tirade. I could see the frustration and anger rising from her like steam. Her body, which had been loose and relaxed before, was now tense, and her jaw was tight.

Dog.

That was the one word a man never wanted to hear, especially on a first date. Respond to a woman that not all men were dogs, and the only thing she'd do is give an evil look, roll her eyes, and suck her teeth. Tell her that you weren't one, and her only response would be, "Not yet, but you will be."

As most women were, Sam was jaded. She'd been burned more than enough times, and the leftover taste in her mouth was bitter. So, what could I possibly say to get rid of the dark cloud that was starting to creep in?

"Do you dance?"

Sam looked up at me and I immediately wanted to retract my question. That's how evil her gaze was. Fortunately, the gaze didn't last for long, as her eyes softened and the easygoing, sexy Sam returned with a smile spreading across her face. "Does a bird fly?"

"Salsa?"

"Love it."

"Let's go."

After paying for the check and leaving a generous tip, we headed to Adams Morgan in DC, and went to a club called

Anzu, where they played salsa, meringue, reggeaton, and reggae all night long. No longer bothering to hide our attraction for one another—due in part to the drinks we'd consumed—we allowed our bodies to touch and our hands to explore. With each step, turn, sway, subtle and not-so-subtle gyration, our lips drew closer together until, eventually, they met.

As a gigolo, I was accustomed to planting soft, gentle kisses upon a woman's lips, but that was just part of the job. For the hour or two that my services were rendered, my duties were to take women places their husbands couldn't or just wouldn't. The woman they presented to everyone else was gone with me, as they were able to let go and become the freaks they longed to be. Uninhibited, demanding, rough, downright nasty; it was a let-go policy when their money garnered my time.

Kissing was always part of the job. Logged into my brain, each woman wanted a different kiss. Deanna, the bitch, wanted rough and sloppy. Tricia, the lesbian, wanted deep and long. Mea Ling, my Asian wanna-be dominatrix, wanted her lips bitten close to the point of bleeding. When it came to kissing, I was an expert. And with it being part of my repertoire, I never felt a thing.

But in the middle of the dance floor, while the music thumped, while people around us moved to the Latin rhythms, I experienced something I hadn't in a long, long time: desire, passion, hunger. My breath was actually stolen with each passing second that Sam's lips danced with my own to a rhythm our bodies didn't need to move to. Our lips conversed through one song and halfway through another before we finally separated and gazed at one another.

We'd just crossed a line that no matter how badly we wanted to, we knew we could never go back over. The attraction felt by both of us, and resisted at the same time, was intense as was evident by the love our lips had just made.

What next?

"Are you ready to go?"

My question had a double meaning. Did she want to leave the club? And did she want more than a kiss?

Was she ready to go?

Was I?

Sam's voice was barely a whisper when she answered. "Yes."

"Home?"

"Please."

We left the club and didn't say a word during the thirty-minute drive back to her place. Every now and then I'd steal a side glance at her, trying to read her body language. What was she thinking? Did she regret what happened between us? Was she upset about it? Upset at me? I frowned and tightened my grip around the steering wheel and cursed myself for crossing the line.

When we got to her home, I parked the car and shut off the engine. For several seconds we sat in silence, and that made me regret our kiss even more.

"Thanks for a great night out," Sam said softly.

"Thank you for accepting."

"I'll tell Kris to thank you for feeding me."

I let out a short laugh. "Don't sweat it. I like for my good deeds to go unnoticed."

"Like a true gentleman, huh?"

"I try."

We both laughed and then became silent again, our kiss and wondering what was going to happen next obviously weighing heavily on our minds.

I fiddled with my dangling New York Giants keychain as Sam fiddled with her dress.

We'd kissed. We'd caressed. Now there was awkward silence.

What next?

I clenched my jaws, irritated by the struggle going on in my mind. This wasn't me. Wondering what to do next with a woman was never something I did. I took a breath, held it, then let it go along with my apprehension, and opened my mouth to say something.

"Are you coming inside?"

I looked at Sam. Looked at her eyes. Had this been a trick question? "I don't know," I said, watching her intensely. "Am I?"

Very easily, very seriously, Sam said, "Yes."

I trailed my index finger over my moustache and down and around my goatee. "Okay."

We opened the door, got out of my Escalade and headed to the door. The moon was out and full, the temperature was a warm 83 degrees with no humidity. I couldn't think of a better way to end a perfect evening if this happened.

"Sam?" I said, taking her hand. She'd just unlocked the front door but hadn't yet turned the doorknob. "Are you sure?" I had to know, had to be sure that she was.

With her back to me, Sam let out a soft breath. "I want you," she said seconds later.

My manhood jumped at the thought of that. "Are you sure?" I asked again. "We've had drinks, and I just want to know that this isn't the alcohol talking."

Sam turned and faced me. "Right here, right now . . . I am."

Nothing more needing to be said, Sam and I embraced and kissed with a passion I don't think either one of us had experienced in a long time. We kissed as though we'd been around the world searching for that perfect kiss and had finally found it. We kissed as though we hadn't eaten for days.

Hungry, feverishly, we kissed, we tongued, and with her back now pressed against the door, we groped. My hands were beneath her dress, caressing her thighs—the outside first, before working their way to the inside—and then moving from there to her very wet and wonderfully trimmed secret garden. Her hands were beneath my shirt, squeezing on my pecs before trailing down and finding their way to my zipper.

"Carter," Sam whispered breathlessly as I kissed and sucked on her neck. "I shouldn't . . . shouldn't want you like this."

Still kissing, still sucking, and occasionally nibbling, I reached around her, wrapped my hand around the doorknob and turned it. "This can't be fought," I said, guiding her inside. My shirt and her thong were on the floor by the time the door was closed.

"The bedroom is up the stairs to the right," Sam said.

Taking the lead, I took her by the hand. When we reached the room, Sam slid out of her dress, lit two candles, and then lay back on her bed. With the room awash in candlelight, I stood at the foot of the bed and took a moment to admire the perfection called her body. Breasts full and firm, with nipples the color of dark chocolate and as erect as I was; legs toned and shapely; perfect hips, wide enough to accentuate her Coke-bottle figure. As many women as I'd been with, none had ever been more beautiful.

The moment gone, I moved to the bed and spread her legs, and just before guiding myself into her, thought again to myself that Sam was definitely The One.

Sam sucked in a breath as she enveloped me into her warmth. In unison our bodies moved; me thrusting downward and Sam thrusting upwards.

"You . . . you should . . . be . . . wearing a . . . a . . . ooooh . . .

a condom," Sam said as I palmed her ass and drove myself deeper.

"I know," I said, running my tongue around her nipples as she opened her legs wider, taking me deeper inside. She was right. If there was one rule I'd never broken, it was that under no circumstances did I ever fuck without being protected. I valued my life too much to gamble on catching an STD, especially AIDS. It never mattered how fine the woman was; no condom meant no fucking. "Do you want me to . . . to stop?" I asked, moving my waist in a circular motion, making sure to hit the sides of her walls.

Sam moaned and dug her fingers into my back. "Oh God . . . no!"

I licked her nipples then pressed my body against hers and drove myself deeper. I know I'd broken my cardinal rule, but what we were doing was so far from fucking.

I continued to pound into Sam's pussy with all that I had until she wrapped her legs around me, held me close, drove her hips upwards and said, "I'm . . . going . . . to . . . to . . . cum!"

Unable to hold it back any longer, I had what was quite possibly the biggest ejaculation I'd ever had. Completely spent, I collapsed onto Sam's beautiful and sweaty breasts and caught my breath.

We lay silent that way for several minutes before Sam cleared her throat. "Carter?"

I propped myself up with my arms and looked down at her, staring directly into her eyes. "Yes?"

She cleared her throat again and cracked a knuckle on her right hand. "I just want you to know that what just happened . . . that never happens." She looked at me with serious intent, wanting me to understand the type of woman she wasn't.

"I know what type of woman you are, Sam," I said reassuringly. "And believe me when I say that I'm not a pro at this sort of thing."

Sam smiled. "Couldn't tell from the way you moved."

My turn to smile. "I said I wasn't a pro at something like this. I never said I didn't have skills."

Sam pushed me playfully. "Whatever."

I could only laugh. "You were . . . you *are* amazing, Sam. I don't know what kind of power you have, but you have worked some kind of black magic on me."

"Why do you say that?"

"Because I've never been this attracted or felt a connection this strong before. It's . . . it's like I've always known you. The kiss we shared on the dance floor wasn't like our first kiss at all. There was nothing unfamiliar about it. The sex we just had . . . we knew just what to do, how to move. Some kind of power or black magic; that's the only explanation I can come up with."

Sam caressed the side of my cheek. "Carter, trust me . . . I'm not the only one working some voodoo."

She wrapped her hand around my neck and pulled me down toward her. Just before planting her lips against mine, she whispered, "Voodoo love."

I couldn't agree more.

Twenty minutes later, we were at it again. I didn't go home until the sun was already in the sky. Saturday night was a repeat, only we never made it to the bed.

Sam

"You did what? With who? How many times?"
I covered my face with my hands and smiled.

Back from her vacation, Kris had come over to give me some big news, but before she could—and only because I couldn't keep my own news to myself—I told her all about my impromptu and very intense weekend with Carter.

The time we spent together had been surreal; the conversations we shared, the dancing we'd done both Friday and Saturday nights, the laughter that passed between us, the sex we'd had. Intense. Deep. I connected with Carter in a way I never had with any other man before. It was as though I'd always known him. Hell, maybe I had, because the man in my dreams at night possessed every single one of Carter's qualities.

Carter.

He was sexy, intelligent, successful, sweet, attentive, down to earth; most of all, he was skillful. I'd never been with a man that could make my vagina sing the way Carter had. I swear he must have designed and custom built it to his length and girth. I never intended to have sex with him on our first night out. What's worse is that I'd never been careless enough to have sex without a condom. Not even with Andre. These were rules I'd sworn by since my high school years, when I'd become sexually active. And they were rules I'd never broken.

Never say never.

After Carter left on Saturday morning, I tried to blame what happened on the drinks I'd had at the restaurant and then at the club. But as badly as I wanted to, I just couldn't. I'd had a buzz, but I hadn't been so far gone that I didn't know what I was doing. I'd never lost control over myself, and from the moment my lips met Carter's on the dance floor, I knew one thing: I wanted him, and I wanted him bad. Although it would have probably happened sooner or later, maybe if Carter and I had not shared that first kiss, things wouldn't have happened so quickly. Maybe instead of Friday night, Saturday night would have been the night. Maybe we would have waited and gotten to know each other more.

Maybe.

But maybe's opportunity had come and gone.

"Girl, you are a freek-a-leak!" Kris said, laughing.

I pulled my hands away from my face. "Shut up. I am not!"

Kris smacked her lips and gave me her palm to look at. "Whatever. You're a freek-a-leak."

"You know what? The door is that way," I said playfully. I couldn't hide my smile even if I wanted to.

Kris started singing. "Freek-a-leak. Freek-a-leak!"

I could only join in her laughter.

"I still can't believe you slept with him, girl!"

I raised my eyebrows. "I can't believe it happened either."

"Looks like I'm going to have to go away more often."

"Why?"

"Because when I'm around, you keep your inner freak hidden."

"Whatever," I said, rising from chair. "I'm getting a refill. You need anything?"

"I'm good," Kris replied.

I stuck out my tongue. "Good, because I wasn't getting you shit." I laughed as Kris smacked my behind just before I walked off. When I came back from inside, Kris was just getting off of her cell phone. "Checking in?"

"Please," Kris said. "More like he was. He just called to see if I needed anything."

"Awww, how sweet."

Kris blushed. "Whatever."

"So anyway, you said you had some news to give me." I sat down in my patio chair beside her.

"That's right. I did, didn't I? Oh well, don't worry about it. It's not that big a deal."

"Tell me anyway."

"Nah. After your news, mine is nothing. Forget about it."

"Come on. I didn't mean to jump ahead of you. I just couldn't help it."

"Sure, sure. I'll give you my news later."

"Just tell me," I demanded. "Wait a minute. You're not pregnant, are you?"

Kris's eyes grew wide. "Hell no! Girl, I got my freak on in Miami, but I wasn't trying to have any babies."

I took a sip of my water and raised my eyebrows, thinking of the condom-less sex I'd had all weekend. "So, what's your big news?"

"It's not that big. Forget it."

"Kris!"

"Okay, okay. But I'm telling you—"

"Kris," I said, adding bass to my voice.

Kris let out an exaggerated sigh, slumped down in her chair, and lowered her Donna Karan shades down over her eyes. "I'm getting married," she said as calmly as the midday breeze around us blew.

I just happened to be sipping some of my water at that particular moment, and after she dropped her bomb, I found myself gagging and spilling water on myself. "What?" I said between gags. "Married?" I coughed some more. "What?" More coughing. "What do you mean you're getting married?"

Still concealed behind her shades, Kris said, "Alex asked me to marry him. I accepted. I told you it was no big deal."

"No big—Girl, were you drunk?"

Kris laughed. "Not on alcohol."

"Are you serious?" I was in shock. My girl, the female who vowed one day that she would always be commitment's sworn enemy, was engaged?

Kris removed her shades, and when she did, I saw tears that had welled in her eyes. "I'm serious," she said with a big smile.

Her tears prompted my own as I got out of my seat and pulled her up out of hers to give her a hug. "I can't believe it! Congratulations. I'm so happy for you!"

We hugged and cried for a little while before parting and wiping our eyes.

"So, what happened to never wanting to be tied down?" I asked, sitting down again.

Kris shrugged. "Girl, I love the man."

"Dayum," I whispered. "I never, ever thought this day was going to come."

"Believe me, neither did I."

"So, how'd he do it? Was he all romantic about it? And where and how big is the ring?"

"The ring is two carats and is being sized right now, and he proposed some thirty thousand feet in the air."

"For real?"

"Yeah. I was sitting there, all into my book, when I heard that fool's voice over the loudspeaker."

My mouth hung open. "No way."

"Oh yes. Right over the loudspeaker he said that he's been in the clouds since we've been together and he never wants to come down. Then he asked me to be his wife."

"Awww," I said, my eyes tearing again. "Did you cry?"

"Cry? Hell no! I cursed him out for embarrassing me like that."

"You didn't!"

"You know I did. Gave him a tap too. Then I accepted. And *then* I cried."

I smiled and wiped my eyes. "Kris, I'm so happy for you. Wow, my girl is about to become a Mrs."

"I know, right?" Kris said, barely believing it herself.

"You tell your parents yet?" I was sure there was going to be some drama there.

"I did."

"And? How bad did they trip when you said you were marrying a black man?"

"Believe it or not, they didn't trip at all. They actually like Alex. Besides, they knew I wasn't going to marry an Asian man."

"Wow." I gave her a playful tap on her arm. "No big deal. Please."

Kris raised her thin eyebrows. "Not compared to your news, freek-a-leak. I still can't believe you had sex with him on the first night. I'm so proud of you."

"Whatever. It wasn't planned. It just sort of happened."

"So, are you going out with him again?"

"Yeah. Tonight. Dinner and then to the movies to see *The Wedding Crashers.*"

"So, this will make four days in a row that you'll be with him?"

"Yeah."

"You're really into him, aren't you?"

I smiled and looked out at the neighboring town-homes. "I don't know how to explain it, but yeah, I am. We just have this connection, this vibe. It's like I've always known him. It's scary how well we seem to fit together. But it's a good kind of scary. I've never felt this with any other man before. Not even Andre."

"I guess you can't be mad at him anymore for messing around then, huh? Because if he hadn't, you'd be making the final preparations before exchanging vows with the wrong man."

"Maybe I should send him a thank you card with a picture of Carter and me." Kris and I burst into a fit of laughter.

"That would be ugly," Kris said. "You should do it."

"I should. Especially after all of the shit he put me through."

"I'll go and get my camera."

We laughed some more and then became quiet for a few seconds.

"Who would have thought?" I said, staring up at the blue sky. "You're getting married."

"And you're in love."

I looked over at her. "Love? I don't know about all that," I said, actually wondering if that were even possible.

"Sam, please . . . Do you want me to go and get a mirror so that you can see the look in your eyes when you talk about him?"

"It's not that serious," I said.

"Oh, yes it is. That brother has you so open, I can smell you from here. And just for the record, let me just say that you are funky."

I gave Kris the finger. She laughed.

Love.

For the rest of the afternoon, although we went back to talking about her wedding and where and when it was going to happen, that word never left my mind.

Love.

Was it possible?

Carter

I was just about to step through my door to head over to Sam's place when my cell phone rang. "Shit," I said, staring at the one number I did and didn't want to see.

Deanna. The bitch with deep pockets.

I thought about not answering it, knowing that if I did, I was probably going to be late picking up Sam. Not only that, but to miss the call meant missing a payday because, as I'd experienced one time, Deanna never called more than once, and no matter how many messages you left her, she never returned a call.

"Shit," I whispered again. I took a look at the clock. I told Sam I'd be at her place by 6:30 so we could make our dinner reservations. She lived twenty minutes away. The most I could spare with Deanna was five minutes. No phone sex for her today. I hit the talk button.

"Hey, Deanna."

"Carter," she purred. "I need you."

I grabbed my Palm Pilot. "I'm open next Monday. You pick the time," I said, my tone all business.

"I need you now, Carter. My pussy needs you."

"You know the rules, Deanna. You have to give me a week's notice."

"I have twenty thousand dollars sitting here for you. I'm horny and stressed. Fuck the rules, and come and fuck me. Hard. I want it to hurt. I want your dick so bad."

I clenched my jaws. Twenty thousand dollars. Two hours tops. Damn.

But I couldn't. Sam was waiting. "Look, Deanna, I already have plans. Can you wait until tomorrow?"

"Fuck your plans, Carter!" Deanna snapped. "My pussy is hungry now. The money is on the nightstand. Come and do your job and collect it. Room 826."

Click.

"Shit!" I tossed my Palm Pilot onto my bed. Twenty Gs. As much as she liked my dick, I knew that if I didn't go, I wasn't going to see that money again, because for Deanna, it was all about control, and the minute she felt she no longer had it, she'd cut ties and move on. "Shit," I said again. I looked over at the clock. I was running a little behind, but I still had time to make it to Sam's.

Twenty thousand dollars.

Laughing at me.

Twenty thousand dollars.

Daring me to turn it down.

Twenty thousand dollars.

"Shit." I cursed with every single name I passed in my cell phone's directory until I got to Sam's name, and I cursed some more when I hit the talk button, dialing her number.

"Hello?"

I didn't say anything right away. Twenty thousand dollars, or dinner with a woman who, in a very short amount of time, was starting to mean everything to me. That's what was going through my mind. Twenty thousand dollars or Sam.

"Carter? Are you there?"

Shit!

"Hey, Sam," I said, my voice filled with disappointment.

"Hey," she said, her tone the exact opposite. "I thought you would have been here by now."

I sighed and clenched my jaws again. "Yeah . . . umm . . . unfortunately, something's come up. I have a client who's in desperate need right now, and because they are my biggest client, I have to cancel our date."

"Oh," Sam said, the lift in her voice dropping.

"Believe me, Sam, the last thing I wanted to do was cancel last minute like this. Hell, the last thing I want to do is cancel period. But unfortunately, I kind of have no choice."

Sam was silent for a few seconds, and that silence only made me hate the decision I'd made even more.

"Okay," she finally said.

"How about tomorrow night? Dinner?"

"Tomorrow's a bad night. We have a lot going on at work, and I'm probably going to be working overtime."

"Why don't you come over after work then? I'll have some dinner waiting for you."

"Although that sounds really tempting, I think I'll have to pass. I'm going to be too exhausted."

"So bring extra clothes with you and you can crash here."

"If I weren't going to be so busy this week, I would. But I know that if I come over there, I won't get any sleep."

I had to smile. She was right. Sleep was the last thing we'd be doing in between my sheets. "So, Friday then?" I asked, hating that I wouldn't see her all week.

"Friday works."

"Okay. Cool. So, I'll see you then."

"Okay."

"I'm really sorry about this," I said, my voice filled with regret.

"That's okay. I understand. You have your priorities. And believe me, that's a quality I like."

"I'll make it up to you on Friday."

"I expect you to."

I smiled. Oh, I would. "I'll see you, Sam."

"Bye, Carter."

I ended the call and cursed again.

Deanna.

Bitch.

Deep-pocketed bitch.

I cursed one more time then headed out the door, determined to give her what she asked for and make her pussy scream.

Sam

"Mmmm. Can you believe we've only been dating officially for three months?"

Carter was lying against me, his back to my chest. We were at his place, in his bathtub, with candles lit all around us and SHAI's CD playing in the background. He let out a pleasant moan as I squeezed water from the body sponge and let it run down his chest.

"It's been a great three months," he said with his eyes closed and a smile on his face. "Feels like it's been longer, actually."

"Yeah," I said with a smile of my own.

It did feel as though we'd been together longer. I could honestly say that for the first time in my life, I was experiencing what I'd heard other people, including Kris, always talk about when they were in love—bliss. Being with Carter was just that. The Will to my Jada, he made me feel whole and complete. Other than my father, no other man had made me feel as regal as Carter did. He took care of me mentally and, of course, physically. The best thing about my relationship with him was that unlike the other men who'd made pit-stops and left behind bad memories, Carter never made me feel as though I had to give up being the independent woman that I am. He allowed me to be me without letting his ego get in the way. That was such a turn-on for me.

With Carter, I was happy, satisfied. It was scary, but my time spent with him was damn near perfect. The only aspect of our relationship that bothered me and actually caused an argument or two, would have to be my feelings over his job. As was evident by the car he drove, the clothes he wore, the places he took me, as well as the spacious three-bedroom condo he owned, his job as a financial consultant paid him very well. Believe me; I had no problem with that. What I did have a problem with was that some of his clients seemed to need him at the worst times. In our three months together, he'd had to cancel more than a few of our dates because a client called him up needing assistance right away. It was a little frustrating at times. The one thing a woman hates is to spend hours primping herself, making sure she looks fine for her man, only to have him cancel at the last minute.

I was okay the first couple of times that happened— maybe the first three times. But by the fourth, fifth and sixth time . . . No one likes to argue early in a relationship, but after those times, I didn't hesitate to voice my displeasure. He hadn't cancelled since.

I squeezed more water onto his chest and kissed the back of his neck, thinking to myself how well we fit together.

And then his cell phone rang.

To my surprise, Carter pushed himself off of me and stood up.

"You're getting that?" I asked, surprised.

"It may be a client calling," he answered, stepping out of the tub.

"At seven o'clock at night?" He was already in his room when I said that.

Twenty minutes passed before I finally got tired of waiting

for him to come back and pulled the stopper to let the water go—just like my mood had gone—down the drain. After showering to wash off the excess dirt and soap, I stepped out of the tub, wrapped a towel around myself and went to his bedroom, ready to let him know how much I didn't appreciate being left alone. I didn't care how bad a client or whoever needed him, this was supposed to be our time, and I was going to tell him just that.

"Cart—" I paused because I couldn't believe what I was seeing. Fully dressed, Carter was sitting at the foot of his bed, slipping on a pair of shoes. "What are you doing? Why are you dressed?"

Carter dropped his chin to his chest, sighed, and then looked up at me with his apology written all over his face. "I'm sorry," he said, his voice subdued. "But a client just called and—"

"And what?"

"And I have to go."

"Carter . . ." I stopped, not even sure how to respond. This was just too unbelievable.

"Baby, this is my top client."

"So? We were just in the tub enjoying a nice, romantic evening. Your client couldn't wait to get help tomorrow?"

"Unfortunately, no he couldn't. He lives all the way on the West Coast, and he's flying back tomorrow."

"And you just have to go help him now? You can't help him over the phone?"

"No, I can't. Look, it's only going to take me about an hour to take care of him. I'll be back before you know it."

"You say that like you expect me to wait on your ass," I said with a nigga-please tone.

"I'll only be gone for an hour, hour and a half tops."

"I don't care how long you'll be gone, Carter. I just can't believe you're actually going to leave."

"I'm sorry," Carter said, standing up. "But I have to go."

"Have to, or want to?"

"What do you mean by that?"

"I mean, asshole, that I bet you're not even really meeting with some client."

"So, who would I be meeting?"

"Don't try to play me for a fool, Carter. What do you have? Some baby momma that you need to go and see? Some girl or wife that you've kept hidden? You may as well tell me the truth now."

"Come on, Sam."

"Come on, Sam, nothing! We were having a nice, romantic evening together."

"I know."

"And yet you're still leaving?"

Carter clenched his fists at his sides. "I have to," he said.

"Go to hell and leave then, you son of a bitch!" I spat furiously.

Carter stepped toward me and tried to take hold of my hand. Of course I wasn't having it, and pulled away.

Carter sighed. "Believe me, Sam, the last thing I want to do is leave."

"Bullshit."

Carter frowned. "It's not bullshit. It's the truth."

"Whatever," I said.

Carter dragged his hand down over his face. "Look, I probably shouldn't ask, but can you be here when I get back?"

I cut my eyes at him. "You're right. You shouldn't have asked."

Carter dropped his head, blew out a slow, heavy breath, then turned and headed out of the room. "I'll call you later?"

"Why don't you lose my number instead?" I said bitterly.

Carter stood unmoving for a few seconds, staring at me, before saying, "I love you."

My response was my middle finger.

Carter frowned again and left. Fifteen minutes and a countless number of curse words later, I was dressed and on my way home. I know I was upset when I said it, but I couldn't help but wonder if I could have been right. Could he have another woman? Having been played for a fool before, I was dead set on finding out if the uneasy feeling in the pit of my stomach was valid.

Carter

"Oh, it hurts, Carter. Hurts so fucking good! Shit. Fuck me harder!"

Pissed, I drove my dick deeper and harder into Deanna, determined to replace the pleasure she was feeling with pain.

"Shit, Carter. Shit!"

Ramming with purpose, with vengeance, I spread her legs wider and fucked Deanna harder with every thrust.

"Ease up a little, Carter," I heard her say. I ignored her, though, and thrust even harder, deeper. I was making her pay for the drama with Sam that she'd caused me when she called and held another twenty thousand dollars over me like a piece of steak, saying that if I didn't come and release her tension, I'd never see money like that again. "Carter, you're hurting me. Stop it!"

"Take it!" I ordered. "You said you wanted it to hurt, so take it."

"Carter!"

I drove my pelvis into hers. She dug her nails into my back. Over the phone, with Sam sitting in the tub, Deanna told me that her pussy needed a pounding.

"I'm in Maryland only until tomorrow. My poor excuse of a husband came to take care of business, but sucks at taking care of business. I have another twenty thousand sitting here for you. Come to the hotel and fuck me."

"We spoke about this before, Deanna. You can't just expect me to come at your beck and call."

"For twenty thousand dollars, I can expect whatever the hell I want, Carter," Deanna said arrogantly.

Twenty thousand. That damn number again.

"I'm busy, Deanna. I can't come right now."

"I don't give a shit how busy you are," Deanna hissed. "I want that dick right now. And, Carter, before you go giving me another excuse, just remember, if you don't show up, you will never see money like this again."

Click.

It had taken all of my willpower to keep my cell phone in my hand and not toss it against the wall, but I had to hold my emotions in check with Sam being in the bathroom down the hall. I stewed for a few minutes, debating about what to do. With every fiber of my being, I didn't want to give in to Deanna. I didn't want to give her the control that she always had to have.

But that damn money. . . . Twenty thousand dollars for an hour's worth of my time was pressing down on my shoulders. Twenty thousand dollars. Let's face it; I'd be a fool to turn it down. But Sam was in the tub, naked and waiting. How could I leave her?

Damn that money. If I didn't leave, I wasn't going to see that money again—at least not at one time. Not like that. Twenty thousand dollars, on the night table, waiting to be in my hands.

Sam was going to be pissed, but this was going to be the last time she would ever have to deal with it, because after the twenty Gs slid into my pocket, I was officially going to retire. Would I miss the easy money? Of course. But I had enough saved up. I could make more another way. Besides, it was time to leave that lifestyle behind and focus on my future with Sam.

I'd actually been giving the career change some thought over the past several weeks. I was smooth with the way I handled my duties while keeping Sam in the dark, but karma was a bitch, and I knew that if I didn't quit while I was ahead, I was gong to get bitten in my ass.

"This is the last time you'll ever have this dick," I said with a thrust. "Don't call me anymore, because I won't come." Another thrust. "Do you understand?"

"Yes," Deanna said, grimacing.

"Good."

I rammed myself into her pussy one more time then pulled out and went into the bathroom. I removed the condom I had on, flushed it down the toilet, turned on the cold water and doused my face and the back of my neck, then looked up at myself in the vanity mirror. I didn't know what she was doing, but if Deanna were calling the police, I wouldn't be surprised. I hadn't meant to lose control the way I had. My emotions had gotten the best of me. Frustration, anger, disappointment, fear; they all blended together and damn near made me a rapist. I dragged my hand down over my face and sighed as I thought about Sam.

I'm not taking your ass back. That was the tone she'd used when she'd told me to go to hell and leave. *I'm not taking your ass back.*

I didn't know what it was going to take, but I had to change her mind. I loved her and I needed her.

I frowned at myself in the mirror then stepped out of the bathroom. Deanna was still on the bed, sitting now, with the sheet pulled around her. She looked up at me as I grabbed my clothes and put them on. Plastered on her face was a look of shock and maybe even mild fear. I can't lie; seeing her there like that actually brought a smile to my face. For once she'd had no control.

After slipping into my shoes, I went over to the night table and grabbed hold of my payment. Twenty thousand dollars. Easiest money I'd ever made. I'd miss it, but I'd miss Sam a hell of a lot more.

Sam

"Come on, Sam. Just give me another chance. Pick up the phone and talk to me, please. I know you're there because I'm now pulling up to your house and I can see your silhouette in the window. And before you say it, yes, I'm stalking you. And you know what? I'll continue to stalk you until you give in. And yes, I said until you give in. Not if. In other words, I'm determined to break you and make you take me back, because I need you, Sam. And this is all new to me, because I've never needed someone before. Pick up, Sam. Please. Fine then . . . I'll just come up to the door and unlike the other times I've come, I'm just going to keep knocking until you open the door."

I tried not to, but I smiled. For the past four days, Carter certainly had been determined as he either called me or stopped by periodically, trying unsuccessfully to get me to talk to him. He'd left me a countless number of apologies on my home, cell, and work voicemails. He'd sent roses and cards. He basically groveled without shame, and while I was still pissed about his leaving me the way he had, I just found his determination to be adorable.

"Come on, Sam," Carter said, doing just as he said he would, knocking incessantly. "Will you just open the door and talk to me?"

"Go away, Carter," I said, moving closer to the door and hoping that I sounded as though I'd really meant what I'd said.

"Come on, Sam—"

"Don't you have a client to go and rescue?" I said sarcastically.

"Sam . . ."

"What do you want, Carter?"

"Open the door and find out,"

"Why should I? So that you can just up and leave me again when a *client* calls?"

"That's not going to happen, Sam. Not anymore."

"So you say."

"I got rid of that client."

"Oh, did you?"

"Yes."

"Why?"

"Because I was tired of being available at his beck and call. Because he almost cost me the woman I love."

"Almost?" I said, loving the sound of his words.

"Sam, open the door. I'm not leaving again. Not because of a client anyway."

I smiled to myself and placed my palm on the door. In a weird sort of way, it almost felt like Carter's palm was at the exact same spot as my own, on the other side. Who knows . . . maybe it was.

Putting him through the wringer had made my week a long and lonely one. In just a matter of a few months, Carter had come into my life and left an imprint that no other man had. I was in love—really in love. But still, and only because my heart demanded it, I had to ask, "Carter, although if there was, you wouldn't really tell me the truth, I need to know—this client wasn't another woman, was it?"

Carter's answer was nothing but silence for a few too-long seconds, and within those passing moments, my heart dropped. But when he finally answered, "There is no other woman, Sam," with strong conviction, my heart leapt and goose bumps rose from my skin.

I opened the door. Carter stood with what looked to be about two dozen roses in his hand. "Hey beautiful," he said with his handsome smile.

"Hey, yourself."

Carter stepped inside, wrapped his free arm around my waist, pulled me close, said, "I missed you," and then pressed his lips against mine. Minutes later, we were making love. I didn't put the roses in a vase until we were finished.

Our relationship was a storybook after that. With each day that went by, our bond grew stronger. While I was helping Kris with her wedding plans, in the back of my mind, I couldn't help but think that someday in the near future, roles would be reversed and she would be helping me.

Carter was my man, my soul mate; my better half, who apologized when he was wrong, and told me when I needed to extend an apology of my own. Because of him, I'd finally spoken to my father after ignoring him for months, and while I still had major issues with him allowing that bitch to—in my opinion—call the shots, at least our conversations stopped ending with me hanging up on him. Well, almost all of them. Talking to him over the phone was the only thing I could bring myself to do since his move to the West Coast. Once or twice a month he'd come back to DC to take care of business, and whenever he did, he'd call me with the hopes of us meeting for lunch or dinner, but I never agreed. The strong father-daughter relationship that we used to have before my mother's death was what he wanted us to have, but because I just couldn't get over his affair and marriage, the twenty minutes once or twice a week was all the time I would give him.

Carter. He'd made that happen. He filled my days with sunshine. He had my heart completely.

He was also the one who would make it impossible for me to trust another man again.

Carter

Two months later . . .

My life is the pits.
I'm unemployed. It's been three days since I've showered. I stink and I don't give a shit. I haven't shaved in almost
two weeks. My place is a wreck. Dirty dishes are overflowing
in the sink. Food is probably spoiling in the refrigerator. The
garbage can has been begging to be relieved of its trash, but
I keep ignoring it. Dirty clothes are scattered in the living
room, the hallway, the bedroom; basically wherever I dis-
carded them. They've long since spilled out of the hamper
in the bedroom.

My Escalade has empty McDonald's and Chik-Fil-A wrap-
pers littered on the floor and seats. Bird shit is splattered all
over it because I haven't been throwing the tarp over it like I
normally do every single day. It needs a wash and wax just
about as badly as I need to bathe and shave.

I'm angry at myself. I'm tired. I'm depressed. I'm frustrated. Worst of all, I'm lonely and heartbroken. Sam was
right. I'm a pathetic, sorry-ass son of a bitch.

None of this was the case two weeks ago. Two weeks ago I was the man—happy, content, clean.

In love.

Life was beautiful, and every day was a sunny-eighty-five-degree-no-humidity-light-breeze-clear-blue-sky-birds-chirping-from-the-trees type of day. Absolute paradise. And then Deanna called and snatched it all away.

"Carter, I need you."

Why I answered my phone that day, I don't know. I let out an irritated breath of air. "I thought I told you not to call me anymore, Deanna."

Deanna sighed. "I know, Carter. I just . . . just . . ." She paused, giving me a second to marvel at how different she sounded. "I just need you, Carter."

"Deanna, I'm not in the business anymore."

After my last appointment with her, I'd contacted my other clients and let them know that my services were no longer going to be available. They were all disappointed, but they understood when I explained my reason for quitting. I was in love, and even though I could have probably continued on without Sam ever finding out what my real occupation was, I'd made the decision, and I was going to stick to it. Those four days without Sam had been more than enough, and I wasn't going to take the chance of being without her again. So why I answered Deanna's call was a question for which I had no answer.

"Carter, please. I need you. Just one more time."

"Deanna—"

"Carter, the last time you fucked me, it hurt. I mean really hurt. I wanted to call the police it hurt so much. But after you left, I lay in the bed and realized something. I realized that for all of the pain I felt, the pleasure was double that. I'd never been fucked like that, Carter. Never been rammed with such force, such anger. I masturbated, thinking about how much you hurt me. I came all over my fingers and cried as I thought about how badly I wanted to be hurt again. It was so good, Carter. So hateful. You hated fucking me.

"Carter, it was amazing. Liberating. There was nothing I could have done to stop you as you damn near raped me. I know you've quit, but I need it again, Carter. I need to be hurt like that again. I need to have absolutely no control."

"Deanna, I told you I'm not in the business anymore." I shook my head. I couldn't believe she had gotten off on the way I'd treated her.

Deanna moaned on the other end and breathed out heavily. She was masturbating. I didn't want to, but I listened. And as much as I tried not to let it happen, blood pumped and I became erect. "Thirty-five thousand dollars," Deanna moaned. "It's yours, Carter. Ooooh. I need to have it. Need to be hurt again." She moaned louder.

Although I wasn't there, I could imagine her body writhing with pleasure as her fingers traveled deep inside of her. I called out her name again, but my voice had been weak. Thirty-five thousand dollars. She wanted to pay me that much. As I listened to her get herself off, I unzipped my pants, took hold of my stiff manhood and began to stroke.

"Thirty-five thousand dollars, Carter," Deanna whispered. "Just come and hurt my pussy again."

I should have stopped. I should have ended the call, but I didn't. Instead, I stood with my cell phone in one hand and the tip of my member in the other, imagining that I was stroking amidst a pile of dead presidents. "Deanna," I whispered, wanting to protest, but saying nothing more.

"Carter," Deanna whispered back, the octave in her voice getting higher. "One . . . time . . ."

"Deanna . . ." I said, my rhythm getting faster.

"Carter . . ." Deanna gasped, her breaths quicker, shorter.

"Deanna . . ." I said, throbbing, nearing the point of release.

"One time, Carter. Thirty-five thousand dollars. I . . . oooh . . . I need it. Oh God, I need it." Deanna let out a squeal as she climaxed. At the same time, I exploded powerfully. Little by little, Deanna's breathing slowed, but her pleading didn't lessen in its intensity. "Please, Carter. I need it."

"I quit, Deanna," I said, squeezing the last bit out of me.

"Thirty-five, Carter. Thirty-five thousand to have your way with me. I'm at the hotel in our room. Please come."

Click.

Thirty-five thousand dollars. The number hung in the air around me as I cleaned myself off.

Thirty-five thousand dollars. One time. Money, more than anything else, had always been a weakness for me. I had enough and always wanted more. Thirty-five thousand dollars, waiting for me, just like Sam.

Thirty-five thousand dollars.

That's all I thought about as I showered, changed, and went to the hotel to collect my pay. I just wish I would have remembered that the bachelorette party that Sam had planned for Kris was going to be that night, at the exact same hotel.

I slumped down into my couch and covered my face with my hands as I thought back to the moment when just before sliding into Deanna, there was a heavy pounding on the door.

"What the—? Are you expecting someone?" I asked, looking down at Deanna.

Her eyes wide, she said, "No."

"Maybe they have the wrong room," I said, but more banging and the sound of my name being screamed let me know that was not the case.

Sam.

At the door, banging.

Sam.

At the door, screaming my name.

Un-fucking-believable.

I looked around the room, my eyes resting on the windows. Had we not been fourteen floors above the ground, I think I would have jumped. Unfortunately, I couldn't fly.

"The door is for you?" Deanna asked, looking at me with confusion and fear.

I sighed and lay on my back beside her, and squeezed my temples. I couldn't believe what was happening.

"Carter!" Sam screamed. "Open this fucking door, you son of a bitch!"

I closed my eyes, wishing that when I opened them, I'd be alone in my bed, just waking from a nightmare. But unfortunately, when I opened them, not only had my nightmare not gone away, my surreal situation only got worse.

"I know that voice."

I looked at Deanna. "What?"

"That voice. I know it."

"What do you mean you know that voice?"

"That's Sam. My stepdaughter."

My mouth fell open. "Your what?"

"My stepdaughter."

"What?" I said again in absolute disbelief.

"I said it's my—"

"I know what the fuck you said!" I snapped. "Oh, shit!" I squeezed my eyes shut tightly and clenched my jaws. "You're the bitch," I said.

"Excuse me?" Deanna asked. "What did you just call me?"

"Shit!" I said again as Sam banged on the door. I looked toward the window again as the room spun around me. Fourteen floors. Too damned far. "You're Sam's stepmother," I said with an incredulous chuckle.

Karma was most certainly a bitch.

"What's she doing here?" Deanna asked.

"She's throwing her friend a bachelorette party," I said, laughing a bit about nothing funny at all.

"Well, go and talk to her, but don't let her inside," Deanna said, dropping her voice to a whisper. "She can't know that I'm in here."

I gave Deanna a look basically saying that she was in-fucking-credible.

She shrugged. "I have more to lose."

I gave her another look.

"Open the damn door, Carter!" Sam yelled, pounding on the door again.

I closed my eyes, kept them closed, and prayed for a way out of my predicament. But without a cape and the ability to fly, or a secret entrance with a pole leading to the basement, I was screwed.

"Carter, I saw you go in there."

I opened my eyes and rose from the bed. My luck had run out.

Karma was a real bitch.

I dressed in slow motion and three minutes later, walked to the door, opened it and faced Samantha Jones. For a few seconds, neither one of us said a word. Quite frankly, I was busted. Words weren't really needed.

Smack.

Right across my face. Both of her hands; two, three, four, five, six times, until I grabbed her wrists and stopped her.

"Sam, please," I said softly.

"Fuck you, Carter! Fuck you!"

"Sam, please," I tried again.

Of course she wasn't trying to hear anything that I had to say.

"Let go of me, you son of a bitch!" she yelled, frantically trying to break free from my grasp.

"Sam! Please just let me explain!" *Or at least try to*, I thought.

"Fuck you, Carter. I don't want any explanations. God! I can't believe it's really you. I saw you walk into the hotel, but I didn't want to believe it was you. I wanted my eyes to have been playing tricks on me, so I followed you up here to this room. I banged on the door and screamed out your name, praying that a stranger would open the door. You son of a bitch!"

"Sam, please!"

"Just let go of my wrists and go back to whatever bitch you have in there."

"Sam . . ."

By this time, people had opened their doors to see what all of the commotion was about. I didn't want to, but I let go of Sam's wrists. The last thing people needed to see was a brother mishandling a woman, even if he was just defending himself. Speaking of which, with her hands now free, Sam laid into me again, only this time her feet joined in the fray as she slapped my face again and kicked my shins.

Because I'd been focusing on the people watching the scene we'd created, Sam's wrath caught me so off guard and off balance that, when I grabbed hold of her, her forward momentum sent us falling into the hotel room.

Perfect.

"Oh my God!"

That was Sam as she looked up to see Deanna, thankfully now half-dressed, standing in the middle of the room. "You? What are you doing here? Is this some sort of joke?"

"Samantha!" Deanna said, hurrying to throw on her blouse. "This . . . this can be explained."

"Explained?" Sam said, rising to her feet. "Carter, this is a joke, right? You're not really sleeping with her, right?"

On my feet now, I sighed. "It's not what you think, Sam."

"Not what I think? What the hell do you know about what I'm thinking? You're in a hotel room with that bitch, who just happens to be struggling to put her clothes on. What the hell could I be thinking, asshole?"

"Samantha," Deanna said, her voice quivering. "Please let us explain. It's not how it seems."

"Not how it seems?" Sam yelled. "Bitch, you're sleeping around on my father with my—" She paused and gave me a vile look. "My ex-boyfriend."

"Sam, please . . . let's just talk about this," Deanna pleaded.

"Fuck you," Sam said, stepping forward and smacking Deanna square across her face. "The only thing we need to talk about is how quickly my father's going to drop your nasty ass when he finds out what you're doing."

"Please, Samantha!" Deanna said with tears welling in her eyes. "Don't tell him. We can work something out!"

"Go to hell, bitch!" Sam spat. "To think that my relationship with my father has been strained because of your ass. Bitch!" Sam hauled off and slapped Deanna again, two times, sending Deanna down to her knees.

And then Sam turned toward me. Instinctively, I backed up a step.

"You fucking coward!" Sam screamed. "You don't even have the balls to stand still and take it like a man."

I put my hands up. "Sam, baby, please. I know this looks bad . . . but just give me a chance to explain." I pointed to Deanna, who was sitting on the edge of the bed now. "*She* means nothing to me. What you're seeing . . . it's not what it looks like."

"Oh, it's not?"

"No!"

"So you weren't here sleeping with her?"

"No! I mean yes! I mean no! Shit!"

"Make up your mind, Carter. You were or you weren't here having sex with her?"

I closed my fists tightly at my sides and clenched my jaws as the frustration of what was going down made my blood boil. I looked from Sam to Deanna. *God damn me*, I thought. All I had to do was ignore the phone call and none of this would be happening.

I looked back to Sam as she stood in front of me with tears beginning to fall from her eyes. I dropped my chin to my chest, as shame and regret consumed me. I'd fucked up in the worst way, and I knew that after this moment, the only thing I would have to hold on to at night would be memories. I took a deep breath and held it for a few long seconds before exhaling slowly.

"I'm a gigolo," I said evenly as my breath escaped.

"What did you just say?" Sam asked in an I-know-you-didn't-just-say-what-I-thought-I-just-heard-you-say tone.

I raised my head and locked my eyes with hers. "I'm a gigolo. Deanna is one of my clients."

"A gig—one of your—" Sam paused, taking in what I'd said. Her eyes were filled with confusion, disbelief and disgust. "You mean you get paid to have sex?"

"Yes," I said in the most defeated tone.

Sam shook her head. "No. No way. You're really a financial consultant. You're just lying, joking, whatever . . . right? I mean . . . you've got to be."

"I'm not, Sam. I wish I was, but I'm not."

"You're . . . you're . . ." Sam paused again as her tears fell harder. "You're a prostitute, a trick?"

"No. I'm a gigolo. There's a difference."

"A diff—Nigga, you sleep with women for money! Oh God! I'm going to be sick."

True to her words, Sam doubled over and vomited right there in the middle of the floor. When she was finished, I went to the bathroom and wet a washcloth to give to her, but when I attempted to hand it to her, she shot me an evil look and snapped. "Stay the fuck away from me, asshole! Don't fucking come near me!" She moved away from where she'd thrown up and looked at her stepmother. "Bitch! How dare you take my father's hard-earned money and throw it away on a fucking whore!"

"Sam," I said, not really knowing what the hell I intended to say.

"Motherfucker, don't you utter one fucking word to me." She wiped her mouth with her top and then furiously wiped her eyes. "I can't believe I fell in love with a whore." She chuckled. "You really know how to pick 'em, Sam. You really know a good man when you see one."

"Sam . . ." I tried.

"So tell me, Carter. Were you planning on making me one of your clients too? I mean was your plan to woo me until I would eventually start throwing money at your feet?"

"Come on, Sam. Don't."

"Don't what? Am I hitting too close to the truth? Is that how he got you, bitch?" she asked, looking at Deanna, who surprisingly said nothing and stared at the ground. "Did he woo you, or were you just a pathetic, desperate bitch to begin with?"

"Fuck you, Samantha," Deanna said, finally speaking.

"Fuck me? Oh no, I think Don Juan here is better equipped to handle that. Just make sure you have enough cash in your purse."

"Sam, can we talk about this, please?" I begged.

She looked at me. "Talk? Why would we do that? Wouldn't

you rather fuck? Oh, wait. I guess we need to work out the financials first, right?" She chuckled then said, "Help people with their money. . . . What a joke," and reached into her pants pocket and pulled out some money. "Here," she said, balling it up and throwing it at me. "I'm not sure how much it is, but it should be enough to render your services. Pig!"

"Please, Sam . . ."

"I hate you, Carter. I hate you for tricking me into ever falling in love with you."

She moved forward to walk past me. I don't know why, but I tried to stop her. All it did was get me a knee in my balls. The last view of Sam that I would ever have was of her back as she left me on the floor, doubled over in pain.

Opting to give her time to cool off, I waited a few days before trying to contact her. Unfortunately for me, when I finally did, I found out that she had not only changed her cell phone number, but she'd also quit her job and moved. I tried my damndest to find her. With Kris regarding me as pubic enemy number one, Deanna not answering my calls, and no forwarding info of any kind, I eventually had no choice but to come to grips with the fact that I'd lost The One.

Like I said before, my life is the pits.

I know eventually I'll break out of the depressed funk I'm in, but for now, all I want to do is sit on my couch unbathed, unshaved, and sing along with Akon's song, Mr. Lonely, which is playing on repeat on my stereo.

So lonely.

I'm so lonely.

I have nobody to call my own.

The Playa Chronicles

A Story by Roy Glenn

Also by Roy Glenn

Is It A Crime
MOB
Drug Related
Payback

Anthology:
Girls From Da Hood
Gigolos Get Lonely Too

1

April

Let me tell you about how it all ended for me. April and I have enjoyed a long and sometimes turbulent relationship. The first time I saw April, she was walking across the yard on her first day at Spellman, and I fell in love with her instantly. April thought I was arrogant, rude and she hated my northeastern accent. Said it was like talking to one of the Kennedys. She couldn't stand me at first, but by the end of fall semester, I had worn her down.

April's from Charlotte, North Carolina, the youngest of Doctor and Doctor Virgil Thompson's six children. She was so fine when I met her, and she still is. She's five-five and slim, but not skinny by any means. April's got what some would consider the perfect 36-24-36 body, with a D-cup. But it was her eyes that drew me to her. Her thick eyebrows and long, seductive eyelashes accent her dark, oval eyes.

I know that over the years, April always assumed I cheated on her, but she never actually caught me with so much as another woman's phone number. But the truth of the matter is that her assumptions were not unfounded. I'd had many sexual encounters with the opposite sex. Some women didn't seem to care if you got somebody. They just wanted a man.

I was honest with each of them about my relationship with April, and I was very blunt about my feelings for her. I loved April. She came first. All they could ever hope to be was second. None seemed to care. So, they'd come and go like women through a revolving door. Each accepted the role gladly and played the part well, until one or the other of us got tired of the situation. Every now and then, a woman would come along thinking she could take me from April, taking a stand, causing controversy and drama. "Me or her?" Trying to force me to choose. But when the smoke cleared, it would always be April, still standing, untouched and unaware of the storm that surrounded her.

I loved April. Sometimes I asked myself why I did it, but I never had a good answer.

I rolled over in bed and reached out, but there was nobody there. I could hear the water running in the shower. I sat up and looked around. "This is the hangover I was expecting." I lay back down and pulled the covers over my head. The sound of running water stopped, and shortly thereafter, the bathroom door opened.

"Good morning," I said from under the covers.

"Ooh! You scared me. I thought you were still 'sleep. Did I wake you up? I tried to be quiet, but I guess there ain't no way to make a shower run quietly. Anyway, how you doin', Rick? And by the way, it's afternoon," Karen said, talking a mile a minute.

"Well, good afternoon then." If it was afternoon, I needed to get out of bed. As much as I hated to, I decided to surface from under the covers. "What time is it, anyway?"

"Quarter to one. Didn't you say you had somewhere to go today? I didn't even think about that when I woke up. I was up for a while before I dragged my ass outta bed and got in the shower. If I had thought about it, I would have woke you up. What time you supposed to be there, anyway?" Karen said as she wandered around the room looking through the assortment of clothes we'd practically torn off one another.

I met Karen the night before at a party Victor and Keisha were throwing. She worked with Keisha and had come to the party with six other women who made me consider asking Keisha for a job. The thought passed quickly. Karen stood five feet six inches tall, pecan tan, and thick. Not fat by any stretch of the imagination. I noticed her watching me while I was talking to Vic and Keisha. After that, whenever I looked around for her, Karen was watching me. All night long, she and her partners were always surrounded by men, circling them like vultures. My opportunity came when she got up to dance. I grabbed Keisha and dragged her out on the floor. I angled my way toward her and explained to Keisha that I was going to leave her the first chance I got. "So don't be mad at me."

When Karen started to sit down, as promised, I left Keisha and went after her. We danced and talked the rest of night. After the party, we went to Hairston's before ending up at my house about four in the morning.

"What are you looking for anyway?" I asked.

"I ain't really lookin' for nothing, I'm thinking about getting back in that bed, but I know I got someplace I gotta be, so I been trying to talk myself out of it." She stopped walking but not talking. Damn, she could talk. "That's why I gotta keep moving, 'cause if I keep standin' here lookin' at you and that tent I see there, I might have to drop this towel and get back in that bed, and I ain't tryin' ta do that. But it ain't like I don't want to, boo, 'cause I'm damn sure thinkin' 'bout droppin' this towel and crawlin' back between them sheets and gettin' some of that dick before I go." She shook her head, started picking up her clothes and laying them out on the bed. "But I gotta go. I tried to wake you up, but you were dead to the world. I'm gonna leave you my number. Call me sometime so we can hang out, but let's go someplace other than Hairston's next time. It was cool since we was both coming this way, but there's too much posing and not enough partying goin' on up in there for my taste." She reached for her bra and I sat up in anticipation of the dropping of the towel.

The towel dropped.

I smiled.

"What you smiling 'bout?"

"Looking at you." She looked good.

"Oh, really." She smiled back. "I guess that means I'll hear from you again, huh?"

"Chances are," I said.

"Chances are? Ain't that a song? Chances are what? Let me find a pen so I can write down my number," Karen said, searching through her purse. Finding a pen, she continued as she wrote her number down on the back of a business card. "I really don't want this to turn out to be just a one night stand. I usually don't do stuff like this. I wanna blame it on being drunk, which I was, but I wasn't that drunk, I knew exactly what I was doin'."

Once she finished dressing, she grabbed her purse. "Get up and walk me to the door, Rick," Karen said, smiling when I got out of bed. "Damn," she said with her eyes focused. "Yeah, you make sure you call me. I don't mean to be pushy, like I'm tryin' to force myself on you or nothing, but tonight wouldn't be too soon. But even if you don't, I had a good time with you last night. You're really a nice guy, so if you don't call me, please don't scandalize my name too bad, okay?"

"I'll call you, Karen."

"Karen! My name is Sharon."

"Sorry. Yes, I'll call you, Sharon."

She kissed me on the cheek. "Don't be callin' my house askin' for no Karen now. The name's on the card. It should be easy for you." She smiled. "You can read, can't you? Anyway, you go and handle your business and hopefully I'll hear from you later or somethin'." She kissed me again, on the lips this time, and left.

"Damn, she can talk."

I walked back to my room, looking at the card she had handed me. I threw the card on the dresser, got back in bed and called Laura at work. Laura's a food and beverage manager at the Peachtree Plaza hotel. "Hospitality, Laura Barnes, how may I help you?"

"Hello, Laura, this is Rick."

"Hi, Rick. I'm sorry about last night. You forgive me?" she asked. I was supposed to go to the party with Laura, but she had to work.

"No problem. You're a very busy woman. I understand that. So, how are you?"

"Running. I had three functions today," Laura explained. "Two at the same time. Then Cathy, one of the other managers, got sick and had to go home, so I have to cover her function in a little while."

"Sounds like you had a hard day."

"You just don't know. So, what are you doing?" Laura asked.

"I'm at home."

"I'll meet you there."

"No, April's gonna meet me here."

"April," Laura said in disgust.

"Yeah, April."

"I guess it's my fault. If I had made it last night, I'd been layin' there next to you right now. No point crying about it. What about tomorrow?"

"Going to a play."

"Don't tell me—with Miss April," she said sarcastically.

I had something that I wanted to say to her, but I wasn't sure whether I should. I decided to go for it. The question had to be answered. Right here, and right now was as good a time as any. "Listen, Laura, I like you. But you . . . That's not fair. Neither one of us have time for the other. Maybe if we did, things might be different."

"You're not trying to kick me to the curb, are you?" Laura asked. "'Cause that's sure what it sounds like. I should be the one kicking you to the curb. But I knew the job was dangerous when I took it."

I thought this was my chance; end it now, before things went any further. I knew that with her work schedule, I would have to spend less time with April to be available when Laura had time to see me. I wasn't willing to do that. I liked Laura, but our relationship was sex and nothing more. On the other hand, me and April had gotten into a real good groove lately. I was spending more and more time with her. We had reached a point where I considered April my best friend. We share everything with each other—well, just about everything.

"No, that's not what I'm saying." I wasn't willing to cut Laura loose either. "All I'm saying is I really like you."

"Well, if you really like me so much, make some time for me. Meet me down here. I'll get a suite. I'll bring a bottle of Moet and we can make love in the hot tub."

"That sounds real nice, but I can't. As much as I want to, I can't."

"I know, you promised little Miss April."

"Exactly, and I'm not gonna dis her. I wouldn't do you like that, tell you I'm gonna spend time with you and dis you for April," I said, even though that's exactly what I'd do. "Anyway, how much longer you gonna be there?"

"I told you I gotta cover this function, so I'm gonna be

here for at least two, maybe three more hours. But you're not gonna call me back."

"You don't know that. I may just surprise you."

"Whatever, Rick," Laura said as she hung up the phone. I laughed and hung up, thinking about dissin' April to be with Laura. I gave thought to the timeline it would take to be with April and still see Laura later in the evening.

"No!" I said out loud. "I'm not gonna start that. If I do, she'll expect it all the time." That would take me down a road I had no wish to be on. But I'd never met anyone quite like Laura. She was a lot like me in many ways.

No, I thought, *April is too important to me to risk our relationship to accommodate Laura.*

2

Donna

It had been a particularly busy day, and I spent the entire day in the office. Around eleven o'clock, I had a free minute, so I called April, but she was away from her desk. I left her a message and I called Victor.

"What's up, playa?"

"Lighten up, Vic. I'm tired of runnin' hoes. I really just wanna kick it with April."

"Hello, who is this? No, I didn't hear a true playa say he was tired of runnin' hoes."

"You heard me, man."

"I gotta stop calling you playa now. But I understand. The game does get old after a while. It did for me, anyway. But I thought you were a die-hard."

"Nah, Vic. I'm gonna get old with April. She's a good girl."

"I know that, playa—excuse me, ex-playa. We were all just wondering how long it was gonna take for you to realize it. I always thought April was too good for the way you treat her."

"Damn, Vic." I knew he was right. I should have realized this a long time ago, but there's something about the game that keeps telling you that you can get her. But what did I have to prove and exactly who was I trying to prove it to? It would be different if I didn't have April and she wasn't so cool about, well, about everything. She was my best friend. I could talk to her about anything and she always understood. Things that I wasn't good at, April was right there picking up my slack. Well if all that was true, what was I doing with Laura? "You didn't have to go there," I said to Vic.

"I know that, man. But, you know, honesty is so liberating. I've wanted to tell you that for a while. I feel like a weight has been lifted from my shoulders." Victor laughed. "So, what you gonna do with Laura?"

"She gotta go."

"Not that I don't believe you, but I'll be interested to see. I know you really dig Laura. Anyway, I gotta go, but why don't you meet me after work for happy hour at the Doubletree on Peachtree Dunwoody."

"Can't do it. I'm supposed to be meeting Laura tonight."

"So I'll see you there, 'cause you know she's lying. Some people steal, some people gotta drink. Laura gotta tell lies. She can't help herself."

"I'll talk to you later." I hung up the phone and got back to work. I skipped lunch for a conference call and ordered Chinese food around 3:00; half eating it between calls. It was 6 o'clock before I realized it. Everyone in the office had gone or was leaving for the day and I still hadn't heard from Laura. *No surprise there,* I thought while I finished my paperwork and called it a night. When I passed the receptionist's desk on the way out, I noticed that there was a message slip in my box. It was from Laura, saying she wouldn't be able to make it tonight.

"She's getting better. At least it was the same day."

I got in my car and decided to meet Victor at the Doubletree. When I got there, Victor was already there and had found a table close to the buffet. As soon as he saw me come through the door, he stood up and started laughing. All I could do was smile and drop my head.

"Okay, so she stood me up."

"Correction, playa. Again. She stood you up again." Victor stuffed another shrimp in his mouth. "She stood your dumb ass up again. I don't know why you bother making plans with her. She'll call you when she wants you."

"Yeah, but this time it was her idea."

"Yeah, but she didn't make it," Victor said as the waitress arrived. "Bring me another Long Island Iced Tea."

"Make it two," I said, getting up to hit the buffet. I got back to the table just as the waitress arrived with the drinks.

Victor and I sat and ate quietly until out of nowhere Vic said, "Me and Keisha been talking about gettin' married."

"Get the fuck outta here!" I said much louder than I should have.

"Well, it's more like Keisha talking and me listening."

"You ready to get married?"

"I don't know, Rick. I really don't know."

"It's not the end of the world. Besides, marriage ain't so bad if you marry the right person."

"How do you know? You've never been married."

"Yes, I have."

"You been married? When? To who?"

"Ten years ago. Her name was Donna. Donna Price. I still get chills every time I say her name, after all this time. It didn't last long."

"Ten years. How old were you then?" Victor asked. I could tell he was shocked. I'd known Victor for a long time, and I'd never mentioned it. Never even told my mother. Didn't want to talk about it, didn't know why I was now. "I was nineteen."

"Young and dumb. How long were y'all married?"

"Seven years on paper. Actually, it was about eight months."

"Rick, I'm serious. I just can't picture you being married. Why'd you get married so young?"

"Thought I was in love. I was more pussy whipped than anything else. Damn, that girl could fuck. She turned me out, Vic, man." Everything I knew about the sex, everything I knew about satisfying a woman in and out of bed, I knew because of Donna. "I moved down here from Boston when I was eighteen years old."

"I know the story. You got here on a Wednesday with two hundred dollars in your pocket and everything you owned fit in your knapsack. Got a room in the West End and had a job working the grill at McDonald's by Monday. Yada, yada, yada. What that got to do with you getting married?"

"Her and her friends used to come by McDonald's. Vic, I'm telling you, Donna was the finest woman I had ever seen. She was the total package. She was beautiful. Pretty smile, with the cutest dimples. She had the kind of eyes that got your attention and looked through you. You know what I'm saying? And a body that makes Tyra Banks look like just another skinny girl from da hood. I caught her eye and smiled at her, and she smiled back a copula times, but I couldn't talk to her 'cause I was always on that grill."

"Can't exactly get your mack on smelling like burgers."

"Yeah, I didn't think she'd wanna be bothered a with a burger boy anyway. She was older than me, and like I said, she was so fine."

"She was that bad, huh?"

"Hell yeah!"

"How old was she?"

"Twenty-two. She lived with her parents a few blocks from me. She didn't really have a job. She just hung out with her girls all day. They used to boost stuff from stores at the mall. One night after work, I'm sitting out in front of the house, drinking a quart of Old E, talking shit with the old heads, still dressed like burger boy, when Donna and her crew walked up. I wanted to run in the house, but I figured why bother? I didn't have no shot at her anyway."

"So, how'd you get her?"

"Well, they start talking shit with the old heads. She had a real sexy voice. So, I sat there quietly, sucking it all up, and after a while she says, 'Hey, why you so quiet over there? I don't trust no real quiet nigga.' "

"What you say, Rick?"

" 'Cause if I was talkin', I couldn't concentrate on lookin' at you."

"Smooth line, Rick."

"Wasn't it? So she says, 'Why you gotta concentrate to look at me?' I said, ' 'Cause you the badest muthafucka I've ever seen, that's why.' Then I stood up, trying to be cool. Drained the quart, nodded my head and walked off. She said, 'Hey, where you going?' I said, 'I'm going to the store, get me another quart.' And I started walking down the street, and she says, 'Hold up, I'll go with you.' "

"You was in there."

"Big time. On the way, she says, 'So, you think I'm fine, huh? Is that why you be staring at me every time I come to the burger stand?' I said, 'Yeah.' I didn't think that she even noticed, much less gave it a second thought. She said she'd been checking me out too. Said I looked kinda cute in burger wear. Picture that. So, we get to the store and she asks me to buy her one too. We get back to the house and her girls are gone. So, we leaned up against a car, talking and drinking and shit. We drained those quarts and went and got two more. On the way back, she asks me if I smoke weed."

"Stupid question."

"Anyway, she says she got a coupla joints. So I said, 'Let's go up to my room.' Next thing I know, I'm tasting all parts of tongue and rubbing tities." Now, I'd gotten some pussy be-

fore I met her, but I swear, I was like a virgin to her. The first
time I fucked her—or should I say the first time she fucked
me?—she put her foot in my chest and kicked me out the
pussy. Told me she didn't know what I was doin', but it wasn't
fuckin'. She was right. I was just poking and stabbing at it.
Donna taught me how to move in rhythm with her. Picture
that. It was Donna that made me understand that there was
more to sex then just busting a nut.

"Take your time, Rick. Get into the actual act," she'd say.
Told me that penetration was fine, but she didn't get off on
just fuckin'. Donna taught me how to do that too; how to use
the flat of my tongue and the tip of it to make a woman feel
different sensations; to pay attention while I was down there;
to listen to her moan and the sound of her breathing; to
open my eyes and look at the expressions on her face. That's
how you know what's working from what's not; feeling her
thighs on my arms and feeling them quiver; the sound of her
toes curling up against the sheets.

"We were married six months later. She was gone eight
months after that."

"What happened?" Victor asked.

"She left me."

"How come?"

"She found out the grass was greener someplace else. We
were living in that little room. She wouldn't work, me working at Mickey Dees. We never had shit. Just fucked all the
time. That wasn't enough for her. She met this nigga who
was ballin', had money and shit, so she left me for him. For a
couple of months after she moved out, she'd still come by
and fuck me. Tell me she loved me, but a girl gonna do what
a girl gonna do."

"Huh. Where have I heard that before? All of them got
that same rap, Rick."

"I know." But it didn't make a difference. Donna was my

first love, and I couldn't keep her. You never get past that. At least I didn't. Never would.

"Don't sweat that shit, Rick. She'd probably kick herself in the ass if she knew how you raised up."

"You're right, she probably would." I used to use her to inspire me. Made me into a hustler. That's the only way a black man can make it. I'm not talking about doing anything illegal, although I'd done that too. I'm talking about being out there taking advantage of opportunities. That's why I used to keep changing jobs, always trying to do better, make more money. I was determined never to let a woman say she wasn't being taken care of. Donna taught me a whole lot more than just how to satisfy a woman sexually. A man has to be the total package to keep a woman. If one thing is lacking, she'll creep on him, every day of the week.

After Donna left me, I spent a lot of time at Mr. George's house. If you wanted it, you could either find it at Mr. George's or find someone there who knew where to find it. He ran a liquor house in the West End. Been doing it for years. Mr. George sold beer, dollar shots of liquor and dime bags of weed. Anytime day or night, there was always something going on at Mr. George's house. It wasn't a big house, just a small shotgun house. Everyone hung out in the living room. There was a long hall which led to the kitchen, bathroom and two small bedrooms. Over the years, he had become the father I never had. I never knew my real father, never even knew his name. When I was growing up and would ask my moms where my daddy at, she'd always say, "You ain't got no daddy. I'm your daddy."

After Donna gave me an education about women, Mr. George educated me about life. He taught me how to hustle. I came to him and said I needed to make some money, mistakenly thinking that if I had some money, Donna would come back to me. Mr. George laughed at me when I told him that.

"Boy, don't you know a young girl like that ain't what a smart nigga like you need? If you wanna make money, fine, I'll show you how to make money, but know the reason you making that money ain't to give it all to some bitch like that," he said.

I was mad that he called Donna a bitch, but I didn't let on.

"You wanna make money to get you a better crib, fine. You wanna make money to buy you a nice ride or some fancy rags, cool. But if you planning on giving it to some bitch, you best get the fuck out my house." He took me in the back room and he put me to work baggin' up nicks. That's how I got over Donna, sitting in that room by myself every night, baggin' it up, thinking about Donna, thinking about the future, making my mind strong, focused.

"Excuse me for a minute, Rick. I think I see somebody I wanna get to know."

"You ain't ready to get married," I said as Victor made his way across the room to the bar, where two attractive young ladies were sitting. After a while, Victor stood up and started waving for me to come over. "I really ain't tryin' to do this," I said and made my to the bar anyway.

"Rick, this is Yvette and this is Beverly. Ladies, this is my friend, Rick. Have a seat, man. Bartender, another Long Island."

"No, man, I'm out," I said, but I could feel Yvette's eyes on me. I could tell she was on me. I turned to get a good look at her, but it was dark.

"Gotta check in, huh?" Yvette said as she looked me up and down.

I considered that to be a challenge. "I don't punch a clock

for anybody. But I do have something to do," I said, trying to stay on task. "Vic, I'll get with you Thursday."

"What's happening on Thursday? I wanna go." Noticing the enthusiasm in her voice, I gave her a second look. Yvette looked away and took a sip of her drink. In the dimly lit bar, I didn't get a good look at her face. All I could tell was that she was dark-skinned with short hair and a bit too much makeup, wearing a red skirt trimmed in black, with a jacket to match. She turned back to me and crossed her legs.

"We're just gonna help a friend move. You look pretty . . . strong. You wanna help us?"

"No," Yvette replied without hesitation. "I'll pass."

"Manual labor ain't your thing, huh?" I handed her my card, more out of instinct than anything else. I really wasn't interested. "Well, give me a call sometime. Maybe we can get together and have lunch. I promise you won't have to lift anything. Nice meeting you, ladies."

3

Yvette

I got into the office at 7:30 Monday morning and spent the entire morning reviewing the last details for the presentation I was going to give later that afternoon. By 11:00, I felt pretty worn out and was about to go outside to get some air when the phone rang. I looked at the display on the phone. It was Patty, the receptionist, calling.

"How are you doing this morning, Patty?"

"Hi, Rick. I'm fine. I have an Yvette Prentiss for you."

Not recalling the name, I asked, "Who is Yvette Prentiss?"

"One of your many women, no doubt," Patty quipped playfully.

Suddenly it hit me. She was the one Victor introduced me to at the Doubletree. I started to tell Patty to take a message. "I'll hang up. Give me a minute or two, then go ahead and put her through, Patty." A little harmless conversation wouldn't hurt. *But that's how it always starts, playa.*

"Okay."

Patty put the call through right away. I smiled and answered. "This is Rick."

"Hello, Rick, this is Yvette Prentiss. I met you at the Doubletree."

Roy Glenn

"I remember. How are you doing?"

"Not bad for a Monday. What about you, working hard?"

"As a matter of fact, I am. I was working on a proposal that I have to present this afternoon. If they accept my proposal, I'll present it to the client in a couple of weeks."

"Oh really?" Yvette said with a hint of excitement and curiosity in her voice. "I was callin' to see if I could take you to lunch today."

"I'd love to, but I can't. I really have a lot to do today, but what about tomorrow?" I said almost out of reflex. I was a little intrigued, but not really all that interested in her.

"Sounds good. What time?"

"Call me tomorrow and we'll see how the day shakes out," I replied, giving myself an opportunity to back out if I changed my mind about seeing her. It was dark when I met her, so I didn't really remember what she looked like.

"Okay then, I'll call you tomorrow. I'm looking forward to seeing you again. Don't work too hard."

"I probably will."

For the rest of the day, I sat at my desk doing my work and thinking about how I would tell Laura it was over between us. It shouldn't be too hard since I'd already laid the foundation. Laura really didn't have time for me anyway. She'd understand . . . No, she wouldn't. She'd think it was about April, which it was.

I picked up the phone and called Laura. As always, I got her voicemail, both at work and at home. I considered taking the easy way out and just leaving her a message that I couldn't see her anymore. But Laura deserved better. After all, her only crime was falling for a man who had someone.

Knowing the kind of person I was, I wondered if I could really be a one-woman man. I was a flirt by nature. I enjoyed talking to women. I preferred the company of women. And all that was fine, as long as I kept my pants on.

I decided a live test was in order, and if she called, Yvette was an excellent subject. I'd have lunch with her and that would be that.

Yvette called the following morning. I made arrangements to meet her for lunch. We planned to meet at 1:30 at Macaroni Grill on Ashford-Dunwoody. I arrived early so I could see her coming.

Yvette got there at 1:30 on the nose and walked straight for me. I looked her up and down as I watched her walk; young girl, maybe twenty-two years old. She was fuckable, but that wasn't why I was here. This was only a test. I would have to keep telling myself that to keep me on task.

She wore a purple suit, buttoned to the neck with no collar. Her short skirt highlighted her big legs. The girl looked good. I stood up to greet her.

"Yvette," I said, offering her a seat.

"How you doin', Rick? I hope you haven't been waiting long."

"Not really. I got here a little early."

"Wanted to see me before I saw you, huh?"

I smiled, knowing that she had busted me. "Something like that."

"I don't blame you. You probably didn't even remember what I looked like. Well, now that you see me, what do you think?"

I started to say, "You're fuckable," but I thought better of it. She wasn't the prettiest woman I'd ever seen, but she was sexy. Very sexy. Her movements were suggestive. That dress fit her, and she wore it well. "You look very nice. That color agrees with you. It highlights your beautiful complexion."

"I ain't too dark for you? I know how y'all light-skinned men get sometimes."

"I ain't light-skinned, I'm brown-skinned." I hated it when people called me light-skinned.

Yvette laughed. "Anyway, y'all want a woman to be skinny as a rail, have long, stringy hair and be damn near white."

"No, Yvette, that's not my type." I paused to contemplate just exactly what my type was. It didn't take long. I compared her to April. "How tall are you?"

"Five-five," Yvette said as the waiter arrived. He introduced himself as Tony and told us he would be our server. We didn't really care. "Who you comparing me to, your woman?"

"Yes," I said, glad that I got to that part early on in the conversation.

"You live with her?"

"No."

"What's her name?"

"April."

"So, how do I rate?"

"I'd say you stacked up pretty nicely." I remembered what Victor said about honesty being so liberating. "I think you wear too much makeup. But other than that, I'd say you rate very highly," I exaggerated, because telling her that April was much prettier than she was somehow seemed a little inappropriate.

By this time, Tony was feeling pretty left out of the conversation. He said that he would give us some time to look at the menu and return. Before he left, I ordered a drink.

"I'll have a Cuervo Margarita. On the rocks, no salt."

"And for the lady?" Tony asked.

"The same," Yvette said, dismissing him with her left hand.

"So what, you work around here, live around here?" I asked.

"No, I work around here. I stay in the swats."

"Where?" I asked.

"Southwest Atlanta."

"Oh," I said feeling a little old, not being up on the latest slang.

"Where do you stay?"

"I live in Decatur."

"I'm out that way all the time. Whereabouts?"

"Off Miller and Covington Highway."

"I know where that is. I got a girlfriend that lives in some apartments out past Panola. I'm out there all the time," Yvette said. She paused a minute. I could tell she was waiting on the casual invitation to stop by sometime. When I didn't offer one, she moved on. "I work down the street at Rivinia. I work for a collector."

"What do you do there?"

"Duh, I'm a collector."

"Have you been here before?" I glanced at the menu.

"Yeah, I come here all the time."

"I always have the Penne Rustica when I come here."

"So do I." Yvette leaned on the table and folded her hands in front of her face. "Maybe it's true," she said, peering over her hands.

"What's that?" I noted her eyes. Very soft eyes.

"Great minds think alike."

"Maybe so." I was starting to dig her. *Pull up, Rick. This is only a test.*

"So, you got a woman, huh? That's too bad."

"Oh, really. Why do you say that?" *Here it comes.*

"'Cause you and I could have done some things."

She set it out. Just like that. Before the drinks even came. Maybe this wasn't such a good idea. I looked at her and the way she was looking at me. She looked good. Now, this was usually the part where I would lay out my program, how we could still do some things as long as she realized what time it was. But that wasn't what I was here for.

"That's a shame. Guess that's my loss."

"Rick, you just don't know."

"So, what's up with you, Yvette? You got a man?"

"No, not really. I mean, I got someone I go out with."

"Sounds like a real man to me."

"Guess you could call him that," Yvette said as Tony returned with our drinks. We informed him of our lunch selection and quickly dismissed him. "Now, what was I saying? Oh yeah. I guess you could call him my man. I mean, he's good to me and all that."

"You mean he spends money on you," I threw in playfully. I might as well have some fun with this.

"Oh, but yes," Yvette responded in kind. "This man don't have no problem spending his money. But he's lacking in very important areas." She smiled. "Let's just say he don't pay me the type of attention I need. Catch my drift?"

"So you creep." It was more of a statement than a question.

"Just keep it on the down low. Nobody is supposed to know."

"I thought it was 'cause he didn't pay you no attention."

Yvette looked at me, kinda cold-like. "Your point is? Look, every woman needs attention. You can define attention in a lot of ways."

"You're a dangerous woman, Yvette."

"You'll never know just how much and in how many ways. But it's all good. I can assure you of that."

"So, you creep because you need attention," I said suggestively, but with a chastising finger, more to stay in character than anything else.

"Don't sound so judgmental. You out here creeping too. If you weren't, you wouldn't be here with me," she said with a finger to emphasize her point.

"I'm here for lunch. I usually get hungry this time of day."

"Come on, Rick. You got *freak* written all over you."

"What makes you say that?" Was I that transparent to her?

"Trade secret. But I knew you were a freak the minute Victor introduced me to you that day, so I know you ain't gonna sit there and tell me you ain't never creeped on your girl."

"No, I ain't gonna say that. But things change." It was more of a hope than a statement.

"See there, you ain't no better than I am. We're probably more alike than you might think."

"Well, so far we do share the same enthusiasm for Penne Rustica."

"Tell me something, Rick."

"What's that?"

"Does it bother you that I'm creeping on my man?"

"No. Why should it bother me? That's between you and your man."

"That ain't what I'm askin' you. Do you think less of me 'cause I creep?"

"It ain't for me to judge you. I'm out here too, remember." We sat in silence while Tony returned with our meal, which he served without a word and faded away.

"You know what I'm saying. If a woman creeps around, y'all think she's a ho or something. But if a man creeps, he's a playa."

"That's because our peer system is different."

"What's that supposed to mean?"

"I mean when you're a man, you get big props if you got a lot of women. Brothers give you dap and call you a playa. Woman got a lot of men . . . uhm, uhm, uhm." I took a deep breath and shook my head to emphasize my point. "Women talk about her bad, call her a ho, call her a slut. Talk about her worse than we ever would."

"Why is that?" Yvette asked.

"You tell me. You're the girlie here."

"See, a woman, well, most women gotta have a reason to cheat, like when your man ain't treating you right, or he's cheating on you. Or he just isn't satisfying you like you need to be satisfied. That's what sends a woman out there. Men send women out there creeping, but y'all will lay down with any old thing that opens her legs."

"I'd like to think we're a bit more selective than that. The problem is there are so many that are willing to open their legs."

"A woman, I mean a real woman could be handling her business, taking good care of her man. He don't care. He'll mess around on her first chance he gets. Why is that?"

" 'Cause women don't care either," I said flatly.

"What you mean we don't care?"

"If I ask you a question, will you answer it honestly?"

"It depends on the question, but yeah, I'll answer you."

"I told you I got somebody." I paused.

"Yeah, and?" Yvette lean forward, pressing me for the question.

"But you're still thinking about it, aren't you?"

"What you talkin' 'bout, Rick?"

"You know what I'm talkin' about. You're thinking about gettin' wit' me, right? I mean, that is why you invited me to lunch."

"I'm here for lunch. I usually get hungry about this time."

"Thought you said you would answer honestly."

"No, I didn't. I said it depends on the question. But yeah, I'm still thinking about it," Yvette said reluctantly. "I been thinking about gettin' wit' you since I saw you."

"See my point now? You don't care. You're more than willing to dis my girl. But you'd be upset if some other woman, or should I say any old thing, did the same thing to you."

"Yes," she said between mouthfuls. I waited until she was finished chewing.

"But you're still out here, trying to get your freak on?" Yvette didn't answer me. She took another mouthful. I couldn't blame her. The food was good.

Yvette rolled her eyes at me, but it was more sexual, than with attitude. She had pretty eyes and she knew it. I had to laugh, because she was a bigger flirt than I was. She knew how to seduce a man with just her eyes. I knew I could get Yvette. I could flip the script right now.

"Yes, I am. Just like you," Yvette said defiantly, like she was taunting me with her sexuality.

"Is that right?" I said in character. I knew where she was going, and I was doing my best not to go there with her. She wasn't making it easy for me.

"So, what you trying to say? That we ain't no better than y'all?" Yvette asked.

"That's exactly what I'm saying. Men only do what women let them do."

Yvette simply stared at me, unsure of what to say. "Maybe I should just call for the check."

"You haven't finished your Penne Rustica. What's your rush?"

"I'm only kidding. You can't get rid of me that easy. So, we aren't any better than y'all, huh? I can't agree with that."

"Why not?"

"Because it ain't like all that."

"You gonna sit there and tell me that women don't want it just as much as we do?"

"More. Especially when you find a man that gives it to you just like you want it, as often as you want it, for as long as you can stand it. Oooh, child, makes you weak for it. Makes you think of it all the time."

"Y'all do the same thing to us. Great sex is hard to come by."

"You have personal knowledge of this or you just taking your boys' word for it?"

"A little, mostly what I read."

"Yeah, right. You're a freak and you know it, Rick. Why you tryin' to play me? Admit it. That's why you're here. You know you want me."

"Maybe I do. Maybe I'm just here for lunch. Actually, Yvette, I don't know why I'm here. Maybe you were right." I flagged down Tony. "Check, please."

I paid the check without another word passing between us. Yvette tried to pay the check, but I wasn't having it. I didn't want her to have any get-back. You know, I-took-you-to-lunch-so-you-owe-me type of thing.

Coming here was a bad idea from the start. Live test my ass. All that could happen here was me getting weak for her and I knew it. The fact of the matter was, I did want her. If I was ever gonna make things work between me and April, I simply couldn't put myself in situations where I knew it could happen.

I got up and walked out of the place, with Yvette close behind. "The least you can do is walk me to my car," she said. I should have ignored her and kept on walking, but I didn't.

"Well, thank you for lunch," Yvette said. "I enjoyed our conversation. Right up until the point where you shut down on me. What was up with that?"

"It was just time for me to go, that's all," I lied.

"Seemed more to me that you were losing control of the situation. Like you was thinkin' about doin' some things."

I didn't answer.

"Well, whatever the case, I enjoyed myself and I know you did too. So, when can we get together again?" Yvette asked, as we arrived at her car. Coincidentally, my car was parked right behind hers.

"I don't think that would be a good idea. At least not right now." I don't know why I had to go and throw that in. I wasn't trying to get with her, and really didn't need her thinking that there was any possibility that I would. Yet there was still a part of me that wanted to get with her. And for what? I was supposed to be laying off, not hiring. She couldn't take April's spot, couldn't even come close. So why? I had to keep telling myself that I had nothing to prove, especially to myself.

Yvette unlocked the car and I opened the door for her.

"Thank you," she said and I started toward my car. "Nice car. I'll see you around, Rick. I'll call you sometime, just in case you change your mind."

"Anything's possible, but I doubt it," I threw out, got in my car and drove away. I was proud of myself, kinda. She set it out and I didn't jump all over it. But I wanted to, and that was the problem.

4

Vanessa

On the way home the next night, I got off the interstate and drove home slowly, trying to clear my head. I hadn't eaten all day and I was starved. I stopped at Kroger to pick up a couple of frozen pizzas and some beer. I walked through the store, picked up what I came for and headed for the register. I got in the so-called express line and waited, thinking what a joke it was calling it express.

Then it happened. The customer at the register pulled out her checkbook and started writing. The lady in line ahead of me had only a box of pre-cooked fried chicken. She let out a sigh. I had been so preoccupied with my own issues that I failed to notice her, which was completely out of character for me, being the accomplished girl-watcher that I am. She was wearing a black dress that she wore well. Hair cut in a sharp fade. She was a nice piece of business, with an ass that could stop traffic.

She looked over her shoulder and rolled her dark eyes at me. She shifted her weight to one leg and let out another deep breath. "This seems to happen to me every time I come here," she said quietly. Her lips were full and extremely sensual.

"I know what you mean. The least she could do is have the check made out."

"Then all she would have to do is fill in the amount," she came back quickly.

"My name is Rick. And you are?"

"Vanessa Howard," she replied with a smile as the cashier scanned her boxed chicken.

"You have a very pretty smile, Vanessa."

"Thank you," Vanessa said, grabbing her bag. "Nice meeting you." And she walked out of the store.

Damn, Rick, is that best you can do? You have a very pretty smile, Vanessa, I scolded myself as the cashier scanned my items. I paid for my stuff quickly and rushed out of the store in an attempt to catch her.

When I got outside, I headed for my car, but the whole time I looked around for her. There was no sign of her. After one last look around, I started for my car. While I was walking, Vanessa pulled up alongside me and rolled down her window.

"Hello again."

"Hey," she replied.

"Check this out. I just bought some frozen pizza and you got some frozen fried chicken. It looks like we're both planning a quiet evening at home in front of the TV. Why don't we go somewhere and have something to eat? Have a drink or whatever."

"Whatever, huh? No, I don't think so. Thanks for the offer, but I really think the quiet evening in front of the TV is what I need tonight," she replied.

"Maybe we can get together some other time."

"Well, give me your number," Vanessa said.

"You got a pen?"

"You don't carry a pen? I thought men always carried a pen. Just in case."

"Just in case, huh?"

"You know, in case they meet someone."

"Yeah well, I usually have a pen, but not necessarily for that reason," I said with a very confident smile. She handed me a pen. I broke out one of my business cards and wrote my cell number on the back. I handed the card back to her.

She looked at it. "This ain't one of your boys' phone numbers or some voicemail number?"

"What you talking 'bout?"

"You aren't married or living with somebody, are you?"

"No, that's my number. No, I'm not married, and I live alone."

"Just checking, I know how tricky men get sometimes."

"No tricks. I'm too old for games. Now, if you'd caught me a few years ago, I might have some game for you. But now, I'm just me."

"So, can I get a rain check on the meal and the drink or whatever?"

"You sure can. All you have to do is call."

"I'll do that. Talk to you soon. Good night, Rick."

"Have a nice, quiet evening," I said as Vanessa drove off. I got back in my car and went home. I drove home thinking about Vanessa. I had just got picked up at the grocery store. She probably wouldn't call.

5

Why, April?

On the way home, April barely said a word. I didn't try too hard to get her to talk to me. I'd known her long enough to know that she would tell me what was on her mind when she was ready. The look on her face dragged me back to my question. Why do I do it?

The thrill of the hunt, the excitement that you only get from the pursuit of a woman. But lately, once they took their clothes off and lay down, the thrill was gone. Once the act was over, I'd lose interest, except with Laura. Somehow, it was different with Laura.

When we got to April's house, she was ready to talk. As soon as we walked through the door, April said, "Rick, you and I need to have a conversation."

"What about?" I asked.

"I think we need to take a break from each other."

"Why, April?"

"Laura," April said, and sat down on the couch.

I sat in the chair across from her. "What about her?" I was so shocked that April knew about her that I didn't even ask how she found out.

"What's going on between the two of you?" April looked

at me. "Never mind, I already know the answer to that. There's no point in you denying it. There really isn't too much you can say to convince me otherwise. I know you. And to be honest with you, I'm tired of playing the role like you got me fooled."

"You're right, there's nothing I can say, so I won't. But I know you ain't nobody's fool, April," I said, trying to do a little damage control.

"I'd convinced myself that as long as it didn't cut into my time, when I wanted to see you, it was cool. But I was a younger girl then. It was cool back then, 'cause we had that kind of understanding. I was going out with other men. Back then, you were struggling, trying to find a direction for yourself, and you didn't have any money to do anything. Remember how we would lay in bed at night and talk about how we were gonna do this and that? And you would tell me all about how it was gonna be once you made it?"

"I remember those days too. Those were good days between us. I know I didn't have much, but I tried my best."

"I know you did. But I still wanted to go places, do things that I knew you couldn't afford. So I did. I did some things that I'm not proud of. Looking back, I can't believe some of the things I did."

"Like what?" I asked, but I really didn't want to know. "Never mind. Even though those were good days, I still remember how it felt sitting there watching you get dressed, knowing that you were going out with another man. But what could I possibly say about it?"

"So, how do you think I felt? That's what sent me out there. You. I'm not saying you made me do it. You didn't make me do anything. But you know, what's good for the goose and all that. And to be honest with you, I never thought that we would still be together after all these years. I never in a million years thought that I would still love you the way I do. And I do love you, Rick. But this has got to stop."

I got out of my chair and went to sit down next to April. "I know you're not gonna believe this, but I been seeing things a lot differently lately. We've been spending a lot more time together and it's been really great. I know that I never want to be without you. I love you, April." I kissed her on the cheek. "But I had convinced myself of basically the same thing that you did. As long as it didn't cut into your time, it was all good. But now I see that it's really not worth it."

"You're just saying that 'cause you got caught."

"No, that's not it at all." I laughed to myself as I thought about something that Mr. George told me once. Mr. George said that until your woman catches you in the pussy and sticks her finger in your ass and says I got you, you ain't caught. You can always deny it. I started to share that little tidbit of playa logic with April, but I knew this wasn't the time.

"I wanted us to start thinking about the future, Rick. Our future, our future together. Not you, me and Laura, or anybody else, for that matter. Just you and me. I wanted to get married one day. I wanted to marry you. But I can't, not like this."

She said it.

Twice.

The M word.

I cringed when she said it the first time, but when she said that she wanted to marry me, somehow it didn't seem as bad.

"I'm not saying that we should run out and get married tomorrow. I know that you're not ready. But all I wanted was for you to show me some respect."

"I do respect you."

"How could you say you respect me? 'Cause you don't parade your women all up in my face? I know Victor knows what you doin', doesn't he?" I didn't answer. "I'll take that as a yes, *playa.* I've heard him call you playa. So, if he knows, I know that Keisha has to know it too. So, how is that respecting me?"

Once again she had me speechless. I hate it when that happens. But all in all, I knew she was right. And so did she. All I could say was, "Okay."

"Okay, what does that mean? Okay?"

"Okay, April. You're right, I've been wrong. But if you give me some time, I'll show you."

"We'll see," April said as she got up and walked toward the front door. She looked back at me. "But I think you should go home. Like I said, I think we need to take a break from each other."

"Don't do this, April. You'll see, I'll change," I pleaded with her, thinking that this couldn't be happening.

"Come back when you've changed and we'll see. But I won't play the fool anymore."

I got up and walked to the door like a beaten man. It felt like I had lost the only thing that was really important to me. And I had.

6

Leaving Laura

"This is Rick."

"I figured I'd find you there."

"How you doing, Laura?"

"Working, baby. But what else is new?" Laura said.

"Tell me about it. I been here every night this week and I'm still not done."

"I'm about to wrap things up here. What about you? How much longer you gonna be there?"

"I don't know, Laura. Another couple of hours, I guess," I replied, even though I was tired and probably wouldn't be there much longer. *Discipline, playa,* I told myself. I had something to prove, not only to April, but to myself.

"That's too bad. I was hoping that we could get together and have a drink. Then we can have this talk you've been wanting to have with me."

"Yeah, well, we do need to talk." I thought about it. Might as well get this over with before I changed my mind. "Where do you want to meet?"

"Why don't you come down here? Meet me at the Sundial in about an hour."

"Okay, Laura, I'll see you in an hour. Don't have me sitting up there waiting for hours. You know how you are."

"Very funny. You just worry about yourself. I got this," Laura said with a bit of an attitude.

"All right now. I'll see you later, Laura." I hung up, knowing full well that it wasn't going to be as simple as that. I finished the projections I was running and headed for the Plaza.

I arrived at the Plaza, parked my car in the garage and took the elevator up to the seventy-third floor. The Sundial was one of my favorite places. The Mose Davis Trio playing and the view of the city was spectacular. The building is round and the floor revolves slowly, so you can see the entire city from there. On a clear night, you can see as far as Stone Mountain. It was also the place that I met Laura.

I was there with this girl named Shelia. Laura was sitting alone at the bar. We made eye contact each time I passed her. Shelia was making her case for me to leave April and "kick it with me full time. I'm getting a little tired of taking a back seat to your girl. I just can't do this any more. I mean, I never had a man to treat me the way the way you do, Rick. Half the time you don't return my calls. Seems like the only time you call me is when you wanna have sex. But that's all you think about. Ain't it, Rick?"

"Sex is not all I think about. It's just all I think about you," I said calmly. I got the line from Victor, who stole it from Prince. I felt funny saying it, since I'm not particular about the Paisley Prince, but the line fit perfectly. Old Shelia, on the other hand, was not the least bit amused. She started trippin'.

Loud.

"You got a lot of fuckin' nerve sayin' some shit like that to me! Who the fuck do you think you are? You ain't all that, muthafucka! Sayin' that shit to me like I'm a piece of meat or something. I ought to slap the shit outta you!"

At that point, I stopped listening.

I knew nothing constructive was coming after that anyway. We made another pass by the bar and Laura. She smiled and shook her head. I smiled back. "And now you got the nerve to be flirting with that bitch at the bar." She stood up and assumed *sistah position:* hand on one hip, finger waving, head rockin'. "You ain't 'bout shit, are you, Rick? You need to take me home. I'll be right back."

When the revolving floor made its way back around to the bar, Laura was standing there waiting. She sat down, introduced herself and handed me her card. "Call me sometime," she said, got up and returned to her seat at the bar. Shortly after that, Shelia came back and I took her home.

Here's the funny part: after all that flip and dip she went through, she invited me in. "Can I get you something to drink?"

"That's cool." And with that, she disappeared. I sat patiently on the couch waiting for what seemed to be a long time just to fix a drink. She came around the corner and she stood before me.

A naked silhouette in the distance.

I smiled.

In her hand was a bottle, the other a glass. She poured and handed me a glass.

"I thought you were mad at me."

"Shhhh," she said. "We're not going to have sex."

"We never do," I replied. "What we have is far beyond what I would call sex."

"Shhhh." Shelia smiled and poured herself another glass. She raised the bottle, a silent offering. I accepted her offer. She filled my glass and looked at the bottle. Noting that it was almost empty, she unbuttoned my shirt and poured the remains on my chest and proceeded to lick and suck it off. I watched in silence as her tongue moved softly across my chest, lingering only at the nipples. I reached for her, but she pushed my hands away. I started to protest.

"Shhhh." A deep, passionate kiss met my objections. The taste of her tongue and champagne was sweet to my lips. She put her glass down and began to run her hands along my body.

Shelia took me by the hand and led me to the bedroom. She politely asked me to take off my clothes and lay spread eagle on the bed. I looked at her strangely, but I still complied with her request. After all, we had taken our sexual encounters to a level that few know of and far fewer live in. Our minds and bodies existed in a sexual utopia, where euphoria is the order of the day.

She sat next to me on the bed and smiled in admiration of my erection, showing her appreciation for its beauty with her hands. Then Shelia proceeded to tie both of my wrists to the bed frame. I started to protest again, but as before, "Shhhh" and a deep, passionate kiss met my objections, and that seemed to satisfy me for a while.

So naturally, I didn't protest when she blindfolded me.

"What about my legs?" I asked innocently.

"Shhhh," she said. "You're going to need them."

The room was now quiet. I called her name. "Shelia!"

It echoed though the house, but went unanswered. It wasn't long before I heard music playing. I called to her again; still no reply. Over the sounds of light jazz, I heard the front door open and close. I was alone, tied semi-spread eagle to the bed, and glad to be there. I did, however, give some thought to the fact that Shelia had cursed me out less than an hour ago.

Suppose she went to get a sharp knife so she could cut my dick off?

I pulled on my bonds to see how tight they were. I was re-lieved when I felt them give.

I wasn't sure how long I had been there or how long I would have to wait for her return and what would happen when she returned. In my mind, I painted a flowing picture of what was to come. My erection faded and returned with each new thought.

I squirmed.

The door opened. I lay still in anticipation. I inhaled deeply and smelled her scent in the room. I called to her, but "Shhhh" and a deep, passionate kiss was the response I received. This time, it was coupled with the feeling of warmth coming from her hands on my body. As I lay on my back enjoying the taste of her tongue darting playfully in and out of my mouth, I thought, *this is it*. Nevertheless, there was something else. Just a feeling, but there was something else.

I heard a noise. The kissing and touching stopped. I called to her, but this time my calls went unanswered. Another noise, and then her scent returned and she resumed her work, kissing me passionately and stroking my erection. The sensation of hands gave way the sensation of her lips, soft and wet, against my chest and then to my now throbbing hard-ness. She straddled my face and I inhaled her scent. Soon my lips and tongue were engaged with her lips and clit, slowly tonguing her lips and sucking lightly on her clit. My excite-ment grew as I relied only on my senses of touch and smell. Each seemed heightened as the sensation of hands gave way to the feeling of soft wetness slowly sliding up and down on my erection. Then she tried to fuck the shit out of me.

When it was all said and done, I said, "I thought you were mad at me."

"I am, and I never want to see you again, but there's no point in passing up good dick."

And they say we ain't shit.

* * *

I got off the elevator and sat down. Not too long after that, a waitress brought me a drink. She told me that Laura said to tell me that she was sorry and that she had to run down to the Underground and wanted me to meet her at Hooter's. *No surprise there,* I thought. I sucked down my drink and left.

On the way down, I thought about just going home. "No, let's get this over with."

It was a cool night with a nice breeze blowing, so I decided to walk. I'm not sure if it was because I wanted to make Laura wait, or because I wanted to give myself a chance to think about what I was about to do. Did I really want to tell Laura it was over? Before tonight, I hadn't heard from her in days. We hadn't seen each other in over a month. The way we were going, things would just fade out slowly. No suspense, no drama.

Fact of the matter was that I really liked Laura. And if that were the case, why was I doing this? The answer was simple. I was doing the right thing.

Right?

I stopped for the light at the corner. I watched the cars go by and went down my list of reasons one more time. I remembered what Shelia told me that last night we were together. She said if it wasn't her, it would just be somebody else. "That's just the type of man you are."

Was she right? Could I stop, just like that? Would I tell Laura it was over and be back at her or some other woman in a couple of months?

Draw the line at flirtation.

Monogamy.

The light changed and I thought about April. Did she really know what was going on? And did it really matter? It wasn't worth losing April. I started walking faster. I knew I was just making excuses, looking for a reason to fail before I ever started. Trying to give myself a reason for backing out. What I had with Laura was sex. It was time to change.

Right?

I ran down the steps to the Underground two at a time, then quickly made my way to Hooter's. I scanned the room. No Laura. "Ain't this a bitch." I looked around for a seat. Maybe she just went to bathroom or something. I took a seat. No sooner had I sat down, a waitress appeared from nowhere. "Your name Rick?" she smiled.

I tried not to notice how good she looked, but it was inescapable. "Yeah."

She set a drink on the table in front of me. "Laura said to tell you she'd be right back," she said and started to walk away.

"Hey!" I called out to her. "What am I drinking?"

"Bahama Mama."

"Thanks." I grabbed the cup and began to stir it up with the straw. I took a long sip of the liquid courage. I began thinking about what I'd say. I would have to be strong and overcome her objections. I was thankful that I was someplace that didn't have a bed. It would make being strong so much easier. I laughed out loud. The ladies at the next table looked at me like I was crazy. I threw them a fake smile and took another big swallow. This stuff was pretty good. I was a Long Island Iced Tea man from way back, but I could get used to this.

Before I realized it, I had finished half of my drink and Laura still hadn't come back. I began to get the feeling that Laura wasn't coming back. Then the waitress returned. "Hey, Laura said to tell you that she had to go to The Hard Rock Cafe."

"You're kidding, right?"

"No, I'm for real. She just called and told me to tell you

that. She wants you come there. She said she'll wait there for you," she said, grinning ear to ear. "You want another drink before you go?"

"No, but thanks." I was pissed, but I tried not to show it. Hard Rock was right across the street from the Plaza. I finished my drink and left. By this time, I knew that she was playing with me. Question is, how long would the game last? How many more places did she intend to run me to? Then came the more important question. Was I going to play the game at all?

I got the feeling that she was leading me back to the Plaza and she was waiting there in a suite. If that was the case, everything changed. I hit the street and made my way back up Peachtree Street. I could see where this was going; bottle of champagne on ice, little finger food prepared by her so-called personal chef, Laura laying there naked.

Every fiber in my being was telling me to forget Hard Rock; she wasn't there anyway. I should get my car and go home. I feared that I wouldn't be able to control the situation if we weren't in a public place. It's always a whole lot easier to turn down pussy when the woman has her clothes on.

I stood outside Hard Rock, trying in vain to walk across the street and go home. But I was weak and I knew it. The whole scenario in the suite appealed to me. I wanted to fuck Laura one last time. I went inside. I didn't bother to look around for Laura. I knew she wasn't there. I took a seat at the bar. I ordered a drink and waited for someone to approach me with new instructions. After a while, I wondered if I had spoiled the plan by sitting at the bar instead of waiting to be seated.

I got up and went to the bathroom. When I came back, there was a room key card and a number written on a napkin lying on the bar next to my drink. I put the key in my pocket and ordered another drink. I don't know why. I didn't need another drink. I just needed time to think about what I was about to do. And besides, the idea of making Laura wait and wonder if I was coming had a particular appeal to me.

I called for the check. I wondered whether I could control my passion, say what I had to say and jet. I could if I wanted to, but I didn't want to. The bartender said the check was already taken care of. When I asked by whom—*like I don't know*—he just smiled and walked away. I finished my drink and left. As I got to the corner, the light changed, like it was giving me one last chance to go home. I knew Laura had been tracking my movements from place to place. By this time, she knew I had the key and would be there soon. If I didn't show now, she'd be mad, but she'd get the hint. The light changed and I headed for the hotel.

I got to the room and let myself in. The room was dim. As expected, she had it laid out. Champagne on ice, tray of shrimp and cocktail sauce, but no Laura. I sat down on the bed. I heard a noise and turned quickly. Laura seemed to appear out of thin air.

"Hello, Rick. I've been expecting you."

"I just bet you have." She was wearing a full-length black silk gown, which left nothing to the imagination. She started walking toward me.

"It is so good to see you. I've missed you so much." She pushed me down on the bed and kissed me. I gently touched her face to end the kiss and sat up.

"Slow down, Laura."

She stood up and went for the champagne. "You want some champagne?"

I stood up. "Yeah, pour me a glass. I'll be right back." I needed to get off that bed and say what I had to say. I went into the bathroom and threw some cold water on my face. I had a good buzz going, and I wanted to have my mind clear for what I was going to say, not to mention to wade through her objections.

When I came out of the bathroom, Laura had made herself comfortable, sitting up on the bed with her legs crossed. I picked up the drink she had poured for me and sat down in a chair.

"What you doing way over there? Take off your clothes and come lay next to me," she said, sipping champagne.

"There something I gotta say."

"Go ahead. You have my undivided attention." She uncrossed her legs.

Wide.

"And you just made it that much harder." I shook my head. Laura smiled.

"What did I do?"

"Never mind. It doesn't matter anyway." This time, it was me who smiled. She knew what she was doing, tempting me, trying to make me weak for her. And it was working. "I've been trying to think of how I could say this. I even had a speech all ready."

"I don't like the way this is going already."

"Laura, I can't see you anymore." I looked at her face, her eyes. Laura looked at me like she could have killed me, or like I had shot her mama. I waited for a response, but Laura continued her cold stare. Finally it came.

"Just like that. Ain't this a bitch? I had a feeling that's what you were going to say." Laura got up. She came over and sat on my lap. She put her arms around my neck. "Why, Rick? What did I do?"

"It's nothing you did. I just can't keep doing this anymore, that's all."

"This is about April, ain't it, Rick? She flex on you or

something? Told you she was going to leave you if you didn't stop seeing me?"

"Laura, I like you. But I love April. I've never made any secret of that."

"I know all of that, Rick. I've heard all that before. What does it have to do with me? What does it have to do with us?" She tried to kiss me, but I stopped her. She got up, pouting like a spoiled child, and lay on the bed.

"It has everything to do with us, Laura. Can't you see that? This isn't fair to either of us."

"That never seemed to matter to you before!" she shouted.

"Well, it matters to me now!" I shouted back.

"Calm down, Rick. No need for all this yelling." Laura sat up in bed and poured another glass of champagne. She drank half of it then refilled the glass, and then she filled mine. "So it's over now, huh? Just like that. It's over because now, all of a sudden, you say it's not fair to either of us. Well, what about me, Rick? What about my feelings? I'm just supposed to say okay and walk away like it never meant anything?"

I wanted to say yes, but I knew better. I was in no mood for her to throw that glass at me. I searched my mind for a better line, but nothing came. "Maybe if things were different, if I wasn't in love with April. Maybe if we had more time for each other, things could have been different." It was the best I could do. Then Laura looked at me.

"I love you, Rick."

Somehow I knew before the night was through, she would say that. Women always come up with the more dramatic lines. What was I supposed to say now? Even if I did love her, I wasn't going to start saying it now. I had no desire to hurt Laura any more than I already had. Saying the "L" word now would only complicate things. "I like you, Laura. You know that. And what's more important is that I respect you. You deserve better than what I have to offer."

"Stop it, Rick, just stop it; trying to make it sound like you're doing this for me. If this was about me, you'd be having this conversation with April."

"You're right. This is about April. It always has been," I said flatly. I stood up and walked toward the door.

"Rick, please don't go. Not like this," she said softly.

"There's nothing else to say."

Before I could make it out the door, I saw Laura grab the champagne out of the bucket. She threw the bottle, but I ducked just before it crashed against the wall. The bucket was next. I ducked that too and got to the door. I saw Laura grab her purse and move toward me. I walked out and quickly closed the door.

I got to the elevator as quickly as I could, hoping that since she didn't have much on, Laura wouldn't come charging down the hall with whatever she was trying to get out of her purse. When the elevator came, I got on and leaned against the wall. I had mixed emotions about what had just happened. I hurt Laura, and I was sorry about that. But at the same time, I felt good. Very good. I did what I had to do and got out of there before we got to the one-more-time-for-old-time's-sake fuck. Maybe there was hope for me yet.

7

She Called Me

It had been almost a month since April decided that we needed to take a break from each other. And I gotta tell you, it sucked. I mean it was like we were but weren't together. We still talked every day, three and four times most days. The problem was she wouldn't see me. Now April was talking about going back to school to finish her masters. Don't get me wrong, I was glad she was finally going to do it. I'd been encouraging her to go for it for years. But now, it would just give her another reason not to see me.

So, I spent my nights sitting in the house alone, waiting for the phone to ring and wishing that April would give me another chance. All of a sudden, the phone rang.

"Hello."

"Hello, Rick. This is Vanessa. We met a couple of weeks ago at Kroger."

"Oh yeah, how you doing?" I asked casually, keeping my enthusiasm in check.

"I'm fine. I guess you thought I wasn't going to call you, didn't you?"

"The thought had occurred to me." She ran me some line about meaning to call but she lost my card and only found it just that minute. I let it pass without comment. I figured she was bored and didn't have anything else to do, so decided to give the new guy a try. I didn't care; she called me.

We talked for a while. Actually, it felt more like an interrogation, with her asking most of the questions, about where I lived and what I did for a living. She was sizing me up, trying to decide whether she wanted to be bothered with me. I knew I'd passed when she asked, "What are you doing tonight?"

"Nothing. What did you have in mind?"

"I was hoping I could cash in my raincheck. You could meet me somewhere, get something to eat, have a drink or whatever. Have you eaten yet?"

"No. Actually, I was just thinking about going to get something to eat anyway." I lied, hoping that she didn't want to go someplace and have a big meal. I grabbed a couple of burgers on the way home, but I could choke down some finger food over drinks and conversation. "So, that's cool. Where do you want to meet?"

"Tell you what; why don't you come pick me up in about an hour?" Vanessa asked and gave me her address.

"Sounds good." I looked at my watch. "I'll see you there." I hung up the phone and headed for the shower, thinking about what the evening would be like.

When I got to Vanessa's house, she was standing outside. "I hope I didn't take too long."

"Not at all, Rick. You are right on time," Vanessa said and got in the car.

Once we pulled off, I asked, "So, what do you have a taste for?"

"You know what? I'm not really all that hungry right now. But it's such a nice night, why don't we just ride? Maybe we'll get something to eat later."

"That's cool." So, we simply drove around, talked and got to know one another. When we passed a liquor store, we picked of a fifth of Alize and continued our trip to nowhere.

"Hey, hey, turn here."

I complied with her request and turned on LaVista Road. I didn't ask why, because I didn't care. That's just the way it was. I'd do anything she said at this point. Go anywhere, talk about anything, 'cause I saw the light at the end of the tunnel. As we passed the Fairfield Inn, Vanessa said, "Pull over here."

"Yes," I said softly. I turned into the parking lot and parked in front of the office.

"Why don't you go get us a room, handsome?"

"I'll be right back." I quickly got out of the car and went inside to handle my assigned task. Even though we could be at my house in fifteen minutes, I thought it best to preserve the spontaneous mood of the evening. Besides, I didn't want her to think I was cheap.

Once we got to the room, I tried to kiss her right away.

"Slow down, handsome. We got plenty of time for all that. Why don't you go get some ice so we can have a drink?"

I composed myself. It wasn't easy.

I grabbed the bucket and went for the ice. I left the room playing out several scenarios of how things would play out. On the way back, my enthusiasm waned. I stopped dead in my tracks. "I sure hope she got some skills. There's nothing worse than getting all excited about the act and having to lay around, rock hard, waiting to see if she can finish the job. And I sure hope she's not a nibbler. Ain't nothing in the world worse than a nibbler."

When I got back to the room, the lights were out. The room was lit only by the television, with no sound. The radio was tuned to the Quiet Storm on V103 and the shower was running. I casually fixed the drinks in the motel-issued plastic cups and got undressed. Then I grabbed the cups and went into the bathroom.

I pulled back the shower curtain and joined her. She was a little caught off guard by my sudden appearance. I handed the cup to her and we stood there sipping Alize and looking each other up and down. I didn't know about her, but I was thoroughly impressed with what was standing before me. And my impression was obvious.

"Hmm," she said, "I hope you taste as good as you look." She stepped away from the water and proceeded to pour Alize across my chest. It quickly dripped down to my impression. She ran her tongue across my nipples and worked her way down.

Showtime, I thought. Time to see if she was a nibbler. She bent her knees slightly, caressing my hardness with both hands. She began to kiss the head.

"Damn, another nibbler," I mumbled.

And then she proceeded to take it all in. I was in ecstasy. I grabbed the curtain rod to steady myself. There was no more question; this woman definitely had skills. Right then and there, I knew I was through.

After what seemed like an eternity, we got out of the shower. We slowly dried off one another, each of us exploring the other's body with the towel, our hands and our eyes. Maybe it was her, maybe it was the Alize, I don't know, but it seemed as though her touch made my head spin. I felt a rush of warmth when she kissed me, like it was all happening in slow motion. I felt myself losing control of the situation, so I pulled away.

"You wouldn't happen to have any baby oil, would you?" I asked.

"No. I don't usually carry baby oil around with me. But I do have some lotion," Vanessa said, walking toward her purse. She dug around and pulled out a small bottle. She held it out in front of her as she walked slowly toward me.

"Why, you wanna put some on me?"

I took the bottle from her and she sat on the edge of the bed. I kneeled down on the floor and poured a little lotion on her legs. I rubbed the lotion in slowly then began massaging her calves and did the same to her thighs, exploring with my tongue, until I felt her body shake. Now she knew I had skills too.

I sat next to her on the bed, applying lotion to her arms and chest. Vanessa took the bottle from me. "Lay down on your back. Let me do you," she said.

I smiled my reply, and again, quickly complied with her wishes. Vanessa knelt on the bed next to me. She poured the lotion into her hands and rubbed them together. She began to massage my thigh gently. She straddled my torso as I looked on with great anticipation. She slid down on me. I exhaled. She moved slowly, up and down, then in circles.

She reached for the lotion and poured it across my chest and began to rub it in with her fingertips. Once she had covered my chest, she leaned forward and kissed me. She moved from side to side, rubbing her chest across mine in beat with the music. The sensation I felt when her nipples rubbed against mine was indescribable.

I ran my hands down her back and across her cheeks as she started to move her hips faster. Then Vanessa sat up and went to work. After a while, she stopped and moved her legs so her feet were on the bed. Then she proceeded to fuck the shit out of me. I felt my head turning from side to side.

She gave me a look I had seen many times but never experienced. It was on.

It went on in that manner for hours. We'd stop from time to time to catch our breath, have a drink and talk some shit.

A couple of times we just stopped and sat there, breathing hard, staring at each other and shaking our heads. After a short nap, Vanessa got up and began to get dressed.

"Get up, Rick. I gotta go."

I looked at the clock: 3:45 AM. I shrugged my shoulders and got up thinking, *no, she ain't married.*

I got dressed and we left the room. As we drove in silence, I looked over at her and shook my head. *Married or not, I got to see her again. She fucked the shit out of me,* was all I could think.

She caught me looking and said, "I'm gonna tell you something and I don't want it to scare you, okay? But I love you," she said and returned to her silence with a smile on her face. I looked away and smiled to myself. She slayed me; now I knew I slayed her too.

We arrived at her spot. As soon as I put the car in park, Vanessa leaned over and kissed me on the cheek. "Good night, Rick. I had a good time tonight." She kissed me on the cheek again and practically jumped out of the car.

"Vanessa," I said and she stuck her head back in the car. "Can I see you again?"

"I'll call you." Then Vanessa closed the car door and walked quickly toward the house.

8

April and Yvette

I hadn't heard from Laura since that night at the hotel. She did send me an e-mail saying that she understood and wished me all the best. Even that pain in the ass Yvette had stopped calling me. I guess I was partly to blame for her persistence. I liked talking to her, so I always took her calls. But she was starting to get on my nerves. "When we gonna get together? When we gonna get together?" How many times do I have to say no? It's not like that. There are some women that you're glad you didn't mess with, and Yvette was definitely one of those people.

Around 3:00, I turned off my computer and headed for home. April had finally agreed to see me. She was supposed meet me at the house around 4:30 and we'd go eat from there.

When I got home, I turned the radio to smooth jazz and went through my mail. I was about to get in the shower and had just started taking off my clothes when the doorbell rang. I looked at the clock on the cable box.

Three forty-five. She's early, I thought, assuming it was April as I opened the door.

"Um."

I was wrong.

"If I had known that you answered the door in your underwear, I would have dropped by a lot sooner." It was Yvette, standing there smiling from ear to ear, looking me up and down like I was an ice cream sundae. She was dressed in black heels, black tights and a man's white shirt that didn't quite make it down past her hips.

"Yvette, what are you doing here? I don't remember inviting you. Or telling you where I lived."

"I got spies everywhere, boo."

Victor. I thought, but didn't say anything.

"Anyway, I was out this way. You remember me saying I had a girlfriend that lived in The Thicket. Can I come in?"

Thinking with my dick, I stepped aside and allowed her to come inside. My first mistake. She rubbed her hip against me as she passed, walked around the house, looking around. She stopped to study the stereo, picked up a CD and looked at it. Then she changed the station to HOT107.9 and continued to walk around my living room.

"Well, I was supposed to be hanging out with her today, but she wasn't home, so I decided to roll around here and see if I could find your house. You know, just to kill some time. I never expected to find it."

"Lucky you," I said, reaching for my pants. I had to laugh at myself. There was a time when a set-up like this would be a welcome addition to an afternoon. I would have said something provocative like, "I was just on my way to the shower. You wanna join me?" Crude, yes, but extremely effective. But now, I was reaching for my pants, getting ready to ask her to leave, and mad at Victor for telling her where I lived.

My, how the mighty have fallen.

"Don't put your pants on because of me, boo. I like a man in briefs, and you have nice legs," she said, staring directly at my crotch, which, by the way, had looked up and had taken notice of her presence.

"Yeah, well, I was about to get in the shower."

"Don't let me stop you. Mind if I watch?" she said quickly and unbuttoned the top button on her shirt.

"Yes, as a matter of fact, I do," I said, laughing at myself again. "Like I said, I was about to get in the shower because I'm going out with April tonight. She'll be here soon." I zipped up my pants and started walking toward the door.

"Oh, I'm sorry. I shouldn't have just come over here like this."

"Well, let's not let it happen again, Yvette," I said jokingly, but I was serious. "I hate unannounced, uninvited guests at my door. We're cool and we can socialize, but dropping by, definitely a no-no."

Yvette started making her way slowly toward the door, hand on her left hip, right hand waving through the air as she continued to walk and beguile me with her overwhelming sexuality.

If I chose to be honest with myself, and I usually didn't at times like this, I wanted to fuck her and I wanted to fuck her now. I had to keep telling myself that whatever she had, it couldn't compete with April. And the more I thought about it, she couldn't. It wasn't just something I had to convince myself of. It was a fact. And the fact of the matter was that April had it going on. Yvette, on the other hand, was just entertainment to me. I know how it sounds and I hate to say it, but she was. When I was at work and I needed a break to clear my mind, or just a change of pace, I'd call Yvette and bullshit with her for a while. The girl was just plain foolish. She'd say anything. She was funnier than the ton of e-mail jokes I got from co-workers and friends, but beyond that, nada; although I was willing to bet she could fuck. In spite of that, I was leading her on. I knew what she was about and I wasn't interested. So, it was my fault that she was standing here now. I shouldn't have let it get to this point.

"But you and I need to get together and do some things real soon. I don't know why you keep playing this game like you don't want me. I can see it in your eyes. You know you want me," Yvette said as the phone rang.

I looked at the display. It was Laura calling from home, on a Saturday, no less—proof that things do change. If a workaholic like Laura could take a Saturday off, then a ho like me could change too. I excused myself to Yvette and answered the phone.

"Hello, stranger."

"Hmm, I should be saying that to you. You're the one who's acting like a stranger. The least you can do is call me sometimes, say hello, how you doing, something. There's no reason for you to just cut me off just because you're trying to work things out with little Miss April. Just 'cause we've stopped being lovers doesn't mean that we can't be friends," Laura said as Yvette angled her way closer to me.

At first, I thought she was going to try to cop a quick feel. When I realized she was looking at Laura's name and number on the display, I stepped in front of her and turned to block her view. "You're right, Laura, and I am sorry about that. I can call you sometime, but, can I call you back? I was just seeing somebody out, and then I'm going out with April."

"You got some other bitch up in there already, don't you?"

"Yeah, I guess you could say that."

"No you didn't kick me to curb for some other bitch."

"No, it ain't nothing like that, but I'll tell you about that when we talk. Okay?"

"Okay, but I'm serious, Rick. Call me sometime."

"I will. I promise."

"Rick."

"Yes, Laura."

"I miss you."

And then she hung up without waiting for me to reply, saving me that uncomfortable moment with nothing to say. I did kinda miss Laura, but it would pass. I turned my attention back to Yvette, who had assumed *sistah position*, hands on her hips, head tipped to the side.

"Who was that? Your other bitch?"

"That's what she said when she asked about you." Amazing how they could call each other bitch and ho and this and that, and it wasn't no issue. But let a man say it, and a woman will lose her goddamn mind. "She's a friend of mine, just like you're a friend of mine."

"Yeah, uh-huh, sure. Friend, huh? Only she got your home number and I don't," Yvette said, nodding her head with her lips poked out. "But I ain't mad at you."

"That's nice, 'cause I ain't mad at you either. But this unannounced, uninvited thing, definitely a no-no."

"That's all good too, boo. And I'm so glad that you ain't mad at me," she said sarcastically.

I resumed my escort run to the door.

"I'm gonna go on and go before your girl gets here, but I'm serious. You need to get with me sometime."

Walking behind Yvette, scrutinizing every movement of her hips, I had to agree with her. I did want her. She looked back and saw me watching. She smiled and began to throw it harder than she normally did. There was a time not too long ago that I would have checked the time, worked out all the logistics, and boned her, even with April on her way. But not today. Man, it wasn't easy, but not today.

"Good-bye, Yvette."

"Good-bye, Rick."

I closed the door behind her and headed for the bathroom. I stopped to change the radio station back to jazz. It's not that I don't like rap, but I wasn't feeling like all that.

I glanced out the window to see if Yvette was gone. I felt a cold chill come over me as I watched April pull into the driveway, blocking Yvette in.

April got out of car and walked toward Yvette. I fought the urge to run out there, looking on in horror.

Whatever Yvette was saying, April seemed to be taking it well. Yvette must have said something funny, 'cause April was laughing like it was the funniest thing she ever heard.

Yvette turned away and April went back to her car and let Yvette out. Realizing that I had no shirt on, I scrambled to put it on before April unlocked the door and walked in.

"Hey, baby, you ready to go?"

"Not yet. I was about to get in the shower when Yvette showed up."

"Who? Who's Yvette?"

"The woman you were just talking to outside."

"Hold up. Something ain't right here. She knew my name and she seemed to know exactly who I was, then she told me her name was Marie and that she came to pick something up for Victor. Now you're telling me that her name is Yvette. So, whose friend is she, Rick?"

"She does know Victor, but she's my friend."

"She made it seem like she was with Victor. Why she lie?" April sat down. "You need to tell me something more than that. Who is she?"

"I was out with Vic one night and he had pushed up on her friend and he introduced me to her. But I ain't interested in her."

"Well, if you ain't interested in her, what was she doing here and why'd she think she had to lie to me like that? If you ain't interested in her, how'd she know where you lived?"

"Victor told her."

"Oh yeah, right. Victor told her. You can do better than that, Rick. Why would Victor tell her where you lived?"

"I don't know why Victor told her. I didn't invite her. She just showed up." She didn't believe a word I was saying, and the worst part of it was, I was telling the truth. I got caught with another woman after all this time, and I could honestly say there was nothing going on, and she didn't believe me. But I was innocent this time, and I had to convince her.

"Victor knows." I looked at April and picked up the phone. "Pick up the phone in the kitchen."

April got up and went in the kitchen. She picked up the phone. "Who you callin'?"

"Victor. Don't say nothing, just listen."

The phone rang and rang. Maybe he wasn't home. I needed Victor to answer the phone. He finally answered on the fifth ring.

"Hello."

"What's up, Vic?"

"Oh, what's up, playa? Oh, I'm sorry, I mean ex-playa."

"Vic, why did you tell Yvette where I lived?"

"I thought about that as soon as I said it. Hey, man, she tricked me."

"When did all this trickin' happen?"

"Last night. I met her and Beverly. I was tryin' to get you to go. Didn't you get my message?"

"Yeah, Vic, I got it. Didn't you get mine?"

"No, I left work early yesterday."

"You got a three-way?"

"Yeah, why?"

"Check your messages."

"Huh?"

"Check your messages, Victor."

"Why?"

"Just do it, Vic."

"Damn! Hold on, playa."

When Victor put us on hold, April came out of the kitchen. "You don't have to do this. I believe you."

"Yes, I do. You weren't believin' a word I was sayin' a minute ago. You just keep listening." Victor came back on the line. Audix told him that he had two messages. The first message was from Beverly.

Victor, Yvette's here wearing me out. I hope you told Rick to come so she could leave me alone. I'll see you tonight. Bye.

April stood in the doorway to the kitchen, looking dead at me. It couldn't have worked out any better if I had planned it. The next message was mine.

Vic, this is Rick. I got your message about tonight, but I ain't gonna make it. I ain't trying to be about all that with Yvette, or anybody else for that matter. Hope I ain't messing up your night. Holla at me.

"I'm sorry, playa," Victor said.

"How'd she trick you?"

"I met them for happy hour last night. I was glad you didn't show. It just gave me a reason to jet that much earlier. Anyway, Yvette told me she was supposed to be hanging out with some girl that lives near you and she might stop by your house."

"So you told her where I lived?"

"No, Rick, chill out. I didn't believe you told her where you lived, and I told her that. She said she'd been there before. Then she starts callin' out street names: Covington, and Miller and whatnot. Then she says, 'What's the name of the street he lives on? You know, Victor, it's got kind of a funny name.' And I just blurted it out. Why? Did she come by there?"

"Yeah, she just left."

"Ooops, wasn't no drama, was it?"

"Oh no, she just met April in the driveway," I said calmly.

"Oh shit. What happened?"

"She told April that you sent her here."

"I didn't send that knucklehead over there, Rick. I swear, she's lying."

"I know she lied, Vic. I ain't mad at you."

"'Cause you know I wouldn't do no dumb shit like that. Is April mad?"

"I don't know. April, are you mad?"

"April's there?"

"No, Rick, I'm not mad. Hi, Victor."

"Oh shit. Hey, April. You been on the phone the whole time?"

"Yes, Victor. I heard everything."

"And?" I asked.

"I believe you."

"So, y'all just used me," Victor said. "Is that what just happened here?"

"Yes, Victor, we used you." April said.

"Thanks, Vic. I'll get with you."

"Now you're through with me, huh? I just want you to know I don't appreciate being used like this. But it's cool. I'll holla at you. You have a good day, April."

"Bye, Victor." April hung up the phone and came out of the kitchen.

"So, you believe me now?"

"I believe that's what happened, but that don't end it. I just have a problem believing that some woman you met once, five months ago, would just show up here and think that she had to lie to me. There must be more to it than that."

"She's just aggressive like that."

"Bullshit. Try again. No, let me put it to you like this: you tell me what you did to make her just come by here and why she had to lie to me."

"Okay, I did go out to lunch with her once. But today was the first time I've seen her since then. We have talked a few times on the phone since then, but that's it."

"So, if that's all there was to it, why did she feel like she had to lie to me?"

"'Cause she knows who you are. I talk about you all the time."

"You're not understanding me, Rick. Even if she knew who I was, why did she lie to me? I can't get past that."

"I guess she thinks she has a chance."

"Now we're getting somewhere. So, what did you do to make her feel like she has a chance of getting with you?"

"April, I swear I ain't doing nothing to encourage that girl."

"What are you doing to discourage her?"

"Huh?"

"Don't *huh* me. Did you tell her that you weren't interested in her?"

"Not exactly."

"Did you tell her that it would be easier to take the cold from snow than to make you cheat on me?"

"Not exactly."

"You see what I'm saying? If you're not doing anything to discourage her, you aren't doing anything but making her think that she can get with you."

I knew she was right, so I decided to say it out loud. "You're right, April."

"I know I'm right. I see what kind of person she is. She talks shit and she's funny as hell. I'm for real. She had me crackin' up out there. And I know you like that about her. But, Rick, you're a flirt. You were a flirt when I met you, and that hasn't changed the whole time we've been together. I accept that about you. What you have to learn, *playa*, is that you can't flirt with everybody."

"You're right, April. I messed up."

"Yeah, you did. Okay, so this time it worked out. But you see the trouble this could have caused?"

"I sure do."

"Suppose Victor wasn't home? Suppose he deleted those messages? We'd be going for it right now, and nothing you could have said would have convinced me that you hadn't just gotten through having sex with her and y'all just got caught."

"And you would have been wrong."

"But all that wouldn't have been necessary. 'Cause it wouldn't have happened if you didn't allow it. Work with me, Rick. That's all I'm saying. I know that you're an attractive man and women are gonna push up on you. But don't put yourself in these positions. Ask yourself if flirting is worth risking us trying to re-build our relationship."

My answer would always be no, so I said it out loud. "My answer would always be no. I love you." But the damage was done. April told me that I wasn't ready and went home. I stood in the driveway and watched her drive away, knowing that I just did more damage to our relationship; damage that maybe I couldn't fix.

This shit sucks!

9

Vanessa's Sex

Vanessa was workin' me. There was nothing else I could say about it. The girl was insatiable. She'd call me just about every day and at all hours of the night.

"I'm coming over."

Always a statement, never a question. But I didn't care, because sex with her was incredible and we were going for it into the early hours of the morning. There were plenty of days when I was surprised that I could stay focused at work because some nights I didn't sleep. Days like this one.

My feet began to hurt, so I sat down on the curb. If there was one thing I hated, it was waiting. I hated missing the beginning of a movie. If I've already missed the beginning, I'd rather not see it, and it was getting dangerously close to that time. I looked at my watch: 8:05. The new Denzel Washington movie was going to start in five minutes, and there was still no sign of Vanessa.

I'd already checked my voicemail. There was no message from her saying she'd be late or wasn't coming. I'd even called myself to be sure it was working. Slowly but ever so surely, I was coming to the conclusion that she wasn't gonna show up at all. And the thought of it pissed me off. Getting stood up was something I'd gotten used to dealing with Laura. I've never done anybody like that. I think that it was just flat out rude to have someone waiting for nothing.

At 8:10, I had a decision to make. I had already paid for the tickets and saw no reason why I should miss the movie because she couldn't tell time. Eight-ten came and left and there I was, still sitting. By a quarter to nine, I declared Vanessa a no-show and stood up. I ripped the tickets in half and started walking toward the car.

I saw a car that looked like hers coming toward me. I ran back and picked up what was left of the tickets, then the car drove past me. It wasn't her. I ripped the pieces again and threw them in the air this time. On the way to the car, I decided that I wanted a drink, but I didn't feel like being bothered with anybody, so I walked to the liquor store in the plaza.

When I walked into the store, the lady behind the counter was busy talking on a cordless phone. She acknowledged me with her eyes.

"Pint of Stoli. No, make it a fifth." I gave her my money and the lady handed me the bottle without a word. "You're the second woman tonight to show me no respect," I said to deaf ears as I walked out. I cracked the bottle on the way back to the car, "No point waiting," and turned up the bottle.

As I drove home, I felt stupid, sitting there all that time, waiting, watching people go in to enjoy the movie I'd been talking about seeing for weeks. She knew how much I wanted to see it. The least she could have done was call and say she couldn't make it. That was the least she could have done. I took another swallow. "No! The least she could have done was show up!" I shouted.

When I got to the house, it was about 9:30, and I was feeling pretty good for somebody who just got stood up. I turned on the television in the living room and checked for messages.

"You have no new messages in your mailbox."

I decided not to be bothered with getting a glass, and continued my assault on the bottle. A third of the way through the bottle, I decided to move to the bedroom. It wasn't too long after I lay down on the bed that I felt a good, drunken sleep coming over me. I didn't try to fight it.

The phone rang. I reached to answer it. "Hello."

"Hi, Rick, are you in the bed?" a female whispered.

I couldn't quite make out the voice, and I really didn't care. "Yes."

"Can I come get in the bed with you?"

"Who is this?"

"It's Vanessa."

I knew then that the answer to her question was yes, but I had to bitch and moan for a while just to keep up appearances. I didn't want her to think that standing me up was cool. "Vanessa, what happened to you tonight?"

"Something came up. Sorry I didn't call, but it couldn't be helped."

"Okay, so something came up. You were too busy to at least call me and say 'hey, I'm not gonna make it, okay, bye.' You were that busy?"

"Yes, like I said, it couldn't be helped," she said boldly, which only increased my level of anger. "Did you see the movie?"

"No, I sat there like a fool waiting for you. I bought the tickets and then I sat there watching people go inside to see the movie I've been looking forward to seeing for weeks."

"When you realized I wasn't coming, why didn't you just go see the movie?"

"I started to. Lord knows I started to, but I kept thinking, hoping really, that you were just late and you'd be there. Why didn't you call?"

"I said I was sorry, Rick. Damn. Let it go. Let me come over there and I'll make it up to you."

"No. I'm in the bed."

"Come on."

"No."

"I'll suck your dick."

"And what else?"

"Anything you want me to do, boo."

"Okay, you can come by for a minute."

"I won't say a word. I'll just fuck you and leave. Would that be cool?"

"How long you gonna be?"

"Twenty minutes, maybe less, so get up and unlock the door in case you fall asleep. Come on now, get up."

"Okay. I'll see you when you get here." I hung up the phone and tried to get up. My head hurt. I looked at the bottle. It was half full or half empty. I couldn't tell which. I looked at the clock. It was a quarter to three. "Shit, I must have passed out."

I practically had to throw myself out of the bed. I staggered to the shower, turned on the water, and started for the door to unlock it as I was instructed to do. I went back to the bathroom, checked the temperature. Not too cold, not too hot. I got in the shower and just stood for a while with my face in the water. Once that got old, I turned around and let the water beat down on the back of my neck. It felt soooo good, I didn't wanna get out. But I had to, just not right away. I was tonight's booty call. *Picture that.* So, I planned on taking out all my frustration over being stood up on Vanessa's all too luscious body.

I turned off the water, dried myself off quickly and got

back in the bed. I looked at the bottle of Stoli and actually gave some thought to getting a couple of glasses. The feeling passed without incident.

I looked at the clock as it rolled up on ten after three. "So much for twenty minutes, maybe less." By a quarter to four, I had once again declared her a no-show and tried to go back to sleep.

No sooner had I said it, I heard the door slam. I rolled over. Vanessa came through the door naked.

"Hello, Vanessa."

She didn't answer.

Without a word, she got up on the bed and pulled back the covers. I lay back and watched as she worked me with both hands until I felt myself getting hard. Once it was standing at attention, she proceeded to tease me with her tongue, making small, circular motions with the tip, around the head and up and down the sides. Vanessa looked up at me and smiled, and I smiled back. She opened her mouth as wide as she could and lowered her head down on me. I watched as it slowly disappeared and reappeared. She began to move faster and faster. I felt my toes begin to curl against the sheets. I was making a sound I'd become accustomed to producing in others, but never experienced for myself. I squirted, squirted and screamed as I grabbed the back of her head. She sat up on the bed and looked at me, smiling. Once I composed myself, I crawled between her thighs and returned the favor.

The sun had been up for a while before we retreated to opposite sides of the bed. I resisted the temptation to roll into the fetal position and say, "Don't touch me." I still had my pride, but facts were facts. She had me, and I was powerless to do anything about it.

It was almost noon by the time I woke up the next morning. Vanessa was gone, but she left an envelope on the pillow.

It had the word *desires* written on the front of it. I sat up on the edge of the bed and opened it. It said:

Dear Rick,

I have something that I want to share with you. I want you, and I have an overwhelming need to satisfy your every desire. I think about it all the time. It consumes me, and at times defines my actions. I can't close my eyes without seeing visions of you and I locked in each other's arms, having mad sex. You've taken me places sexually that I only dreamed of. Now I can't stop myself. I have to feel you deep inside of me. Not just physically, not by any means. I need to feel you deep inside my mind. You have taken over my mind and body. You make me cum uncontrollably. I get so excited when I feel your presence. When you touch my body, it quivers. When you kiss me, I cum. And penetration drives me insane. I want to caress, lick and suck you while you feel my flow. I wanna do it with you all the time. I have become a slave to your passion, and it is my passion to satisfy you.

Just so you know

V

I sat there smiling as I read her words. Just reading it excited me, and it was evident by my hardness. My mouth was dry and I felt dehydrated; the combination of Vanessa's sex and Mr. Stoli, no doubt. I went to the kitchen to get something to drink, and read the letter again on the way. When I got to the kitchen, I was shocked. Vanessa had cleaned the kitchen, washed and dried all the dishes, by hand no less, and put them away.

"Damn," I said, as I poured water into a clean glass. "All this and pussy too. I wonder if she does windows."

10

April's friend zone

Things seemed to be improving between me and April. We'd gotten to the point where April would at least spend some time with me. Only we didn't have sex. She wouldn't even let me kiss her. But every once in a while she still wanted to cuddle. April said that sometimes she missed being close to me and wanted to cuddle. Cuddling sucks, especially when you know that the chances of it leading to hot, butt naked sex are slim and none, but I did it. I'd do anything if it meant getting back with April.

In spite of that, it was sorta working out. I was working on my relationship with April; she thought it was going very well. "Since you cut loose all of your other women, we're finally spending some real time together." And why wouldn't she think that? I didn't do anything; I was home whenever she calls, so I always had time for her. No more having to make up excuses about why I couldn't see her, like having to work late or hanging out with Victor. I was always there for her. "And I like that," she told me. The problem was the reason I was always available.

Vanessa. I was home because I was waiting for Vanessa.

She only came out at night. Never before midnight, so I had plenty of time for April.

On this particular day, April had come by and we sat around and watched movies on TV. Oh, and by the way, this was a cuddle day.

The phone rang. I rolled over and looked at the display. It was Laura. With no intention of answering, I rolled back toward April. She sat up and looked at the display.

"If you don't answer it, I will," she said.

"Be my guest."

"Just answer it, Rick," April said, smiling as she hit me with her pillow.

"Hello, Laura. How've you been doing?"

"I'm fine. How are you?"

"A little tired," I said and winked at April, who was all up in my mouth. "But I'll live. What's up?"

"I'm not interrupting anything, am I?"

"No, I was just watching a movie with April. It was watching us, actually." April hit me lightly on the arm and mumbled something about her not needing to know all that.

"Oh." She sounded disappointed, but I needed everyone in earshot, especially April, to know it was over between Laura and me. "Anyway, do you know somebody named Prentiss? I don't know what her first name is, but it begins with Y." I knew she was talking about Yvette.

"Yeah, I know her. Why?"

"Rick, she is getting on my last nerve, calling my house at all hours of the day and night, calling me at work, talking about how she's the one, and how I need to step aside and let a real woman have you. At first she was polite about it, talking like she had some sense. So I tried to explain to her that it was over between us and that I hadn't seen you in months. But she wouldn't stop. I got tired of it and started blocking her calls. What I wanna do that for? Since then, these last few days, it's like she's lost her mind, calling me at work, cursing me out, and now it's all about *bitch this* and *ho that.*"

"I'm sorry about all this, Laura. I didn't know all that was going on."

"First of all, who is this fool? How did she get my number and how does she know where I work, Rick?"

"She was over here one day when you called. I guess she memorized your number. I don't know how she found out where you worked." But I had a good idea. Yvette was a collector. It was her job to find people and harass them. Professional pain in the ass.

"It doesn't matter how she found out. You just need to do something about it. I don't need this!" Laura said and slammed the phone in my ear.

I hung up the phone and closed my eyes. I knew that when I opened them April would be looking dead at me, with questions, valid ones, but questions I didn't feel like answering. I could feel her eyes. I lay there waiting for her to get tired of waiting for me to say something. I thought about how honest I was going to be about it.

"What did she want, Rick?"

Then it hit me. "You remember Yvette, don't you?"

The whole truth. Answer all questions honestly and without hesitation.

"Why?"

"Laura says that she's been calling and harassing her."

"Why?"

"Yvette wants her to step aside and let a real woman take over."

"Take over what?"

"Me."

April had a sorta half smile on her face, so I knew it was

no big deal to her. I had the feeling lately that April had started to believe that I was really trying to change and she was willing to give the process time. I appreciated that. A lot of other women would have a hard time dealing with this whole scenario and would be taking every opportunity to express themselves. I was fortunate and I knew it. I took the time to think about how I had done nothing in my life to this point to deserve a woman like April.

"You're kidding, right? Why is she calling Laura?"

"Why don't you ask her?"

"I'm serious, Rick. Why would she be calling her, telling her to step aside?"

"Do you really want to know?"

"Tell me why. This ought to be good."

"Because she knows that you're not going anywhere."

"She knows this, huh? 'Cause as far as I know, I have gone somewhere."

"Let me put it this way: As far as I'm concerned, you're not going anywhere. I've never tried to hide you from anybody. I've never made a secret about how I feel about you."

"And how is that?"

"I love you."

"You just had this funny way of showing it."

There was a point that April wanted to lead me to, but I didn't want to pursue that point with her at this time. I knew she would get back to it if it was important to her. And I had a feeling that it was.

"Anyway, knowing that, Yvette is probably thinking that the reason that she can't get any play is because of Laura."

"You said there was nothing going on with you and Laura anymore."

"There isn't. But Yvette doesn't see it that way. She was here one day when Laura called. She asked me who Laura was and I told her that she was just a friend of mine."

"When was this?"

"The same day you caught her over here. She said something about how Laura must be a better friend than she was, because Laura had my home phone number and she doesn't."

"And from that she decided to start harassing Laura? So Laura would leave you to her?"

"Exactly."

April looked at me, rolled her eyes and lay down. "I know there's more to it than that, but as long as she doesn't start that foolishness with me, I'm not gonna worry about it. You sure know how to pick 'em. I hope to God you didn't have sex with that girl."

"I told you that I didn't."

"I hope not. And I hope to God that you're learning something from all this."

"Yeah. I'm learning a lot."

"Like what?"

I wanted to say something deep and philosophical, but nothing was coming. Then I remembered what she'd said when all this started coming down. "That I can't flirt with everybody."

"That's right." My answer took away some of her steam, but it just gave her an opening to get back to her point. "Can I ask you a question?"

"Go ahead."

"You said that the fool knows how you feel about me."

"Right, she knows I love you."

"How can you say you loved me and still mess with other women?"

"One had nothing to do with the other."

"I beg your pardon?"

"One had nothing to do with the other."

"How can you say that? If you really loved me like you say

you did, how could you have messed around on me for as long as you did?"

"I don't have to be in love with somebody to want to have sex with her."

"You're not understanding what I'm saying, but we'll get back to that in a minute. Did you want to have sex with Yvette?"

"No." Then I thought about it. "I knew that I had no intention of having sex with her, but I knew that I could if I wanted to. She set herself up to get tossed up. That's all she was about. To be honest, that's the real reason I went to lunch with her."

"Because you knew you could? I don't get it. Why would you put yourself in that position if, as you say, you had no intention of fucking her?"

"That's exactly why I felt like I had to." April looked at me like I was from another planet or something. I smiled at her. Women have a hard time with male logic, just like men have no clue when it comes to female logic. And women never understand playa logic. Sometimes I don't understand it, or how that logic has led me to do some of the things I've done. That unwritten rule that says *find and conquer as much pussy as you can.* That one rule has led me to have sex with so many women, some I didn't even like and knew that I had no use for once I was done.

I started to break that point down for April, but decided against it. All it would do was force April to ask for more details, and she didn't need to hear all that. It would only destroy the trust we were trying so hard to build.

"Because I had to know. I had to know for myself if I could be in that type of situation and not capitalize on it."

I looked at the blank expression on April's face and I knew she still didn't get it, so I broke it down. "Nobody knows better than I do that I am a flirt, and what I was capable of doing. I knew that I'd be in that type of situation again, and I had to know if I could even draw the line, much less not cross it."

"Okay, on some twisted level that makes sense. But once you saw that you could draw the line and not cross it, why did you keep talking to her?"

"She was just fun to talk to."

"Fun, huh?" April folded her arms across her chest. "Now you see what that fun got you?"

"Yeah, yeah, I see what it got me."

"Didn't you see how she was?"

"Yeah, after a while I knew she was a pest. That's why I stopped taking her calls. That's when she came here."

"That's what scares me, Rick. A normal woman with some sense would see that you don't want to be bothered with her and move on, find a man of her own."

"She got a man."

April's eyes narrowed and her face contorted. "Then why is she at you?"

"He ain't on his job."

"So she wants you to be her part-time lover." April smiled.

"I don't like the song, but yeah, she just looking for a fuck buddy."

April laughed and kissed me on the cheek. "Look, Rick, I appreciate you being honest with me about all this. But the more I find out about you and how you were, the farther you slip into the friend zone."

11

Will She?

Will she show up? It's a question I had to ask myself far too many times. It was like I never knew with Vanessa. It had been a couple of months since Laura called about Yvette stalking her, and since then I'd seen less and less of April. It had gotten to the point that now she didn't even return my calls. Ain't that a bitch? I cut everybody loose to get with April, and now she wasn't tryin' to get with me.

I would have liked to spend more time with Vanessa, but that wasn't happenin'. I finally learned not to make any plans with her. The only time I knew that she was gonna show up was when she called me and said "I'm on my way." And even then, it might be a while before she got there. So, I just sat around every night, waiting. Hoping, really, that she'd call me.

At least the odds were in my favor. She'd show up at least four nights out the week. I tried to act like it wasn't bothering me when she didn't show. But it bothered me—bad, some days. I should have just put a stop to it. Yeah, gave her an ultimatum.

I reached for my new friend, Mr. Stoli, and poured another shot. I lost count of how many I'd had. The television was on and the remote was in my hand, but I wasn't watching anything. Just like last night.

What was I doing?

What was I thinking?

Give her an ultimatum?

You sound like a fuckin' fool. What was I supposed to say? "Please spend some time with me. Why don't you ever have time for me? How come the only time I see you is bedtime?"

I turned the glass up and hit myself again.

Is that all I'm good for? Am I just a cheap trick to her?

"If that's the case, you need to start droppin' some money on a bill or something." I laughed out loud. The words sounded so familiar, but I'd never said them. But now it was me that was turned out.

She had me in ways that nobody, including Donna, has ever had me. Sitting here like a fool. I flipped the channel again: animal programs. For the next forty minutes, I sat there watching the king of the beasts. Now, that is a true pimp. All he does is sit around fuck all the lionesses in his pride and fight off other lions that want to fuck them. He doesn't even have to hunt for food. He sends the lionesses out to stalk and kill their prey.

Sweet.

Every once in a while, I'd look over at the phone. A dumb English comedy came on, so I turned the TV off. Sat in the dark, feeling around for the stereo remote. Something told me to put an end to the suspense and turn on the light, but I resisted. Common sense finally got the best of me, and I turned it on. With that small task out of the way, I raised my glass, tilted my head back, opened my mouth and poured the contents of the glass into my mouth to celebrate my triumph. Another trick I'd mastered lately. I turned the stereo to some mellow oldies; Smokey Robinson's "The Love I Saw in You Was Just a Mirage" was playing.

"Thanks for telling me, Smokey, but I already knew that."

I turned off the radio and stood up a lot faster than I should have. It was the moment of reality when you realize that you're drunk or pretty close to it. I wandered around, turning on lights, looking for something.

"What was I looking for?" I tried to retrace my thought process. "I was going to lay down. I got up. I said, 'Damn, I'm fucked up.' Then I thought about Vanessa. If she did make a cameo, I'd be too drunk to do anything. I know what she comes for, but I ain't saying nothing. I was going to take a shower. Then what?"

I wandered around for a while, thinking that if I saw what I was looking for, I'd remember I was looking for it. I went into the bathroom and turned on the shower. What if she called while I was in the shower? Then all of a sudden it hit me. "The phone. I was looking for the cordless phone." Now that I knew what I was looking for, I resumed my search. Forty-five minutes later, I still hadn't found it, but the house was cleaner than it was when I started.

I got in the shower, thought about Vanessa, and tried to focus. The water was hot. I liked it that way. There is nothing better than a hot shower to clear your head. Makes you see things clearer, gives you a new perspective on things. If there was something that demanded a new perspective it was this—I started to call it a relationship, but that wasn't what it was that we had, Vanessa and I. We had sex, great sex, fantastic sex, mad sex. Might as well call it what it was. Sex. In a relationship, people do things with each other. I had to get to that state of mind, for my own peace of mind. If I didn't, I knew I was going down. Going down slow, and for what?

For Vanessa?

Well now, let's think for a minute. I didn't know anything about her, not really. I didn't know for sure where she lived. I wasn't really sure if the she actually lived at the house that I dropped her off that first night. Any time I called her, no matter what time of day or night it is, the same female voice answered, with that same *Why does your dumb ass keep callin'? You should know that she ain't here* voice that always pisses me off.

Why was she playing this game with me? I was keeping it real. Maybe she was being real about it from her point of view. I mean, she never gave me any indication that she had any other purpose for me other than to make her cum. And if I got mine in the process, that was all the better. Maybe I was the one who wasn't being real with myself about it.

I stood there, thinking about every time we'd been together, and for a while, I lost myself in the rhythm of water. I really enjoyed being with her. For me, it was more than just her sex, which was a formidable force to be reckoned with, to say the least. It was the way we were together. I dug talking to her. She was funny and she could talk intelligently about anything. The few times when we did actually go somewhere, we—or I should say I had the best time. I could only hope that she felt for me the way I felt for her. I watched the soap roll off me and I knew that wasn't the case. I represented one thing to her.

I got out of the shower, dried myself off and lay across my bed. Staring at the phone still, willing it to ring, and hoping that it was Vanessa doing the ringing.

I was getting too comfortable with my depression and I could see where it was leading me. I was drinking more than I should be and not focusing on business. I wondered what it was going to take to make me see that I was traveling quickly down the wrong path, and the reason was Vanessa.

I should break it off with her. What a concept.

But that would be too much like right. And besides, I knew sooner or later she would come around and we might be able to have something. Was I fooling myself into thinking that this was something more than good sex to her?

"Yes!" I screamed out loud.

But nobody heard me, not even myself.

On the way home from work the next day, I stopped at the liquor store and picked up another bottle of Stoli. I hadn't finished the one I had at home, but I didn't want to run out and have to take a chance on leaving the house and missing Vanessa's call.

It was getting close to 8 o'clock before I realized that the only thing I'd eaten all day was bag of chips. I dug up a coupon and called Pizza Hut for delivery. They told me that I could pick it up in thirty minutes, but it would be at least an hour before delivery. I didn't care. I wasn't leaving the house. I turned the TV to A&E, poured a drink and watched *Biography*. Halfway through *Investigative Reports* and my third shot of Stoli, my pizza came.

I ate a slice and took a shot, a pattern I continued until there were only two slices left. A little after 11 o'clock, the phone rang. "About time."

I snatched it up on the first ring. It was Victor. He said he called because he hadn't heard from me in about three weeks and just wanted to make sure I was all right.

"Three weeks. Has it been that long?" I rushed him off the phone, and I felt stupid for doing it. All this for a woman who wasn't interested. Not really. Not interested in anything other than getting tossed.

"You got to pull up. Put a stop to this, one way or the other. 'Cause this ain't it for you." I turned off the television and began walking around the house, listing all the reasons why I should stop this madness, one more time. I knew all the reasons why I should. I could only think of one reason to let her stay.

I stopped.

"Is that enough for you?"

I stood completely still and thought carefully about an answer. I fought the impulse to yell "yes" out loud. 'Cause I was just as preoccupied with fuckin' her as she was with fuckin' me.

I walked to the couch and lay down. If that was the case, what needed to happen here was that I needed to get a grip on myself and take this thing for what it was worth. Stop trippin' about what she was gonna do and get a life.

Then it hit me. If I was gonna get a life, why did it have to include her? I had one before I met her, and she was the reason I didn't have one now.

No that was a lie and I knew it. I was the reason I didn't have a life anymore. But the fact of the matter was she had to go. There was no reason for me to believe that things would ever change between us. And if it did, it wouldn't be anytime soon. If I allowed her to stay, I knew that even with a refreshed attitude on her part, I would still want more.

"She gotta go!" It felt better saying it loud, so I said it again. "She gotta go!"

I got up and went to bed. Every once in a while I'd say it again. The more I said it, the more pumped I got. The next time she called I'd lay it all out for her. Tell her . . . what would I tell her? That I didn't want to see her anymore because she turned me out and I couldn't take it? That she got me so turned out that I just sat around here and hoped that she'd call?

I don't think so.

I'd just say that I wasn't not interested in dealing like this then hang up. And what if she called back and asked me to explain what this meant? Let her catch voicemail.

Coward. Be a man and face that woman.
I said it again. "She gotta go!" and that's all there was to it.
I rolled over and the phone rang.
"Can I come over?"
"Come on. I been expecting you."

12

The End

Things couldn't be any worse. April finally got around to calling me back. She called to say that as much as it hurt her to say it, she couldn't see me anymore.

"You'll never change, Rick."

So, in spite of the fact that I really had changed, it was over between me and April. I couldn't honestly say that I blamed her. I did dog her for years. And to make maters worse, I hadn't heard from Vanessa in weeks. I guess she moved on too.

So now I was alone.

I sat at my desk, staring out the window at nothing in particular, when the phone rang.

"Rick, you need to get down here right now and do something about that fool before I have to hurt her," Laura said excitedly. She was mad, shaking mad. I could hear it in her voice.

"Calm down, Laura. What's Yvette doin' down there?"

"About to get her black ass kicked, that's what she's doing down here. You just need to come get her."

"All right, all right. Just chill out for a second, Laura, and tell me what happened."

"It started yesterday. She just walked up to me in the lobby and introduced herself, get this, as your new other woman. Then the fool just walked away. But for the rest of the day, she would just be there every time I turned around, with this stupid-ass grin on her face."

"Why didn't you call security?"

"I did. But by the time they'd get there, she'd be gone. So, this morning she calls me, mad 'cause I put the 'poo-lice' on her. And all morning, I've been getting pages to call a number, but when I called, nobody there paged me or there's no answer. I know it's her."

"How do you know she's down there? She's probably calling from somewhere else. I don't think she's stupid enough to come back down there when she knows security is looking for her."

"Rick, you just don't know. That bitch is crazy. I just saw her at the escalator. I called security and told them what she was wearing, but they won't catch her. This is a busy hotel. She'll just blend in with the rest of the crowd. You need to talk to her and get her to stop bothering with me."

"I'll call you back." I hung up with Laura and tried to call Yvette. When I didn't get her, I called Laura back.

"Did you talk to that crazy bitch?"

"No."

"Why not?" she asked, laced with attitude.

"I tried callin' her at home, but the number is disconnected. I called her at work, but they said she doesn't work there anymore."

"Probably found out she was crazy and fired her crazy ass."

"I don't see what good me coming down there is gonna do."

"Look, Rick, I'm tired of this chile bothering wit' me. You just need to come on."

"Okay, Laura, I'll be down there." She slammed the phone down in my ear, which was becoming her custom, especially since the only time I heard from Laura was when she complained about Yvette.

On the way down there, I thought about what kind of mess I was driving myself in to. "The mess you created, playa," I said out loud.

Laura was right. Yvette was out the box and it was my fault. There are some women that you're glad you didn't fuck with, and Yvette was definitely one of those people. And now, I wish I could actually say that about her, but I can't. I know, I know I said I wasn't gonna fuck her. But I did. I fucked her.

I was supposed to meet Vic one night at the Doubletree, but he was a no-show. I sat at the bar by myself and had a couple of drinks until I decided he wasn't going to show. I paid my check and walked right into Yvette.

"Hey, Rick. I didn't see you inside." She looked good. As always, her outfit hugged her and showcased her legs. Yvette really did have pretty legs. Pretty body, really. It was the type of body that you just can't wait until she comes out of them clothes so you can see it, because a black woman's body is something to behold. Nothing compares to their beauty. Sometimes that's all there is.

Anyway, I told Yvette that I was getting ready to leave. She said she was leaving too.

I started lying to myself at that point.

I offered to walk her to her car. She said she took the train and asked if I'd take her home, and I said yes. That was my first mistake. I should have lied and said anything to get outta taking her home, but I didn't. I said, "Sure, come on."

During the ride to her apartment, the lying continued. Those lies allowed me to live in the delusion that some bizarre scenario existed where I would drop Yvette off at her door, say good-night and go home. I kept telling myself that

I wasn't gonna fuck her. I was just gonna drop her off and go home.

As soon as we got in the car, Yvette unbuttoned her top buttons, exposing a delectable view of cleavage, which only made the lies more complex and harder to support. I reminded myself that this was supposed to be the great project. I reminded myself of the reason I went out with Yvette in the first place: to prove to myself that I could be friends, just friends with a woman. A woman I wanted to fuck.

Traffic was heavy on the way to the west side. Yvette commented that she had to use the bathroom and that she might have been better off taking the train. Sensing an opportunity, I offered to take her to the nearest train station. But she wasn't havin' it.

"Oh, but no, Rick. You gonna finish what you started tonight." My delusion allowed me to believe that her comment wasn't laced with sexual innuendo.

Traffic finally broke loose and we made it to her apartment. I was hoping that since she had to go, she'd jump out of the car. But that wasn't gonna happen either. I pulled up in front of her building and looked over at her. She called me on it.

"Come on, now. You need to see me safely to my door." She was right. If it were April, I would have jumped over the car to the open the door for her. But she wasn't April.

Yvette walked quickly, and I followed behind her. She opened the door and headed straight for the bathroom.

Yvette came out of the back about ten minutes later, wearing a big T-shirt and red sweat pants. She turned on the radio and asked me if I wanted a drink. I accepted. What it was didn't matter. I thought about the consequences of what I was about to do. I sat watching Yvette. The view was fascinating. I would have to justify this with myself. Or could I just take a shower and shrug it off? But by the time we finished our drinks, we were naked and on our way to her room. It didn't last long. The girl had no skills at all. I hate it when that happens.

When I got to the Plaza, it was on. As I walked in the lobby, I saw that Laura and Yvette were being separated by security. By the look of their clothes and their hair, I could tell they'd been fighting. By the time I made it through the crowd, Laura had calmed down enough for security to let her go. Yvette, on the other hand, was still wrestling to get free. That wasn't gonna happen. Herb is too big a boy.

"Rick!" Laura said.

Almost immediately, Yvette calmed down and stopped fighting with Herb. "What you doing here?" she said to me, her entire demeanor changed—until I walked over and stood near Laura. Her eyes narrowed as she looked at Laura.

"You called him, didn't you, bitch? Tryin' to embarrass me in front of my man, huh?"

"Yvette, I ain't your man!" I yelled.

"That was your last mistake, Miss Laura Barnes."

"Just get her out of here!" Laura yelled and walked away.

I watched as Herb and the boys escorted Yvette out without anymore drama. I caught up with Laura at the elevator. She had been crying, but she stopped when she saw me.

"Are you all right?"

"That's a stupid question. No, I just had a fight on my job. In the lobby, on my job, because of you, Rick. All because of you."

I felt like shit.

"I need a drink," Laura said with a disgusted look on her face.

We sat in the Sundial, where it all began for us, and talked. Well, Laura mostly talked and I mostly apologized. What else could I do? Everything she was saying was true.

". . . because of you."

It was the way she spit out *you* that dug the knife in a little deeper. The expression on her face turned the knife slowly.

After a long silence, Laura finished her drink and stood up. "I'm not gonna be any good here for the rest of the day. I'm going home." I went with her to get her things and to let her boss know she was leaving. Naturally, she knew all about what had happened and insisted that Laura go home and take a day or so off, which Laura gladly accepted.

We took the service elevator down and went out the employees' entrance.

"Time to die, bitch."

Yvette pointed the gun.

I pushed Laura down.

Yvette fired.

Instinct got the better of common sense and I jumped at Yvette. I felt something burning in my stomach. We hit the ground and the gun fell out of her hand. With both hands free, she proceeded to punch me repeatedly about my head and shoulders. I closed my eyes and accepted every blow she had to offer. I felt like I deserved them. If Laura decided to join in and start kicking me, that would have been cool too.

Finally, Herb and the boys showed up, then the police arrived shortly after and took control of the situation. I looked around for Laura. A small crowd of employees had gathered around her.

"Are you all right?" I said and reached out for her.

Laura pushed my hands away. "Don't touch me, Rick! She just tried to kill me! Because of you!" she yelled. "Get away from me!"

Laura turned and walked away. I tried to go after her, but her co-workers closed ranks to block my path. What would I say anyway? I'm sorry?

Pretty lame at this point, don't you think, playa?

That's when I felt myself getting a little lightheaded and the pain shot through my stomach. I grabbed my midsection and felt the blood on my hands. My legs gave out on me and I fell to the ground.

I looked up in time to see the cops drive away with Yvette in the back seat. She tried to kill Laura, over me. Laura's words, "because of you," rolled around in my head. I tried to make sense of it, but it didn't matter. No matter how I sliced it, it was my fault. Yvette was going to jail for murder.

Mine.

WHO'S YOUR DADDY?

Jihad

Also by Jihad

Street Life
Baby Girl

1

Vernon

I would be every lying muthafucka in the book if I told my boys I had a threesome with Li'l Kim and Janet Jackson. Hell, if I wasn't getting licked and sucked by one while I was knee-deep in the other one's pussy, I wouldn't believe it my damn self.

And to think it wasn't costing me a dime. Periodically, I smiled for the cameras I had hidden around the hotel luxury suite where we were getting our freak on. The covers were on the floor and one of the king-sized mattresses was on its way.

"Uh-huh, harder, harder, baby. Oooooo-ooo-ooo, yeah, like that, baby. Right there. You hittin' my spot, got-damn. Ooooh shit. Fuck this pussy."

That's all the motivation I needed to start Superman-pyle-driving that wet pussy. "Who's your daddy?" I asked while slappin' that soft ass.

"O-O-Oh, you-you are. Slap my ass harder, baby."

"Whose pussy is this?"

Scrunch, scrit, scrot. Her wet pussy was making noises as if it were answering my question.

"Yours, Daddy. Oh my God. Fuck me, Daddy. I'm about to cum all over that big dick."

Cheyenne should have never told me that Shemika was curious about being with a woman. To no avail, I'd been trying to get Cheyenne to have a threesome with me since we met over the phone after Trey got locked up six years ago. If I didn't have it so good at home, I would have slipped her a mickey and made her fuck me and another ho.

So, it wasn't all my fault that I had Shemika on all fours, ass tooted up in the air, pussy juice flying everywhere.

I was sitting on my legs, my back was flat on the bed, my biceps were bulging, and sweat was rolling down the ripples of my stomach muscles as I curled and lifted my wife's best friend up and down off of my diamond-hard dick. Five years of doing yoga made it so I could comfortably fuck and cum in positions that most women couldn't even imagine.

"Does the good reverend fuck you like this? I asked while changing gears and speeding up."

"Oh-oh, I'm cummin'. I'm cummin' again." Her back muscles tensed up, her legs started shaking. "Cum with me, Daddy."

I couldn't see shit. I had sweat in my eyes. My heart was pounding. I tried to ignore the cramp I was catching in my left foot. I felt her pussy contracting.

"Oh-oh-oh, here it is, Daddy. You feel it, Daddy? I'm cummin'!"

She lurched forward, trying to get away. My dick almost came out. "Oh, hell no you don't. You ain't getting away from this dick yet. No, not 'til I bust," I said while wrapping my arms around her waist. I was about to explode any minute.

"You feel all nine inches? Huh?" I gritted my teeth as I banged in and out.

"Ooooooo, I'm cummin' too. Oh-oh, oooooh," what's-her-

name said, between sucking Shemika's nipples and playing
with herself with the vibrator I took out of the goodie bag I
kept in my trunk. My goodie bag was like the American
Express card; I never left home without it. I never knew
when I was gon' get lucky.

The inventor of Viagra should get the Nobel Peace Prize.
Fuck, I'd be their national spokesperson for free. All I took
was half a pill, and it seemed my shit stayed hard forever.

I flipped Shemika over on her back and threw those long,
dark chocolate sprinter's legs over my shoulders. Shemika
was a cleaned-up ghetto ho, and Cheyenne was an Ivy
League prude. I couldn't see what she and my wife had in
common.

The way what's-her-name was swallowing Shemika's titties
and pushing them back out of her mouth was making me
lose my mind. I could only imagine those lips wrapped
around my dick.

Not even five minutes ago, what's-her-name wiped my
face with a towel, and I was already dripping with sweat
again. I was toying with Shemika, barely inserting the head
of my dick in and out while what's-her-name licked clit, balls
and all with a Halls cough drop in her mouth. I felt like I was
the king of the world the way Shemika moaned, creamed
and screamed for mercy. Oh, yeah, Shemika was a screamer.
The whole seventeenth floor at the W hotel was probably listening outside our door.

Finally, what's-her-name scooted from under me on the
bed and went back to running her tongue around Shemika's
pinkish-brown, marble-hard nipples. All of a sudden,
Shemika started gyrating. I didn't think that pussy could get
any wetter, but it did. She wrapped her legs around my slip-
pery back. My legs were up under me as I lifted that tight little ass off the bed and began my stroke in Mississipi, swooped
through Louisiana and Alabama before my long stroke was

deeply imbedded in that pussy. What's-her-name had one hand between her legs, and her arm was moving almost as fast as my pyle-driving motions were. For the sixth or seventh time, Shemika was letting the world know she was cumming.

That was my signal. I took a quick, deep breath and went to King Kong fucking her. "Whose pussy is this?" I repeated. And every time, she replied, "It's your pussy, Daddy." Sweat was flying everywhere. I was tired, breathing hard, and I was about to call it a wrap.

My back straightened, I got all bug-eyed, and I started to shake like the vibrator that was up in what's-her-name before she stuck her tongue in my ass.

"Ohhhhhhhhhhhh, shit-shit-shit. What the—?" I came so hard I thought I was peeing.

Fuck that, I thought as I whipped my dick out of Shemika, hot white cream flying everywhere. Shemika was busy convulsing and moaning in ecstacy when I turned to what's-her-name.

I didn't plan it. No way, especially not without a condom, but by now I was out of my mind. After this little sexy hood rat damn near made me lose my mind, I had no choice but to try out her hot, shaved pussy. It was as bald as a newborn baby's ass.

None of us had any condoms, so I definitely wasn't planning on banging what's-her-name. But I also didn't plan on her lips and tongue having me jerking like I was being brought back to life by a defibrillator. Shemika was safe. She'd been married to Reverend Poo-nanny for a few years, so I wasn't worried about catching shit from her. What's-her-name smelled clean, and with a pretty pussy like hers, she had to be straight. And hell, the Viagra wasn't showing any signs of letting up, so why should I?

I turned what's-her-name on her back, pulled her up on all fours, and I let her pull me on in. She felt like hot butter.

In his stand-up routines back in the '70s, the king of comedy, Richard Pryor, used to always talk about the elusive snapping pussy—pussy that will make you disown your own momma. Well, I'd found it, was exploring its cave, and I didn't ever wanna go home. Her face was uglier than sin, but that pussy was heaven.

A while later, she came, I came, we all came, again and a-damn-gain, and I owed it all to Cherry. That's it, her name was Cherry.

Shemika had been giving me fuck-me signs for far too long. I was scared to act on them just in case Cheyenne was setting me up. I mean, I just couldn't imagine how Shemika could play her best friend like that, especially as close as they were. I knew I had to find a way to test that fine-ass Shemika, and I had.

Yesterday, Cheyenne was home taking care of her motherly duties when I walked into the TGIF after-work live jazz set at the W hotel. Every Friday night I hoped to get lucky, but I never expected to hit the poo-nanny lottery.

It was still early, around six. People were still getting off work and fighting that crazy Friday Atlanta rush hour traffic. The weather was beautiful. The sun was shining, and there was just enough wind to keep the sun cool.

Life was beautiful. I had a successful wife, a beautiful three-year-old daughter, and I'd just flim-flammed another wanna-be real estate investor.

I lived in pussy paradise. There was a seventeen-to-one men to women ratio in Atlanta. With all the gay dudes running around, I'd have to say it was really more like twenty-five-to-one. And I was always updating my top twenty-five. That was why I was out now, like I was every Friday.

Friday was recruitment day for me and my brother Trey. It was boys' night out, and I needed some new pussy. I mean something brand new and in the wrapper. I wanted to get an early start, so I made my way up I-285 before the traffic started.

My twin brother, Trey, wouldn't be here for another hour at least, I thought as I looked at my mother of pearl-faced Movado and noticed that it was only 6:30. A few minutes after walking into the spacious ballroom of the W hotel, I grabbed a seat near the stage.

I was minding my own, sipping on a Grand Marnier and Coke, listening to the Soul Factory warm up when my hodar (radar for hoes) went off. Her back was to me, and her ass was screaming for my help. I mean she looked like she had a basketball under her AKA-green, damn-near-waist-high skirt.

I was out of my chair and on my way over to the bar where she was posted up in a wide-legged stance. I closed my eyes and imagined walking over to her, pushing her head into the bar's countertop, lifting that skirt up and thug-fuckin' her right there.

She was just like I liked them: short, petite, and all-out fine. As I got closer, I noticed the imprint of a thong. It was exactly where my tongue would be if I played my cards right. From what I could see, it was all good. Her shoulder-length, African fake-ass braids and long, green-painted fingernails, along with her outfit screamed ghetto fabulous, brainless, and most important of all, easy new pussy.

I took my wedding band off and replaced it with the 14-karat gold-plated Superbowl ring I had made at the flea market last year. From what I could see, Ms. Sexy looked like the groupie type.

"Excuse me." I lightly touched her arm. She turned to me. I was momentarily at a loss for words.

"Yes," she replied.

Ugly wasn't quite the word to describe her face.

Still, I flashed my million-dollar smile. "My name is Jamal,"

I lied while smiling and slowly shaking her hand, making sure she saw my ring. "Can I buy you a drink?"

She sucked her teeth. "Your name ain't no damn Jamal. Oh, so you don't remember me, huh?" she asked with her hands on her hips.

I had never seen this ho in my life. I'd remember an ugly muthafucka like this, with such a fine-ass body. She must've thought I was Trey. I had to think fast. I saw all hopes of being able to ride this ass like a horse jockey fading right before my eyes.

I opened my arms. "Babycakes." Before he went to prison, Trey always called his hoes Babycakes. "Where you been?" It worked. I could see her face softening up. "Come on now. Give Trey-love a hug." I stepped closer, pressing my dick against her, hugging that soft, hourglass body.

She sniffled. "I missed you. You never called. You never gave me your number. I even went to the Motel 6 we stayed at both times to see if I could get a number, an address, anything."

This was definitely the old Trey. The new Treyvon would not have played a ho like this.

"Honestly," I licked my lips, "Babycakes." I took her hand and looked her straight in the eyes. "I've been through a lot. I was strung out on crack. I went to prison, did four years for some shit I didn't do, and I just got out a few months ago."

She put her hand on the side of my face. "Ahhh, poor baby, you been through hell."

Did God put dumb bitches in this world to be played or what? The sympathy shit works all the time. Shit, I might even shed a tear for the ho. Whatever it takes to get a nut.

2

Cherry

Yeah, you been through hell, but not nearly the hell I'm going to take you and every muthafucka that gets in my way through. I was young. You told me you loved me. You promised to take care of me. I had the abortion you wanted, knowing that if I did, I wouldn't ever have children. But you told me that it would be okay, that we could adopt. You fucked me, but not nearly as hard as I am going to fuck you.

To get the bartender's attention, he used the same finger he used to play with me.

"Bartender, I'd like a shot of Grand Marnier." He looked at me with those dreamy, evil eyes. "And the lady will have . . ."

"Jack and Coke with a cherry, light ice, and a shot of tequila with a cherry." I know he said a drink, but fuck it. I was thirsty, and I might as well be right for what I had planned for his ass.

"And your name is again?"

Asshole Joe really didn't remember me. I wonder how many women he fucked over; how many women he lied to; how many women he promised the world to; how many women he left after they had an abortion that almost cost them their lives. I'd play his game, and we'd see who won this time. The difference between him and me was that I played for keeps. I'd be the whore he wanted me to be for just one night. That's all. One night was all I needed.

"Luscious, but e'rybody call me Cherry," I said, looking at that fake-ass ring he wore. I bet some airheads were awed by shit like that. I bet he was thinking I was some alley rat straight out of the projects, that I was a dope girl. You know, some dope boy's play-toy. He had no idea.

"So, how'd you get the name Cherry?"

"My ass."

"Huh?"

"Everyone be sayin' it's shaped like a cherry. I love cherries, so I started callin' myself that. I can't go around introducing myself as Luscious. Men might get the wrong idea and think I'm a ho."

3

Vernon

Someone needed to tell her that it wasn't the name that had brothas thinkin' she was a whore.

"I ain't really feeling this place. I ain't into music without no singin'. I just came here 'cause they be talkin' 'bout this place at my job," she said.

"So, what are you doing with yourself now?" I asked.

"I work down the street at the Super 8. I'm in housekeeping. It's just temporary until I get my demo out there."

"You sing?"

"You don't remember? Oh, that's right, you been through a lot," she said.

Smart aleck-ass bitch. She think Trey dogged her ass out. I was going to half fuck the whore, get a quick nut, get some head, nut in her mouth, and kick the oom-foo-foo-jungle-looking bitch to the curb.

"Nah, I rap and write poetry. I'm also writing a book of poems."

"That's cool. I do a little spoken word myself. You'll have to recite some of your work to me sometime." I smiled.

"We'll see. So whachu do for a livin', pretty eyes? Still getting high?"

"I see you got jokes. It's all good, though. I love a woman with a sense of humor." I smiled. I almost fucked up and said I played pro football. I nearly forgot that I was Trey and this bitch was from his other life. No telling what he told her.

"I own a real estate and land developing company."

"That's nice."

That's nice. What did she mean, that's nice? A car was nice. My credentials were off the chain. Oh, she was good. I know she was impressed, but she remained passive, as if my credentials didn't get her wet.

"So, are you open minded, Ms. Cherry?"

"Very."

"Oh, really?" I asked.

"What is that song the band is playing?" she asked.

"You like it?"

"Yeah. Now, that shit is tight to death."

"That is Morris Day and the Time's old school jam, 'Gigolos get lonely too.'"

"Do they?" she asked.

"Do they what?"

"Do gigolos get lonely too?"

I shrugged. "I wouldn't know."

"Save that for some otha dumb chick. I know a playa when I see one."

"Nah, baby, you got—"

"Ah-ah-ah-ah." She waved one of her green glitter finger-nails in my direction. "You came up to me because you saw my ass. And from the beginning, your intention was and is to be," she pointed to her crotch, "up in this. Go 'head, lie. Tell me I'm wrong."

You hit it right on the head, bitch. What did she expect me to say? Whatever I said would mean the difference between me getting to home plate or striking out.

"Whatever I say can and will probably be used against me,

so," I smiled, "I'm going to plead the fifth, at least for the moment. But I will answer your question before we part company. Is that fair?"

"Whateva." She rolled her neck. "I already know the answer. I was just seeing how real you was gon' keep it."

"All right, babycakes, you wanna keep it real? Let's keep it real."

She smiled and put a hand on my wrist. "Pretty eyes, I don't think you know how."

"Can I ask you a question?"

"You been askin' me questions."

This smart-ass Cro-Magnon cave-lookin' bitch was lucky she was fine.

I leaned in so close that I could feel her breath on my mustache. "What's the most spontaneous thing you've ever done?"

Real calm and nonchalant-like, she said, "Met a chick and her dude at a Publix grocery store and fucked them both in the store's restroom."

"You win," I said, throwing my hands up. "I need you in my life, right now, tonight. What's up?"

"Where?"

"I'll get a room here. Matter of fact, why don't we have a threesome?" I said.

"Where is she?"

"I don't know, but I can call her. I'll introduce you two. You have to do the talking. I know she's down, but I can't proposition her."

"Why not?" she asked.

"She used to be friends with my ex-wife."

"How does she look?" Cherry asked.

"You ever watch that show *Girlfriends*?"

"Every black woman has seen that show at one time or another."

"She looks like the broad married to the white guy, and she has a body like Angela Bassett," I explained.

"Ooooooooookay, why you ain't got her on the phone?"

"You ain't said nothin' but a word," I said with my cell phone already in hand.

4

Shemika

Oh, the hate. For the last three years, I had to put up with the snobbish, old-ass deacons' wives. They had me pegged as a gold digger. The old, crust-bucket haters were just mad because I dug for gold and hit a diamond mine. One even called me a floozy, to which I kindly told her old, no-tooth ass to go kill herself and make the world a better place. I couldn't help that I was twenty-nine and the bishop was fifty-nine. The old biddies had to take that up with God.

But the old busybody bitches were part of the reason I loved Sunday mornings. It had nothing at all to do with church. Hell, church was a business. It was work, and being the first lady required much more than I had expected, but the benefits well outweighed the shortcomings.

After the church benediction, the lights dimmed and the stage lit up. The twenty-foot center aisle oak double doors would electronically open. The church orchestra's percussion section would start its drum roll. One of the junior ministers would read a scripture from the Bible and afterwards, he compared it with what my husband, the Bishop Dr. T.J. Money, was doing or saying before finally introducing us to the concert-hall-like church.

Sunday was my time to shine. And shine I did. Everyone was standing and applauding. The purple-and-gold-robed choir would be singing the word "walk."

Every week was a fashion show, and the red carpeted middle aisle was the runway I strutted my five-eight, size eight figure down wearing Prada, Dolce and Gabana, Armani, or some other top French or Italian label.

While walking down the aisle arm-in-arm with my husband, I smiled at the sea of faces in the pews and the balcony. Each Sunday, my heart sped up with anticipation as I climbed the stairs to the stage. I could hardly wait to smile at the twenty-seven ancient, fat, wig-and weave-wearing grandma wives of the deacons as I made my way to the first lady's throne in the center of the humongous stage.

Oh, believe me, they did all they could to prevent us from marrying. Haters. They would have been successful if I hadn't been planning our marriage even before the first time we met.

I met Bishop five years ago at a private wake for his wife, who'd fought and lost a long battle with breast cancer. It took some doing, but I got on the guest list to attend and view the body. I had a short but tasteful black dress altered just for this occasion. The wake was held at his million-dollar Mexican villa estate home in the Atlanta suburb of Stone Mountain.

Two ushers led me down a long hall and into what I was told was the solarium. The room was breathtaking. I'd never seen an eight-sided room with all the walls made of tinted plate glass. Talk about a sun roof, the whole ceiling opened up like something out of a movie. This one room was larger than my whole apartment. Oh yes, this was the life I was destined to live.

Finally, Bishop was alone. I walked up to him and gently

took his hand. Without a word, I led him to a rear corner on the opposite side of the room where his wife's body rested in her bronze metal casket.

Speak slow and fluid, girl. Proper and prim, just like Cheyenne. No slang. Proper and prim.

"My name is Shemika Morton. I'm a therapist and a very big fan of yours. I must admit I pulled some strings to get in here," I looked toward the crowd standing around his wife's casket, "but I just had to say my goodbyes to Portia."

"You knew my wife?"

His breath. Oh my God. This old fart must have just eaten a fried shit sandwich.

"Well, sort of. I met her at Grady Hospital. My aunt was in her last stages of intestinal cancer, and your wife sat with her and me before she died. It meant a lot to me, especially since she, too, was suffering from cancer."

He touched my shoulder. I held my breath and stepped in closer. He let his hand linger.

"I'm so glad you got in," he said.

If he was in Iraq, Bush would've been dead to right sending the troops in. The bishop's breath was a weapon of mass destruction.

"I am too." I squeezed his hand. "If there is anything, and I mean anything I can do to make your time of grief easier, please don't hesitate to give me a call."

"Do you have a business card?" he asked.

I reached in my purse.

"What type—?"

I put my other hand over my nose.

"Are you okay?"

"Yes, I'm just having a moment. Your wife . . ." I said before sniffling.

He went on. "I was asking what type of therapist you were.

I may need some therapy myself," he said with a sly grin on his face.

Fucking dog.

"I'm a sex therapist. I help couples who are having trouble with their sex lives."

"Oh, really now?"

I smiled. "Yes, really now," I said, handing him one of the cards I printed up at Kinko's a couple days earlier.

He studied it a moment. "I'll give you a call." He nodded.

"You promise?"

"Bishop, there you are. Oh my Lord, God, Jesus, Mary, Joseph, and Paul, I am so sorry." Some geriatric woman stepped her fat ass between us and interrupted without even acknowledging me.

I mouthed the words *call me,* before I turned and left with his eyes, no doubt, on my ass.

Early the next day, he called. He wanted to get together later that evening after the funeral. Men like him were exactly why I didn't feel bad about being a player. Of course I turned his offer down for that evening. Even if he didn't respect the dead, I did somewhat—

I didn't let him take me out until the night after the funeral. That was also the same night I put Annie poo-nanny on his old ass. I took him to heaven and fucked the hell out of him all at the same time. At one point, I made his dick disappear in my mouth while my index finger made figure eights on his dark brown nipples, and the index finger from my other hand was plunged up his butt. The way the nigga went to screamin', I thought he was gon' keel over and have a heart attack. The man called on Jesus, Moses, God, and some others before his eyes rolled into the back of his head. Before I went home at three in the morning, I had ol' Bishop speakin' in tongue, sprung, and straight strung out like a crack head.

For six months, I sparingly rationed out my sex and my time. I had to bide his and my time. Whenever I did give him a taste of Annie poo-nanny, he lost his ever lovin' mind.

After the third month, I surprised him and brought another woman into the bedroom. Instead of joining us, he just stood over his king-sized bed with a jar of Murray's grease and jacked off while we got our groove on.

Many times, he tried to give me money and gifts, but I turned them down. He was the only gift I wanted—at least his money was, all of it. If I took the diamond tennis bracelets or the car he offered to buy me, then he would have control. This was my game. I made the rules. I had to always maintain control so as to keep him coming back until I got what I wanted.

At the six-month mark of our relationship, he started using the "L" word. It was about time, because I was running out of money. If I didn't trap him soon, I'd have to move back home with my cousin Joanne in the projects.

Speaking of my cousin, her and her dyke girlfriends informed me that the bishop hadn't fucked around on me in two months. Hell, that had to be some kind of record for him. He might just be in love with Annie poo-nanny for real. At least that's what I began to think until a week later. That's when he went back to fucking any woman with a big ass and a small waist in and outside of his congregation. It was hard to believe he hadn't been exposed for the whoremonger that he was.

People were so stupid, I thought. How could you follow a man with the name Money? And to top it off, he had three ATMs inside the church, and he even had a drive-thru ATM machine and a drop box for those who wanted to tithe or just give but didn't have time to make one of the church services.

The man was filthy rich. Every Sunday after the last service, two armored trucks picked up the Sunday offerings. One truck was just for the love offerings Bishop Money received every Sunday. All that money and he still had the nerve to charge for all church workshops and the numerous activities the church offered.

For six months I tried to convince him that he didn't need to use a condom. He wasn't hearing it. I told him I was on birth control, but that didn't matter. He felt that his juice was sacred, that it would only be shared with his wife. I didn't trip. I just took matters into my own hands. Desperate times called for some desperate shit.

After two visits to an infertility specialist, I started getting a fertility shot once a week. Right after my first injection, I started taking the condom off of Bishop after he'd spent himself. Surprisingly, not once did he seem suspicious.

After removing the condom, I grabbed my purse and went to the restroom. After opening it up, I got out the funny-looking oversized needle-less syringe, stuck it in the condom and extracted the juices left inside. Next, I put one leg over the toilet and plunged the bishop's cum deep inside of me. So anyway, it was in March, eight months after I'd met Bishop when I popped up pregnant.

We were sitting on the dock in his backyard with our feet in the water. His private lake sparkled as the sun started to set. We were enjoying each other's silent company when I burst out, "I'm pregnant."

He shook the cobwebs from his head. "Uhh, say what?"

"I'm pregnant with your child."

"My child." He patted a hand on his bare chest before he burst out laughing.

I took my feet out of the water and stood up, placing my hands on my hips. "What's so damn funny?"

"What you just said."

I couldn't stand a muthafucka laughing at me.

*Control, girl. Control. Don't let him see who you are. Keep your
Cheyenne voice on. You've worked too hard and too long to go
Shemika on him. Keep the hood, inside of you, like you have for eight
months.*

"And what does that mean?" I said.

He climbed to his feet.

*Amazing how one word, specifically the big "P" word, could make
a player's steel-hard dick immediately turn into soft rubber.*

We were standing naked, facing each other.

He smiled. "Sister Shemika, if you are pregnant . . . and if
you say you are, I believe you, but me being the father is impossible. Number one," he counted on his fingers, "I always
use protection. Two, I have a low sperm count. And three, if
there is a baby in your stomach and you haven't been with
anyone else, you better get used to being called Mary, and
you better start calling me Joseph."

I crossed my arms. "One," I counted on my fingers, "you
are the only man I've slept with since I met you. Two, you
have a low sperm count, not a *no* sperm count. And three,
seventy percent of condoms have microscopic holes in them.
And four, I will not name our son Jesus, because there is
nothing miraculous about this baby I'm carrying, Daddy." I
rubbed my stomach.

A month later at his request, we took a DNA test. Once
the results came back, he offered me fifty grand to get an
abortion. I thought about his offer for two seconds before
turning it down. He was worth millions, and I had to have it.

So he wouldn't be exposed for the whore that he was, he
had to marry me and do it quick. We were married a week
after I was introduced to the church.

Now three years later, I was still depressed. Although I
hadn't wanted a child, I still came to love my son. Enlarged
heart or not, he was my baby. I could never go through this

again, I thought. After little Jake died, I lost track of everything. I almost said fuck it and walked away, but my girl, Cheyenne, was there to get me back on track.

It had been a year today since my son passed. Bishop was old, but he was in good shape for a 64-year-old man. And he wasn't half bad-looking, with his salt-and-pepper short, wavy hair and thin mustache. He was only five-eight, but he had a little somethin'-somethin' to work with. He just hadn't figured out how to use it to the best of his ability. I tried to teach him after we got married, but he got offended and I said fuck it.

I knew he was trying to find a way to get out of this marriage. He was still fucking every fine piece of ass he could trick out of her panties. Well, that is every fine piece of ass but me. He thought he was being slick, but I didn't give a flying fuck what or who he fucked. I was only concerned as to why I wasn't getting any. I mean we hadn't had sex in three months.

My pussy was on fire. A tree branch got me wet these days. Women were cool, but a tongue and a strap-on just could not replace a sweat-glistening, live, shit-talkin', tall, dark, strong, handsome, big-dicked black man. My panties were wet just saying the words *big* and *dick*.

I loved to cum, especially with the aid of a dick, and I was the freak of life, but I was also very cautious who I introduced Annie poo-nanny to. The haters were still there, lurking in the shadows, just waiting on me to slip.

My safest bet was to fuck that fine-ass Vernon. I know he was my girl's husband and I usually made it a rule not to cross those lines, but I was stressed and depressed, and if I didn't get a king dick in me soon, I was going to lose my mind. She knew I wasn't getting any. Hell, she wasn't fucking him. Why else would Cheyenne tell me how big his dick was?

Just this morning I awoke on the verge of having another orgasm. I'd been dreaming of that tall, mocha-fine, electric-brown-eyed thug in a suit, Vernon Van Gant.

It was night outside, pitch dark. The rain was warm on my skin. The only light we had was from sporadic lightning. I know we were near a busy street, because between hair-raising bursts of thunder, I heard the humming of cars speeding by, splashing puddles of water, probably on some sidewalk nearby. I think we were in an alley. I don't know and I didn't care. The only thing I cared about right then was the orgasm that was building up inside of me. We both were naked as the day we were born.

Vernon was standing straight up, like some black Roman warrior about to go into battle. My legs were wrapped around his neck and back like two pythons. He had me backed up to a mattress that was pinned against the wall of some building. The warm rain started to pour.

His strong, big hands palmed my ass cheeks like a basketball. His tongue was long, wet, hard and thick. He worked it like a young Ali in a title fight—jab, jab, uppercut, over tongue, right. I could feel it not only on my clit and inside of me, but I felt it in every pleasure nerve ending of my body. The man was playing my body like a concert jazz sax man. Oh got-damn, the man was makin' it do what it do. He had my pussy humming.

I thought I would drown in ecstasy when, in the middle of a gut wrenching orgasm, in one swift motion, he spun me around, dropped to his knees and gently placed me on that same mattress. The only thing was it was on the ground now instead of the wall. Rain got in my nose as I tried to catch my breath. All of his Mandingo, Zulu warrior manhood was deep inside of me. He hit walls inside me I didn't know I had.

I opened my eyes to see his chest and arm muscles dancing as he did push-ups in and out of me. The only part of his body that was touching me now was his long, thick, hard, C-shaped, tree trunk dick.

Hell, I was about to cum again just thinking about last night's dream when the chirping ring tone on my cell phone brought me back to reality.

"Hello?"

"May I speak with Shemika?"

"This is *Shemika.*"

"Are you alone?" the soft female voice asked.

"Who is this?"

"You don't know me, but I'm in the grand ballroom of the W hotel having drinks with this sexy man who goes by the name of Treyvon, and he has my thong soaking wet telling me about his fantasy of having his dick in you while my tongue is playing with the ball on and around your clit."

Trey . . . oh shit. Vernon's twin brother. No way. I tried to give him some pussy the day he got out of prison. Nigga ain't had no pussy in four years and he turned me down. We ain't had two words since I cursed his ass out and called him a faggot in front of everyone at his coming home party. I could let bygones be gone if he could. Shit, that nigga looked just like his fine-ass brother. Yeah, he could definitely get it.

Without even thinking, I put two fingers in my mouth before I lifted my skirt, pulled my panties to the side and started to finger myself while listening to this sweet, sweet-sounding woman.

"Are you still there?" she asked.

"Yes," I paused, "I'm here."

"Well, that is a problem. We want you here. If you can come, we all can cum over and over and over."

Ooh, she sounded so sexy. A threesome with tall, dark, and well-endowed.

"Give me an hour. I'll be there."

"We'll text message you the room that we are in."

"Don't get started without me. I'm on my way."

"Too late. I have lotion on my hands and I'm jacking him off under the table we're sitting at while he has two fingers inside me in a room full of people. Oh yeah, girl, I hope you can take dick, because his dick feels like veiny flesh over a curved microphone," she said.

I had my skirt and bra off, and I was in the shower in no time.

Oops, I forgot to take off my panties.

My nipples were so hard, pink and tender, it hurt to wear a bra as I raced out the driveway in my Black Lexus SC400.

5

Trey

"I'm about to invent a new sucker, and I'm going to name it after you: Ho Savers."

"Man, forget you," I said, waving Vernon's comments away.

We were identical, but our looks are where the likeness ended. I wasn't a saint, believe me. I did my dirt, but I always kept it real, and I respected the black woman and the sanctity of marriage. Now, there was a time when I was as big a ho as Vernon, but that was when I didn't know who I was, let alone who the black woman was.

I looked at my watch. I could hardly believe that it was already eighty degrees. It was only 8:30 in the morning. Vern and I were stretching, about to start our five-mile morning run around Stone Mountain Park.

"So, Captain Save-a-Ho . . ."

"You the only ho I'm trying to save. And tell me." I stood up and took off my T-shirt. "Why does every sistah have to be a ho? Why can't she be a queen, or just simply a sistah?"

"There you go with that bullshit. You went to prison, did a little time, read a couple books, and now you a holier-than-thou, Captain Save-a-Ho pussy prophet. Man, prison fucked you up bad."

"How you figure that? I mean just because whenever I look at a black woman I see Momma. I see a woman who is or probably will be a mother, and if things were different, I realize the woman you call *bitch* could have very well been our mother."

I shook my head. "No, bruh, the four years I served made me re-evaluate my life and my value system. I dialogued with some old heads that got me to see shit I've always taken for granted. I started reading about struggle, and I saw that my shit was gravy compared to what others before me had gone through, especially sistahs."

"Come on, dog. I ain't trying to hear that, not for real, for real. You still fuck hoes just like you used to."

I wrapped my T-shirt around my waist and put on my shades. Next I turned my stopwatch on. "Let's go," I said before I took off.

"Yeah, I get my groove on, but I'm always straight up with a sistah. I don't pull no punches or play games. I let them know up front that I'm not looking for anything more than a friend, but if something more comes out of it, well, that's all good."

"And that makes you better than me?" Vern asked.

"No, I never said that. I know I ain't living right, but at least I'm giving the sistah the choice to deal with my shit or go on and try to find someone that is looking for the same things she is." I turned around and jogged backwards, jabbing a finger in his chest. "And I don't screw married women."

Vern sped up, turned around and jogged backwards. "Ladies, you are looking dashing this morning," he said to a couple of sistahs getting their speedwalk on. "Look at those asses. Them hoes didn't need to walk. They needed me up in that ass."

I just shook my head.

"You missing out, bruh. Married women are less drama. I won't say no drama, but I will say less."

"Man, that's just bad karma," I said, running up the steep hill near the two-mile mark.

"Slow the fuck down, man. Shit, I can't talk and keep up this pace," he said as we ran up another hill.

"I'm trying to finish in under forty minutes. You know I have to pick up Ariel by ten-thirty to get to First Afrikan Presbyterian on time. This is my Sunday to speak on addiction."

"Oh, I forgot."

"You should go with us. You need God in your life."

"I got God in my life, and I appreciate all the pussy he endows me with. Besides, I ain't trying to hear that jungle oom-gaba-oom-baba ancestral shit you talk about at that church."

"I know. That's why you should go. Get back to your roots, find out who you are and understand what your mission in life is."

"I know what my mission is."

"I'm scared to ask."

"Since you are, I'll go ahead and tell you. It's simple. Fuck 'em all, don't hurt 'em all. Hurt only the pussy that's begging to be punished.

"It ain't like I'm selling drugs or robbing folks. I'm just getting pussy, and besides, I make my hoes feel good, so I'm giving back in my own way. A few times, I fucked a three-in-the-morning, last-piece-of-pussy-in-the-club ho in the day-time. If that ain't a charity fuck, I don't know what is."

We were coming up on the third mile. I thought I had problems. Vernon was paid. He got married and had parlayed his wife's money into real estate, and in less than three years, he was doing million-dollar deals. He was the dumbest genius I knew.

I never regretted turning myself in, taking the rap for the bank my soft-ass twin robbed with a water gun. At that time, I didn't give a damn. I'd already messed up my life; I didn't want him to ruin his. I knew his pretty boy soft ass couldn't handle prison.

I had his looks, but I had always been the one with heart. No one messed with him when we were in school because they couldn't be sure it wasn't me. I was the athlete of the family, while he was the one always trying to make a quick buck.

School was easy to Vern. He could have been or done anything he wanted, but he was lazy, always trying to take short-cuts, getting over on folks. And I was always there to fight his battles.

I looked at my watch.

"Time?" he asked with his hands on his knees.

"Thirty-nine minutes and forty-one seconds."

He fell to the grass. "You gon' have to carry me to my car and take me home. I can't move."

"The only place I'm carrying you to is church. After the way you are screwing over Cheyenne, you need some spiritual upliftment."

"Uplift these nuts," he said, grabbing his crotch.

"Don't get beside yourself. I'll still put my foot up your ass. No need to get mad at me. I'm not the one with a wife and kid at home and out fucking my wife's best friend."

"I'm gon' quit telling you shit. Man, you swear you got all the answers, but you be right up in the club every Friday night with me."

"Yeah, because I need to watch out for you and try to get

my groove on. I'm not married, but if and when I find my queen, I promise I will treat her like one."

"But until then?"

"Until then I will get my groove on. Man, I gotta go. Hit me later on," I said before jogging over to my Chevy S-10 pickup.

I never let anything come between us, especially a woman, but now I wish I had. I met her at an NA meeting about six years ago. The only reason I went to the group meeting was to keep getting a check from the NFL.

Our meetings were held at the old Butler Street YMCA in downtown Atlanta. It must have been twenty of us sitting on the floor in a circle, sharing stories of why we got high, the effect it had on our families, yada-yada. It was hard for me to listen to the group, being that the Y was right around the corner from the John Hope Homes projects. All I could think about was my next blast. My eyes would get glassy and my nose would start to run just thinking about the end of group, when I could jog on over to a crack house in the projects and buy me a fifty-dollar slab.

So far gone and off in my own world, I didn't pay any attention to her at first. But once I looked up, I was mesmerized. Not by her beauty, but by the passion she had when expressing herself. She was different. No one had been able to completely hold my attention in years. She spoke as if she had used or was an addict at one time herself.

Dr. Jamison was a clinical psychologist. She was filling in for our group leader, who had fallen ill. She was vibrant and vivacious, speaking about "the *you* in you that we don't know."

And once we locked eyes, I knew there was something between us. I couldn't explain it, but it was there. It was almost like the electric shock a dead person gets from the defibrillator that revives them.

After group, I sat outside on the stair railing counting the cars that went by for almost an hour. Not once did I think about getting high. Once she came out, we embraced. I can't explain what I was feeling. I just knew I didn't want her or it to ever go away.

I felt very comfortable with her as we walked all over downtown Atlanta talking about ourselves. After about three hours, we ended up at the high-rise condominium building where she had an apartment. She hugged me like someone saying good-bye. We kissed as if it were our last. She invited me up, but I turned her down. I didn't want what we had between our thighs to ruin what we were sharing in our hearts. At least not yet.

I didn't have a cell phone, so I gave her the number at Vern's crib, where I was crashing and in return, she gave me her office and cell phone numbers.

I was so high on her, I never wanted to get high off anything else ever again. The sun was coming up by the time I'd walked about ten more miles to Vern's apartment.

"Man, where you been?" he had asked.

"Heaven."

"Man, are you high?"

"Yeah. But not on no dope."

"Say what?"

"I met a woman. I know it sounds crazy, but it was like . . ." I looked up at the ceiling. "Like some modern-day Romeo and Juliet thing. We fell in love. I mean for real. I know without a doubt I'm going to be with this woman for the rest of my life, Vern."

"Look." He put his hand on my shoulder. "I have something to tell you."

For the first time since I got in, I looked at him. He was looking crazy. Something was wrong.

"I love you, man. I did it for us, but shit got all fucked up.

Man, I was trying to get some money so I could help you get straight. Help you get clean so you could go back and play ball," he cried, while hugging me.

"Police, open up!"

Next thing I knew, the front door came crashing down. It was all a blur from there.

"Treyvon Gant?" a cop said.

Did Vern point a finger at me? No, he wouldn't. I was slammed against a wall and cuffs were put on my wrists.

"What the—"

Next thing I knew, I was downtown watching a surveillance camera of my dumb-ass brother flirting with a teller before handing her a note and pointing to a bulge in his pants shaped like a gun. A minute later, he was running out of the bank with a bag of money that was turning blue as he ran. Once he looked down and saw the bag drowning in blue, he dropped it, pulled a red watergun from the front of his pants and slammed it onto the bank parking lot pavement.

The two detectives in the room with me were having a ball, cracking up. This would have been Vern's third offense, which meant a life sentence, so I took the rap. Vern had never had to do time for robbing the Pizza Hut delivery boy, or for the drug case he caught. Both times he got off with probation and community service. I'd fucked up my career, but he still had a chance. I probably would have gone back to getting high anyway, ruining my chances of ever playing in the NFL again.

At the time, none of that mattered. The only thing that did was her and Vern. I'd always taken care of him, even through my crack woes. But Dr. Jamison was a different story. She took care of the night before.

The first six months on lockdown, I was sick to my stomach every day, thinking about not being able to ever share the same space and air with her again. I had her phone number etched in my memory, but I never called. I couldn't. She was at the top of her game, a shaker and a mover, and I was at the bottom of mine, a two-bit crack head loser.

I had been on the inside for about six months. I was reading all types of books finding out who I was and I was beginning to understand the meaning of life, when I got the letter. I was crushed. I didn't eat for three days. In the letter, Vern told me that he'd gotten married and his wife was having a baby. His wife and soon-to-be mother of his first child was Dr. Cheyenne Amarie Jamison.

6

CHEYENNE

*I*t would be so easy to pull the trigger. Just do it, girl. Get it over with. Lift up the covers, put your free hand in the slit of his boxers, pull out his penis, put the barrel right up to the head and BANG!

If it only were that easy, I thought while I stared at his filthy, naked frame sleeping peacefully under my white satin sheets. I turned and looked at the clock hanging above the 60-inch plasma TV built in the wall in front of my—and I put emphasis on *my*—bed.

It was 4:00 in the morning. Suddenly I felt a chill. I hit the remote on the nightstand built into the wall on my left, slowing the stainless steel blades of the three fans that hung from the ceiling all around the room. I don't know if it was the cold, white marble floor, anticipation, or fear that had me trembling as I climbed onto the platform that my bed rested on in the middle of my room.

The gray sweats and the white wife-beater tank I had on were damp with perspiration. This must have been the—I don't know, maybe twenty-somethingth time I stood over him, gun in hand, pointed at his crotch while he slept. And each time, my eyes burned with tears of hate and rage. If it weren't for my daughter, Ariel, I wouldn't blink twice before pulling the trigger.

She was one of only two bright spots I had in my life. I had earned my doctorate and I was in private practice by the time I was thirty. I made nearly $300,000 a year working a three-day week. I was fit, healthy, married and I had the three-quarters of a million-dollar dream home we lived in built from the ground up. You would think I was happy, right? Wrong.

I was miserable. Oh, I failed to mention that I was married to Satan. Hate couldn't even begin to describe the way I felt about Vernon Van Gant, my husband of five long, hard years. I despised him way before we were even married.

I never understood why he would want to ruin my life by marrying me. He could have gotten anything he wanted. I would have given him over $100,000, every cent I had at the time if he would have just disappeared.

Love was my downfall. It was my own fault. Six years ago, I met a man, sort of a patient. I was speaking at a Narcotics Anonymous group session when our eyes locked. Such passion, I thought, as his orbs burned a hole in my soul.

Against my better judgment, I agreed to go for a walk with him after group. It was a warm but mildly breezy Wednesday evening. The downtown Atlanta we walked through was alive with silent lights and car engine, horn, and pedestrian noise.

For four hours, we basked in each other's company, laughing, talking, listening, and just enjoying moments of sweet silence together. Before the end of the evening, I was sure, without a doubt, recovering drug addict or not, this man was my soulmate.

He had such a gentle and soothing spirit, yet he was waging a war with some inner demons that seemed to contort his soul. Demons that I would have to exorcise from his heart and soul so I could comfortably enter.

I felt like a silly teenager the next day at work, picking up the phone and dialing a couple of digits before hanging up. I did this several times throughout the day. I checked my cell phone as many times, and each time it did ring, my heart skipped a beat, only to return to normal once I answered and it wasn't him. Finally, around three in the afternoon I pressed *67 to block out my number before I dialed the number he had given me.

On the fourth ring, he answered. We made small talk for a few minutes before we set a date to meet on the boardwalk at Piedmont Park in Midtown later that evening.

I remember walking up to him and thinking that his whole demeanor seemed different: sort of cocky yet reserved, but much more aggressive-looking.

I lightened up and let my guard down when from behind his back he brought forth a large brown wooden picnic basket with a blue blanket covering the top.

We'd just dined on peanut butter and jelly sandwiches, Pringles potato chips, and Concord grape juice. His back was against a large oak tree overlooking a dark pond. I was at ease, lying on his lap, listening to the wind sing and watching the leaves dance in the invisible night breeze.

I trusted him, and I needed him to trust me. In hopes of getting him to open up, I began telling him about my own past personal experience with drug addiction. Only God, myself, and my girl, Shemika, knew about my drug problem before I opened up to Treyvon.

I told him the whole story about how I'd started off taking Percoset and Valium to relax, study, and work the long hours I had while in med school. I was writing my own prescriptions, forging physicians' names before I was a doctor myself. By the time I went into private practice, I couldn't get by for a couple hours without my meds.

I remember crying and him holding me when I explained

that I'd kicked my habit, went cold turkey when I was informed that one of my patients had died of a heart attack. It was because of me. I'd prescribed the wrong medicine. This wasn't the first time I'd written out the wrong prescription, but it was the first client I had that died. And she was only thirteen.

The little girl's parents were so devastated that they never even thought to have me investigated. I made some calls and paid a heavy price to have the autopsy results altered.

I told him that I never had, nor would I ever tell anyone this. I remember taking his hand and squeezing it. "I will spend the rest of my life trying to save the lives of children. I will never forget that little girl," I said.

Not long after I bore my soul, we passionately kissed and against my wishes, he rolled over on top of me. I looked into his eyes, and it was then that I knew I'd made a big mistake telling him my innermost secrets.

He had my arms and legs pinned to the ground. He was too big, too strong. There was no need to struggle. I knew his type. Struggling only aroused the rapist and made him more violent. I'd evaluated and counseled rapists and victims in the past. I never imagined that one day I would be a victim.

All his weight was on me as he managed to pull down his sweats to his knees. He grabbed my panties and yanked, ripping them off in one swift motion. Next, he forced himself inside of me.

"Ugh," I grunted. He was too big. I was dry. I silently cried as he started slow and hard. He lifted my legs and bent them back past my forehead before pounding himself in and out of me so fast and with so much force I thought I was going to pass out from the pain.

What he said after he finished hurt me much more than the actual rape.

"Right before the police busted in my crib, taking Treyvon away for some shit I did, he couldn't shut up talking about you. He went on and on about this fine-ass, down-to-earth sistah he met last night. And if I do say so myself, you are fine as all outdoors."

This may sound crazy, but a few minutes later, after I let his words soak in, I was relieved. Relieved that I hadn't misjudged the man I met the day before. He told me that he had a twin. Treyvon explained how he had to get himself together, get re-instated to play football so he could take care of his twin. He told me that he'd taken care of Vernon since they were fifteen. That's when their mother's boyfriend shot and killed their mother and father in a jealous rage. From what I understood, Treyvon's father didn't even know their mother was having an affair.

Ever since then, Treyvon had taken on the role of father, mother and big brother, sacrificing his time to make sure Vernon was well taken care of. And again, he'd sacrificed himself to protect his brother. If he only knew.

Vernon got a kick out of telling me things that he knew I wouldn't repeat. Things like how he'd called the police while Treyvon was out with me. How he'd told the cops that his brother Treyvon Gant had robbed the bank to support his own crack habit. He went as far as telling them where he and Treyvon lived. Vernon even asked them to send someone over to the apartment complex to lay in wait for Treyvon. And when asked why he was being so helpful, Vernon explained to the police that he just wanted his brother to get help, and that he didn't want to have any problems since he himself was on probation.

If I ever said anything to Treyvon, Vernon threatened to have me arrested for the murder of the 13-year-old girl that I'd killed. I offered Vernon money, sex, and my condo; anything to leave me alone. He told me if I gave him a baby, then he'd be out of my life for good.

Reluctantly, I got pregnant, and when I was five months along, he said I had to marry him, so his child would not be born a bastard. I did.

After he moved in and the baby came, I fell in love. Not with Satan, but with my beautiful little chocolate angel. Needless to say, Vernon had lied. He never had any intentions of leaving. And next thing I knew, I was where I am now, standing over him, wanting to blow his big, pinkish-brown-headed black penis off.

Now, five years later, I was still madly in love with my husband's twin brother. The only time I became moist was when I thought of Treyvon Octavious Gant.

Even now, after serving almost five years in prison and only knowing her for a few months, he was closer to his niece than her own father was. And my little Ariel loved her some uncle Trey. In a few hours, my heart would skip a beat when he would come over to get her and take her to church.

I was surprised when Trey told me that he'd be taking Ariel to the One World Faith superdome church. But after he explained that he was speaking, I understood. On any other occasion, he wouldn't be caught dead up in that church. It was no secret how he felt about my friend, Shemika, and her husband, the Bishop T.J. Money.

7

Bishop

Every light in the church went dim. Every one except the spotlight, which was on me as I raised my arms to the clouds. My stare went from the congregation to the stained glass dome ceiling. Suddenly, a loud burst of thunder erupted inside the church walls. The congregation gasped.

"Praise the Lord! For all who fear God and trust in Him are blessed beyond expression. Yes, happy is the man who delights in doing His commands. He himself shall be wealthy, and his good deeds will never be forgotten. Psalms 112:1-3." My voice echoed over one hundred speakers throughout the church compound.

It had cost me nearly one hundred thousand dollars, or rather it had cost the church one hundred thousand for the sound effects and the custom designed podium that doubled as my soundboard. The damn thing was so complicated with all the knobs, buttons and screens, I had to take classes to thoroughly learn how to use it. By all the ahhs and the gasps that could be heard coming from the congregation, it was well worth it.

I nodded my head and smiled as I thought, *I'd like to see Chicago's New Dimensions top this.*

I hit the lights. "Now, family, as we know, the wisest, I said the wisest man in the Bible wrote Psalms. Am I right?"

"Yes sir, Bishop!" John Jacobs spoke out. He was one of the junior ministers who sat behind me.

"Sho' ya right!" someone in the congregation shouted.

"Now, let me help you understand what God was saying when He bestowed this message unto Solomon."

"Preach!" came another voice from the congregation.

I pointed to the sky with one hand, and with the other I hit the button on the podium that paged my choir conductor. "For those who praise Him."

"Praise Him," the choir sang.

The lights dimmed and the spotlight was back on me. "For those who," I pointed a finger to the ceiling, "praise Him."

The spotlight jumped to the choir. "Praise Him," they sang.

"Praise Him," I said.

"Praise Him," the choir sang.

We went back and forth like this for a good three minutes. The congregation joined in, singing His praises and shouting His holy name.

I brought the spotlight back to me. As quick as it started, it ended. The church became silent.

The building brightened up as the church lights came back on. I braced both arms on each side of the podium, leaned forward and looked out into the vast congregation. I smiled as I noticed so many beautiful ladies, ones I hadn't privately had in my council.

"The scripture I just read is simple. How much plainer can it get? Scripture reads, if you praise God," I shot a hand in the air, "and trust in Him, not your boyfriend, girlfriend, wife, husband, mother, father, or even me. Trust in Him," I banged a fist on the corner of the podium, "and only Him, you are blessed. Blessed beyond expression." I pointed to the congregation. "Listen to me, family. God said," I paused. "I don't think y'all hear me." I threw both hands in the air. "I said, God said, you are blessed beyond expression. That means words can't describe how bountifully blessed you are." I paused for a moment, gathering my thoughts.

"Scripture goes on to say happy is the man who delights in doing His commands. He himself shall be wealthy, and his deeds will never be forgotten." I brought my hand down, grabbed the microphone and walked away from the podium and down the stairs, so I could be face to face with the congregation.

I put the palm of my hand on my chest. "I own a million-plus-dollar home. I've recently purchased a fifteen million-dollar private jet, and I drive around town in a three hundred sixty thousand-dollar Phantom Rolls.

"The naysayers call me the pimp in the pulpit, Player Preacher, Black Caesar, and I'm sure most of you have heard other names."

"I love you, Bishop." A pretty little sistah, blessed with a body that would make a gay man go straight, stood up and spoke right in front of where I stood.

Uhm, uhm, uhm, Lord Jesus, give me strength. Good Lord, this little sistah is fine.

"I love you too, sistah," I said.

I'd have to find out who she was. Yes, sir, uhm-hm, she sho' nuff needed some counseling.

I continued, "I'm here to testify before you today, family. I'm your brother in Christ, Bishop Terrell Joseph Money." I paused. "Love Him. Praise Him. Fear Him. And I trust only in Him." I closed my eyes, embraced myself, and smiled. "And I'm ecstatic, excited, and more than delighted in serving Him."

I opened my eyes and said, "For my loyalty, my Father has

rewarded me with wealth as He told Solomon He would. He has blessed me beyond expression.

"So who are they that cast stones, but dwellers of glass houses? Those same stones will boomerang back and shatter the very foundations from which their stones were cast."

Thunder exploded, the lights went out, and a streak of what looked like lightning struck the ground where I stood. The spotlight came on and was shining on me. Both of my arms reached for the heavens. "For God is my rock, my force field. He shields me. Not even lightening can harm me as long as God's arms are wrapped around me. So those that stand in judgment of me, beware, for God's wrath is mighty, and it comes without warning."

As I climbed the stairs back to the stage, I glanced at my watch. I had a half-hour before I could find out who the beautiful sistah was that rose up and interrupted my sermon. My member was rising under my purple robe just thinking of the counsel I'd like to give her.

I smiled as I looked over at one of those naysayer haters, Treyvon "drug-addict-prison-convict" Gant. I had my secretary invite him to speak today. He was a thorn in my finger, but a thorn that was growing. I had to show the congregation that I was the bigger man, and at the same time I had to put him and everyone like him in their places. He didn't realize that if I wanted to, I could crush him like the roach he was. Although it was his twin brother I had on tape screwing my wife in a room at the W hotel, I could easily put a spin on things, making it look like him.

It had taken that idiot a year to get my wife in bed. Vernon had no idea what I was about to do. If he did, he would have charged me way more than ten thousand dollars to record and screw my wife.

Speaking of that Jezebel, she was through and didn't even know it. She thought she was playing me. The dumb whore was about to get a lesson in pimping 101. I'd been in the game far too long to have some two-dollar whore take half of my shit. They'd find her in some alley dumpster with her throat cut first.

She got me good, getting pregnant. There wasn't any question about that. I had to lick my wounds and give in for a while. When our son died, I was somewhat disheartened, but Shemika's suffering pretty much alleviated the remorse I felt.

She was devastated. God don't like ugly. This was lesson number one, and she didn't even see it. She had been smitten by God. No way would He let me, one of His chosen, be taken in by a Jezebel. The child was conceived out of deception. He was not pure. So, it was God who had my seed returned back to the earth from which he came.

Now it was time for lesson number two, and the final lesson, but first I had to deal with Mr. Gant, both Mr. Gants before, Vernon found out what I'd done to him.

8

Vernon

"Who's your daddy? Huh?" *Pop*. I asked while smacking that ass with a metal pancake turner.

"You are, Papi. Ooooohhh. Poooooo-towwww. Fuck me, Papi. Harder, Papiiiii. Give it to me, papi chulo." Meila cooed and ooed as I had all nine point three inches of crooked dick up in her tender, young, wet pussy.

There wasn't anything like low-mileage, young, wet, tight pussy. Oh, she wanted it harder? O-motherfuckin'-kay.

I grabbed hold of the sink's round nozzle and pushed her Puerto Rican ass all the way in to the counter. I could see my house out the kitchen window in front of me. Her bright yellow 38Ds were bouncing around in what looked to be fresh dishwater.

I curved my back and wrapped my free hand around her waist. My legs tensed up, calves tight, quads bulging. I lurched forward like a rocket, pulling the sink's nozzle and her ass in to me at the same time.

"What's my name, got dammit? What's my muthafuckin' name, be-otch?" I asked, trying to break my dick off in that pussy.

Suddenly, she did some ole *Exorcist* bullshit. Her head spun around.

"Who's your daddy?" her—I mean his—deep voice asked.

"Oh shit! Hell nah," I said, backing up, slipping and falling.

"Vernon! Vernon!"

The bitch had a mustache and a beard. She wasn't a bitch, she was her daddy. But how?

"Vernon? Are you okay?"

I shook my head. The room came into focus. I looked up into my wife's eyes.

"You were having an erotic nightmare."

Got-damn. I damn sho' was. Thank God.

I put my hand under the covers and on my dick. *Fuck, I didn't even bust.* My dick was harder than Chinese arithmetic.

"Cheyenne, come on over here, baby. Get into bed with big daddy." I sat up and patted the mattress.

"Three words. Are. You. Crazy?" She put her hand on those curvy hips of hers. "You will never," she closed her eyes, "ever get this again. You just keep screwing all your nasty little whores, including the little high school, eighteen-year-old Puerto Rican that lives across the street. The one you were just dreaming about."

I turned my head to one side. *Who the fuck did she think she was talking to? I mean who the muthafuck—oh, hell double no.*

"I hope her father catches your child molesting ass," she said, turning to leave with her hands on her hips.

"Bitch, you gon' respect me. I'm still the dick in this damn house," I said as I rolled off the bed so fast I almost slipped and fell. I lurched forward, grabbing her long-ass, reddish-brown wavy hair.

In the five years I'd been married to the bitch, I'd never

put my hands on her. She had lost her everloving mind. She didn't know her damn place.

"Get off of me! Let me go, Vernon!" she shouted while hitting me with a barrage of blows.

"This is my pussy. Woman, I own you." A wild blow landed on my nose. I lost it.

"Bitch, you hit me in my got-damn face." I picked her up and slammed her on the marble bedroom floor. I pulled up her dress and off ripped her panties. She didn't move.

"You haven't given me any since Trey got out seven months ago. You fuckin' my brother? Huh? Woman, you still my wife, and I'm gon' have to show you who's your daddy."

9

Cheyenne

I didn't care. I was in pain. I didn't know how bad I was hurt. He could do whatever he wanted.

As soon as I closed my eyes to try to block everything out, my mind drifted back to the night in the park. I didn't fight him. Something told me it wasn't right then. Although I'd just met the man I was in love with, I knew that the man on top of me wasn't him.

No, I did care. If I had fought, I'd be free. I'd likely be in prison, but I'd be free—free to love and free to express my feelings of love to the only man who has ever had my heart. It was time I got off my back. It was time I stood up.

"Ahhhhhhhhhhhhhhhh!" I screamed as I jerked and turned, throwing him off balance. I violently brought a knee up into his groin.

"Ahhhhhhhhhhhh!" He doubled over in pain. "You crazy-ass bitch. I was, I was about to, to nut. Come back here." He somehow managed to reach out and grab hold of my leg as I tried to crawl out of the room.

I kicked and screamed. "Not in me! Not on me! Not around me! Never again will you or your nasty penis touch me."

"Oh, yes the fuck I and it will," he said, dragging me to him.

I gritted my teeth. "You have to kill me first," I said, bringing my arm around and raking my fingernails down the side of his face.

"Got-damn, motherfuck, shit! Bitch, I'll kill your fuckin' ass!" he cried, grabbing his face with the hand that had my leg a second before.

I ran down the winding metal stairs that led to the kitchen. I grabbed the keys to his Rover off one of the islands in the middle of the kitchen. Then I went to the coat closet, opened it, and grabbed a coat to cover me. I ran barefoot down the hall and through the great room. I had my hand on the handle and was about to open the door leading to the garage.

Hell no. Why should I leave? This was my house. I built it. I'd lived in fear far too long. It was time I faced my fears. If he went to the police, I'd just have to deal with it. I was in prison already. At least my conscience would be clean if he did. I'd finally be free.

Besides, I wouldn't have to worry about my baby. Treyvon loved Ariel like she was his own. And God how I wished she was. I'd give anything to have that man's child. He'd make sure Ariel was well taken care of.

Since I'd probably spend most of my life, if not the rest of my life behind bars, I might as well go for double murder.

I felt like an elephant was lifted from my shoulders as I sat on the edge of the eight-foot granite fountain that took up one wall of the great room.

He could go to the police if he wanted. As a matter of fact, I wished he'd go. That would give me even more motivation to send him to hell.

"You still here, bitch?"

"This is my house. I am not leaving."

He laughed while waving a DVD at me.

He looked like a boxer on the losing end after a championship fight. He had on a blue velour Phat Farm sweat suit. His nose was swollen. His eyes were red, and the left side of his face was scratched up pretty bad. He had a hand on the wall of glass that overlooked the pool and the tennis court in the backyard.

His attempt at being cool wasn't working. I smiled, knowing that I was taking back my life. No longer was I scared of him or his threats.

He was maybe ten, twelve feet away from me. It would only take me two or three seconds to run him and me through the glass. Knowing my luck, he'd survive the thirty-foot fall, and I'd be dead.

"As for the nasty little whores you say that I'm fucking . . ." He smiled, holding the disc in the air. "I happen to have one on this that you may want to see. Then again," he shrugged, "maybe you won't want to see this," he said, throwing the DVD at me.

I dodged, letting the disc crash against the fountain wall.

"My keys?" He took a step toward me.

I didn't miss, hitting him in the nose with the keys.

"You gon' make me kill you, woman."

I shook my head and crossed my legs. "Not if I kill you first."

"Are you threatening me? Have you forgotten the little piece of information I have that will put you away for life?"

"No, I haven't. And no, I am not threatening you. I am making you a promise."

"What promise?" he asked, walking toward the door.

"Put your hands on me again and I'll show you."

"Fuck you," he said right before slamming the door leading to the garage.

After I heard him speed off, I jumped up, went to the theater room and inserted the DVD.

10

Trey

The Bishop T.J. Money. Man, he was good. Now, if he was white, he'd be a shoe-in for the presidency. He had what it took. He was conniving, deceitful, evil, very well spoken, distinguished-looking, and he was even intelligent. If I didn't know any better, I'd be a devout follower of his.

Somewhere, I'd read that Satan will come at you from the left, right, front and back. He knows the Word better than you. He will use it to lure you in and control you. He will make you think that it's fine to covet money, worship the golden calf as the people of Moses did. The faces of dead presidents printed on legal tender were modern-day golden calves.

After my gracious snake-tongued host, Bishop "ATM" Money introduced me, I went to the podium and explained how the ancient Africans, known then as Cushites or Abyssinians, had been so successful in ruling the world for over five thousand years without war. I told the One Worlders how their system of communalism and tribalism worked; how there was no class divide, no rich, no poor; how everyone was of the same family, and no one person had more or less than anyone else.

I knew I was speaking of a concept that most couldn't conceptualize, but at the end, I tied the Cushites' ancient Ausarian religion directly to their politics. Church and state weren't separate, they were one. And all the different gods that European ideology had us believing the ancients worshipped was a grave misconception.

The church was deathly quiet as I explained how the ancients used symbols and names to describe God's power in several aspects of nature and conscious thought. This was done so the Cushites could see God with their own eyes and in all of His creation.

I summed everything up with the God concept of nothing being new under the sun, and that this concept didn't start with the birth of Jesus. I left it at that. If I went any further, I knew I would have lost them and really alienated myself from Bishop's people.

I was in my pickup on my way home to cook my little princess lunch when she interrupted my thoughts.

"Uncle Trey?"

"Yes, princess?"

"What is a bitch?"

She caught me so off guard I forgot what I was doing for a second. I turned my head to her. "Where did you hear that word, princess?"

Beeeeeeeeeeeeeeeeeeeeeeeeeeeeeeeeeeeeeeeeeeeep!

I looked up just in time, cutting the wheel hard and speeding up, barely avoiding a collision with a black Hummer. It was my fault. I ran straight through a red light. My heart was beating a mile a minute.

"Do it again. Do it again, Uncle Trey," Princess said as she bounced around in the passenger's seat. I 'bout had a heart attack, and she was laughing like she'd just come off a ride at Six Flags. Kids.

A few minutes later, I pulled over to the curb in front of my home.

"Uncle Trey, I asked Mommy, but she told me I was too young to understand. But I am a big girl. You know I am. If you tell me what that word means, I promise I won't tell nobody," she shook her little braided head, "that you told me."

I undid my seat belt and grabbed her little hands. "Where did you hear that word again, Princess?" I asked.

"Daddy. He calls Mommy that all the time. I know it's bad because he only says it when he's mad."

"He says the B word in front of you?"

She shook her head up and down. "Sometimes, but mostly when they are arguing somewhere in the house where I'm not."

It had taken me a long time to see, and I guess it was always there, but I was blinded by love. My brother was an asshole. I had to bite my tongue, I was so angry. I couldn't believe—no, yes I could. He treated all women the same. Even his wife, the woman I loved, the woman I'd never stopped loving. But how could he so blatantly disrespect his own babygirl?

"Princess, a bitch is a female dog," I explained.

"Ohhhh, like a little puppy," she said as if she completely understood.

I need a goody powder. I massaged my temples before I got out of the truck. No sooner than I'd walked to the other side, I saw a shadow out of the corner of my eye.

"Uh, hey sugar, you got a square I can borrow?" Some made-up little girl who had obviously come from the abandoned house next door asked. She couldn't have been older than fifteen, and she was asking for cigarettes. Uhm, uhm, uhm. I just shook my head. This shit didn't make no damn sense. She was just a baby.

"Nah, baby." I shook my head. "I don't smoke."

"You think you can loan me three dollars then?" she asked, sticking her little chest out at me. It was hot outside, but not that damn hot, I thought, as I looked at what she wore.

She was a little bitty thing. She couldn't be no more than about five-two, and that was with her black three-inch heels on. She had smooth, butter-yellow skin. She wore a dusty, used-to-be-white mini-skirt so small that you could see her reddish-brown pubic hair. And a purple, bra-like top supported her grapefruit breasts. When she turned her head to the side, I could see the new growth in her extensions starting to cause her braids to unravel.

"I'm sorry, sweetie, I don't have any singles," I said as I grabbed the handle on the passenger's side door.

"I can suck your dick for ten dollars, or you can fuck me and I'll suck you off for twenty."

I let go of the door handle, turned and took a step closer to her. "How old are you?" I asked.

She licked her lips. "Old enough to suck, fuck, and make you nut."

I reached in my back pocket and took out my wallet. "I tell you what. Tell me how old you are and I might let you take care of me," I said.

"Seventeen."

"Okay, it's like that," I said, turning around and stepping back to the truck.

"It's like what?" she asked.

I turned my head to her. "You playin' games, little girl." I shook my head. "I don't play games."

"Ain't nobody playin' no games."

"Telling me you seventeen is playing games. You know you ain't even close to being seventeen. I don't care how old you are. I ain't the po-po. I don't carry a badge. You ain't got to fake the funk with me."

"I'm fourteen, okay." She put her hands on her little curvy hips. "So, can I take care of you now?"

I shook my head.

"We can go right in there," she said, pointing to the abandoned house next door.

"Does your mother know what you doin'?"

"Uh, yeah."

"I bet she does," I said with a hint of sarcasm.

"Come on up. She's in the house. What? You want both of us? That'll be forty, but for you, we'll do you for thirty. I bet you ain't never had a threesome with a mother and her daughter."

And I never will. I thought I'd heard and seen it all. How could a mother turn her own teenage daughter out?

I looked at the chipped concrete stairs leading to the house next door, where she and her mother would trick. The steps were covered with knee-length weeds and grass, but I could still see the two fresh, clear-blue crack sacks between the first and second stair. I knew they were new because I'd just swept up the ones from last night before I left for church this morning.

At this point, I was at a loss for words. My princess was probably burning up in the truck. I just reached in my wallet and gave the child a twenty. "I don't want your body, I want your mind. Now, go clean yourself up and get you some food in your system."

"Thank you, uh . . ."

"Trey. They call me Trey," I said to her back. "Oh, and I'll be watching you," I shouted.

My brother Vernon. Boy, was he something, I thought as I held Princess's little hand as we walked up the two sets of stairs leading to the front door of my house. He tricked me into buying a crack house that was in desperate need of repair. I was fool enough to believe his story about the Atlanta University Center being in the process of buying up the land on my street and the next two streets over. He said they were going to fix up the abandoned houses and turn the others into boarding houses for students. I believed him because the university was right up the street, and they had already started building apartment-like student housing on the other side of Spelman. It wasn't until a few days ago that I'd made some calls for myself and found out there were not now, and had never been any plans to buy up the area where I lived.

Half of the houses on my street were abandoned crack houses. Before I got the loan to buy it, my house was the largest crack house on the street. It was a yellow five-bedroom Victorian manor. The only reason Vernon still had all his teeth was because after I started working on the house, I fell in love with it.

My street would be real nice if someone came in and cleaned up all the trash, got rid of the dealers and the addicts, landscaped the yards and rehabbed the homes.

"Uncle Trey?"

I had forgotten all about Princess. She was sitting at the table reading a Little Bill book while I cooked pancakes, eggs and turkey bacon, all her favorites, and mine too. Thank God, because it was about all I could cook.

"Yes, Princess."

"That girl you were talking to when we was outside, was she a bitch?"

Oh Lord, what have I started? No, what has Vernon started? That little girl outside thinks she is nothing more than an animal. It's obvious by what she is doing to herself. That little girl next door could be my niece, she could be my daughter. Did her father call her mother a bitch so much that she started acting like one?

I was getting hotter by the second. *No more.* Unh-uh. No longer could I let Vernon disrespect the woman I loved or my daughter—I mean his daughter.

"Uncle Trey?"

After placing the food on the table, I sat down across from my little princess.

"Come'ere," I said, beckoning her to me. "Girl, you getting too big to be up in your uncle's lap."

"Them big ole muscles you got, I'll never be too big."

"In response to your last question, Princess; no, baby, that young girl I was talking to is a princess in disguise." I pinched her cheeks and smiled. "She is just like you. She is so very far from being a bitch, and your mother isn't one either." After I put her down and ushered her back into her chair, I scarfed down my food. This couldn't wait. I had to straighten Vernon out once and for good.

After we washed the dishes, I hurried her to the truck. I was moving so fast, that after accidentally slamming the passenger door, I slipped and almost fell. If I hadn't grabbed hold of my mailbox, I would have busted my butt. As soon as I let go of it, it came crashing down on the pavement, causing a week's worth of mail to scatter.

I'd been so busy training clients at three different gyms, and tiling my bathroom and kitchen floors, I'd forgotten all about my mail. I gathered up the mail and the mailbox and carried them up to the porch. I was about to place the mail inside my door when a dark blue envelope caught my attention.

I had it with me after I returned to the truck.

"Is that a birthday card?" Princess asked.

It was hotter than Hades inside the truck. I couldn't get the key in the ignition fast enough so I could turn the A/C on blast.

I turned the envelope around. "I don't know, but I doubt it. You know when my birthday is."

"Yeah. It's the same as Daddy's, in April. Are you going to open it?" she asked.

"Later, after I get you home."

"Well, can I open it?"

"Go 'head," I said while pulling away from the curb.

A minute later, I glanced over at her.

"Surrrr . . . Sur . . ."

"Surprise."

"Sur-prise," she repeated.

It was a very colorful card with the word *surprise* running from top to bottom at an angle. I noticed that there was no return address on the envelope. Any ol' nut could have sent it. No tellin'.

I reached out. "Sweetie, let Uncle Trey read it."

"Unh-uh, I wanted to read it."

"I'll let you read it, but let your Uncle Trey read it first," I said in a calm tone, "Okay, Princess?"

"Oooooooo-kay." She was reluctant to give it up, but after she did, she sat there with her arms crossed and her lip stuck out.

A few minutes later, we pulled up in Cheyenne's horse-shoe-shaped cobblestone driveway. I parked in front of the stained glass double front doors before pulling the card from under my leg.

My eyes got wide and I brought my hand to my mouth. I read the card four or five times.

Oh shit. No she didn't. Please, Lord, tell me this is a joke.

11

Shemika

Just this morning on our way to church in the Rolls, without saying a word, Bishop smiled at me as he slid the DVD into the dash. On all four ten-inch screens inside the car you could see and hear my ass getting dicked down righteously by Vernon while my nipples were being tongue-jabbed by some ugly freak-nasty little skank named Cherry.

Before he put the disc in, my panties were already wet. Now I had to squeeze my legs together and concentrate on something else just to keep from cumming all over the beige calfskin seats. Instead of being nervous and worried, I just wished he'd hurry up so I could slip into a church bathroom and masturbate. Fuck.

Bishop kept looking over at me with a wry smile on his face.

Like he's really done something. Arrogant son of a bitch.

I smiled right back at his ass. If he knew what I had planned for his ass, I bet he wouldn't be smiling.

God, I can't believe that punk-ass nigga played me out of pocket like that. If that nigga's dick wasn't so good, I wouldn't have hesitated to make my cousin Jo off his punk ass too.

As we pulled up to the church parking garage, my cell phone buzzed. I reached into my purse and took it out. Speaking of punk-ass niggas, Vernon had just text messaged me to meet him at his new apartment after church. He said he got the place just for me and him.

My nipples were hard and tender as ever. Just because he was every punk-ass nigga in the book, that didn't mean I didn't want to feel his pink-headed, one-eyed black python deep inside of my lava-hot, faucet-dripping wet, swollen pussy. But this was just wishful thinking, or shall I say lusting. With everything that was sure to be going on for the next few days, it wouldn't be wise, and I'd be pressed to find the time to get me some.

This was my big day. I was a little nervous, but I was ready.

I wore an eight hundred-dollar Versace loose-fitting platinum-belted white dress, matching open-toe white heels, and a string of white pearls adorned my neck. The pearl-beaded tiara I wore helped keep my hair in place. I had to look my best for the cameras later on, or so I thought.

But nooooo. Murphy's law had bit me in the ass once again. I was mad as two broke-dick dogs in heat. Right after church, I caught up with my cousin Jo. Instead of crying over the bishop's fallen ass, or having Vernon's big-ass dick knee deep in me, I was going off on my dumb-ass cousin.

We'd planned the shit for months now. This was the Sunday he was going to fuck everybody up with light shows and special effects during church services. Everyone was going to be so caught up in the show that no one would actually see what happened.

Jo was in the projection room under the balcony. I spent $5,000 on the high-powered rifle and the infrared scope. She had a clear shot several times. But what happened? Abso-fuckin'-lutely nothing.

"You fucking idiot!" I waved my hands and arms in the air. "You fat fucking idiot! You supposed to be so hard and shit, but when I need you, you bitch up. You kill a poor, hustlin'-ass nigga over one of your pie-face-pussy-lickin' bitches, but your big, scary ass chokes when I give you a real chance to come up and make some cheese."

I could not believe this shit. My cousin, Joanne, and I were inside the restroom of my office in the church administration building. The dummy had been in and out of girl school and prison her whole fucking life. She ain't never had shit, wasn't shit, and if it hadn't been for me she would be shit.

"I'm sorry, Meeka." Her big, bull-dyking, man-looking ass shuffled back and forth while she spoke. "I-I just couldn't do it. He did something to me, he was speakin' some real good shit about haters and niggas that ain't got shit try'na judge mo'fuckas. I felt what he was sayin'," she put her hand over her heart, "right here. I just couldn't bring myself to burn him. It ain't even 'bout no money. It's about my soul."

"Your soul." I was all up in her face with my hands on my hips. "Bitch, what fuckin' soul? I own your got-damn soul. I bought that shit last year when I paid the Jones brothers twenty grand to spare your bald-headed ass after you smoked that boy that worked for them."

"I told you the Jones brothers didn't want none of me. If I ended up dead, it would have started a war, and they couldn't afford that. They was makin' too much money in the projects. A war would make they dope traps too hot.

"Mike Jones was lucky I gave him the two hundred I took off that puppy-piss, weak-ass nigga of his before I smoked the mo'fucka. The Jones brothers should have paid me for killin' the bitch-made nigga."

I shook my head. "I don't understand you. We grew up in

the same fucking rat-infested projects, slept on the same pissy-ass mattress. We like sistahs, and you kill a nigga 'cause he slapped one of your hoes, but I," I put a fist over my heart, "tell you the muthafucka I married be kicking my ass whenever his dick get hard, and I even tell you I'ma hit you off with a hundred grand after the muthafucka stops breathin', and you shit me." I looked her up and down. "I thought we were family, but now I see you ain't shit."

She shrugged her shoulders. "It ain't even like that, cuz."

Ignoring her, I turned my back and walked out of the bathroom.

"Meeka?" She shouted while following behind me.

I opened the office door and headed toward the elevator.

"Meeka? Meeka?" she cried out as I sped up.

I had my finger on the open button as I yelled, "From this moment forward, I ain't got no family. Make my name taste like shit in your mouth whenever you think about using it."

She stood at my office door looking like she'd just lost her mother.

I smiled after the elevator started going down to the first floor. I'd always known how to push her buttons. Loyalty and family were the most important thing to her. Her big ass was probably sitting on the floor outside my office, boo-hooing her ass off. And after she finished, knowing her, she'd go back to the projects, stop by Pookie's, cop some of that killa Bin Laden weed laced with X, go upstairs to her apartment, put some T. I. or some Li'l John in the CD player, turn that shit on blast, take off her clothes, roll up some of that Bin Laden in a blunt, then get whichever dyke ho that's crashing at her place to eat her pussy while she blazed one and thought about how she was going to smoke Bishop. Damn near the same shit she'd done when I paid her five grand of the two hundred I'd received from the life insurance policy after I made her off that jive-ass nigga I married fifteen years ago.

I just hoped she'd take care of Bishop before it was too late.

I was too stressed to deal with this shit right now. I had to get right. I reached in my purse as I made my way to the parking garage. Thank goodness I had my key to the Rolls. Fuck him. He'd have to get home some other way. I got into the car. Not even fifteen minutes later, I was outside of Vernon's studio fuck pad.

Hell, I was still pissed as shit, and although the nigga had played me, I wasn't going to let that shit stop me from cumming all over that big, black buck dick of his.

I was playing him out of some dick just like niggas played hoes out of pussy. I knew when to open my legs and close my mouth. Just because everyone in my circle was dumb as fuck didn't mean I had to be.

I had everyone fooled. My girls thought I was like them, even Cheyenne. She was cool, I liked her, and I was there for her, but she didn't know the real me. I don't think anyone did, except for my cousin Joanne. And her ghetto ass didn't count. They thought I was a little rough, ghetto sort of, but classy and refined. They had no idea that I was that gangsta hood bitch you saw on the rap videos and in the movies. Only thing was, I was for real, live and in 3D like a mutha-fucka.

I played the game well. I didn't curse around them. I pronounced t-h-e "the" instead of "duh." I said "ask" instead of "ast." I carefully enunciated my words. And best of all, my southern accent was barely noticeable.

I even changed the way I walked. Instead of walking slouched over, I walked like the queen of England, back straight and head held high. I took long, gliding strides.

The only thing I didn't change was the way I fucked. Getting my pussy licked was fine and good, but after some little pretty, soft body got the juices flowin', I needed some eight-inch plus, steel-beam hard, blue-collar, Mandingo dick.

I slid my panties off and put them into my Coach purse before I rang the doorbell. It sounded like he had company. They were making a lot of noise. I hoped they hadn't started without me.

12

Cheyenne

I carefully inserted the funny-looking bullets into the maga-zine. Going to hell was a vacation compared to what I'd make Vernon Van Gant suffer. The black 9-millimeter felt warm and titillating in my hands. He raped the wrong woman for the last time. I didn't know much about guns, but I knew enough to put my hand over the top of it and pull the thingy back to load a bullet in the chamber.

Killing him would be easy now, I thought as I kissed the picture of my daughter that I carried around in a plastic holder on my key chain. After I taped the note on the front door, I got in my Jag and took off.

So careless. Did he think I wouldn't find out or was it that he just didn't care? Why would he use a check from our joint account to pay the deposit and first month's rent for an apartment?

The only reason I hadn't reacted or said anything up to now was I hoped he'd spend even more time away from home.

And his other women . . . *Please,* I could care less about them. Heck, I didn't care anything for him.

I gripped the steering wheel so hard that my knuckles were turning red as I sped through the wrought iron security

gates and over the speed bumps of the Paradise Island luxury apartment complex.

One thing I didn't do was blame him for fucking my best
friend. No, that was all on her. Vernon was part rat, cat, dog,
and snake. He was a scavenger. It was his nature to fuck anyone and anything.

A tear trickled down my face as I backed my Jag in next to
his Rover.

"Why? Why? Why?" I said, thinking out loud while banging my fist on the steering wheel.

*We were friends. All we've been through together and she stabs me
in the back. My girl. Out of all people . . .*

Finally, I took a deep breath, grabbed my purse, got out of
the car and started walking until I found apartment 1132. I
stood at the door. *Should I knock? What if he asks who is it?
What if he looks through the peephole and decides to act like he's not
there? What if he tells me to leave? Should I just shoot the damn
lock?*

I was running out of should I's and what ifs when I heard
and then saw the doorknob turning. I rammed my shoulder
into the door as soon as it began to open.

"What the hell?" He jumped back like he'd seen a ghost.

I stepped in and slammed the door behind me.

He stuck out his arm. "How did you—"

"The check you wrote to the apartment complex with the
address on it. That was real smart," I said as I took a step toward him.

"Wh-what-what are you gon' do with that?" he stuttered.

"What do you think?"

After running out of room to back up, Vernon fell into
the black leather couch against the wall.

"Turn around!"

"Huh?" he asked.

I popped the safety off the gun. "Turn. The. Fuck. Around.

Now, Vernon!" I spoke in a slow, calm, but serious tone. He must have sensed the urgency in my voice, because he rolled onto his stomach without another word.

I took the cuffs out of my purse. "Hands behind your back!"

It was difficult putting the cuffs on him while holding the gun in one hand. The shackles I took out of my purse were much easier to put around his ankles.

"Roll over and look at me." I frowned and pointed the gun at his crotch.

"No you didn't pee on yourself." I looked at the wet yellow stain in the middle of his white linen pants. "Disgusting!" I shook my head. It was hard to believe that this was the same man who had forced his dick in me a couple hours earlier.

"So, you gon' kill me? I-I mean right here with all these people living around me. All the noi-noise the gun will make."

I smiled and brought the gun from his crotch back up to his head.

"Say something!" he pleaded with tears in his eyes.

"There is nothing left to be said. You've said it all. You've done to me what you've wanted to do for these last few years." I tapped the middle of his forehead with the gun's barrel, leaned in and whispered in his ear. "The only thing to do now is pull the trigger, love."

"Wait! Wait! Wait!"

I pulled back and shook my head from side to side.

"Why? Why are you doing this?" he cried.

I put the safety back on, turned the gun around so the handle was pointed toward him. Ignoring his cries, I reached back and swung for his nose, but he turned and I gashed the back of his head.

"Why did you trick me into believing that you were Trey the evening I met you?" I hit him again. "Why did you rape me that night in the park?" This time, his shoulder felt the butt of the gun. "Why did you set Trey up, having the police lay in wait for him? Answer me!"

"You know why."

This time I caught him off guard. I turned my head and looked toward the kitchen before hitting him in the ear with the gun. My heart skipped a couple beats the way he screamed. There was some blood, but not as much as I thought there should be. After rolling off the couch and banging his knees on the floor, he started mumbling.

"Speak up, Vernon, and if you say one word that doesn't have a ring of truth to it, I'll come crashing down on your other ear twice as hard as I did the left one."

He started a little choppy, but after I raised the gun over my head, he spoke as if he were a college professor lecturing to an auditorium full of students with a broken microphone.

Ring! Ring! The door bell chimed.

I turned my head to the door. Had someone called the cops on me? I turned back to him.

Ring! Ring! "Vernon, baby, it's wet and ready. I'm answering your call."

I knew that stank coochie heffa's voice anywhere. No she wasn't at Satan's door when she should have been in God's house with her husband.

I frowned as I put my finger to my lips, gesturing for him to be quiet.

"I hear you in there, baby. Mommy is so wet out here. Don't you want to come take a dip in my pool?"

I slowly walked backwards, keeping my eye on him while heading to the door.

"I'm taking off my panties," she sang. "I have one, two, three, four fingers where your dick should be."

Horny, no-account heffa. To think I took this stray dog in my home.

I unlocked the door and turned the knob.

"Take my dick out of her and come put it in Mommy. And afterwards, we'll fuck—"

"Fuck who? Fuck me?" I reached out and grabbed her dress near the neck. It ripped when I snatched her into the apartment.

She tried to catch her balance, but failed, falling onto the carpet as I closed the door.

"Bitch!" she screamed.

I looked her up and down as she held her ankle while she sat on the floor. "You already did. You," I looked over at that sorry excuse of a man, "and this piece of shit." I turned back to her wide-eyed, dressed-up behind. "Both of you fucked me." I shook my head. "No, sistah. Unh-uh. The fucking isn't over yet."

13

Shemika

High-yellow, light-bright, close-to-white-ass bitch was the first thing that came to mind after she made me bust my ass on the got-damn hard-ass floor. What the fuck did her proper, prim ass mean by "the fucking ain't over yet?" Yeah right, like she was really gon' get gangsta up in here.

I was sitting up trying to rub the soreness out of my left ankle when I looked up to see the wrong end of a black-ass Glock staring back at me.

"What the fuck?" I looked at her. Her face may have been an expressionless statue, but her eyes were on fire. This was not the Cheyenne I'd known for the last eight years.

What the fuck was going on? I turned my head as if Vernon had some answers. If the situation wasn't so fucked up, I would've laughed at his six-foot-two, wanna-be-so-hard, punk ass sitting on the carpet, crying like a little be-otch.

I winced at the sight of all the blood on the side of his head.

She fucked that nigga up. Oh, this is definitely a different Cheyenne.

His hands were behind his back, his ankles were in shackles, and he had his head in his lap, probably so we couldn't see the tears that were sure to be running down his face. She fucked his ass up for real. Still, I wasn't fazed. After eight years, the chick really didn't know me.

"You better pray to God you ain't made me sprain my got-damn ankle." I turned back and looked at her. "Ho, don't you know I will kick yo' muthafuckin' ass?"

"I'm right here, sweetheart." She placed a hand on her chest. "There is nothing standing between us but air and opportunity."

I pointed. "Air, opportunity and that thing you have aimed at me."

"I don't need this to take care of you. What I need are some rubber gloves. That's what I wear when I take out the trash."

"Trash! Trash, bitch!"

No she didn't. I started getting to my feet. I was a little wobbly and sore, but my ankle wasn't sprained. "You married your man's brother and you call me trash?"

"That's a different story, one you don't know and one I'm glad I never told you.

This dumb ho had fucked up and let me get to my feet. If only I could get her to wave that thing at Vernon for one minute.

"Different story my ass. You's a ho too, but the difference between me and you is that I'm a smart ho, bitch. I married money."

I looked over at Vernon, my eyes going from his head to his crotch. *Please don't tell me he pissed on his self.* I just shook my head in disgust.

"Look at what you married: a broke dick dog that'd fuck a tree if it had a hole in it." Turning back to her with a quizzical look on my face, I said, "And I'm trash? That nigga didn't have shit but a big-ass dick when you met him."

Vernon cut in, "You wasn't talking that shit when you was on your knees sucking the nut out of this big-ass dick."

I looked back over at him. "Nigga, psss, shut your scary, half-a-man, down-low ass up before I tell your wife how hard you cum when I stick my dildo up your ass."

"I thought we were friends," she said with a sad look on her face.

"We are. I mean we were. And you shouldn't let a dick come between us."

"That's the way I expect low-life trash to think."

"Trash?"

"Is there an echo in here? Did I stutter?" she asked.

I balled up my fist and closed my eyes. *When I get my hands on her . . .*

"Still, Shemika, I'm married to," she waved the gun at him, "that dick."

"So the fuck what? It ain't like you love his ass. I'm married too. But you think I give a damn who Bishop screws? Hell no."

"Loving him or being married to him is not the point," she said.

"So, what is?"

"The point is that you were my girl. We been through hell together. We were both strung out on drugs. We helped each other pull through. No rehabs, just us and group.

"You were naked, stoned and out of your mind, bent over a toilet with some fat pig ramming himself inside of you when I came and got you out of that frat house bathroom before the other twenty or so guys had their turn with you. Or how about the time I took you to the emergency room when I found you in an empty apartment, half-dead from smoking some bad dope?" She shook her head.

"And now you're worse off than the crack-whore trash you

were when I met you. At least back then you got ten dollars to open your legs and your mouth. Now you've stooped so low as to screw your ex-best friend's husband. For what, a few minutes of pleasure? An orgasm?"

I butted in. "What's so wrong with that? You the one told me about his big-ass dick in the first place. You don't fuck him," I shrugged, "so I fucked him. All he is to me is a dick and a tongue. I married money, so I don't have to get it from elsewhere. All I need is a dick on the side and occasionally a wet tongue and I'm straight."

I put my hand out in front of me. "So, don't go judging me for having multiple orgasms with the nigga you givin' all your money to without getting shit in return.

"A nigga can have the best dick and give the best head in the world, but that shit don't pay no damn bills. But dumb bitches like you do pay the bills and carry," I turned, "niggas like him. But I'm trash. You married and support trash, so what does that make you?"

"You—"

Before she could get out two words, I said, "A trash can. You can't even see the nigga only with you because of your money and your standing in the community. Yeah, he making cake now, but he still ain't clockin' like you."

"I know all of this," she said.

"I can't tell you know." I rolled my eyes and put my hands on my hips. "Hell, you married the punk-ass, dildo-in-the-bootie nigga."

"I had to!" she shouted.

I took another step forward when she lowered her head.
Stay calm, girl. You're getting close. Fuck, I'm still a step or two too far away.

Cheyenne looked up and shook her head. "You don't understand. I had to," she repeated.

"Bullshit! You ain't got to do nothing in this life but be black, live and die."

"I already did." Her voice, so loud and vibrant a minute ago, had now dropped to barely above a whisper. "I died the night he raped me, the first night we met. Now I'm about to be reborn," she said in a trance-like state, looking at him and taking a step toward me.

As soon as she turned her hips and pointed the gun at Vernon, I lunged into her mid-section. The gun made a clanging sound as it dropped to the floor. I was too busy rolling around on the carpet with Cheyenne to see where the gun had fallen.

"Ahhhhhhhhh," I screamed. The ho was trying to pull all the tracks out of my head. I was on top of her, but I couldn't hit her good the way she had my hair wrapped around her hand.

"Where is that ass kicking you promised me?" she asked while landing a flurry of wild blows to my back and neck. "I loved you like a sister," she cried.

Right as I got a hold of her neck, she bucked her hips and snatched my head in the opposite direction, rolling me off of her and onto my back.

"Ho, you done snatched my hair out." I snarled, kicked and bucked. I couldn't get her off balance. She had a bunch of my hair wrapped around her fist while she hit me in the face. I tasted blood. I couldn't see shit.

"I loved you, Shemika. You betrayed me."

My hands and arms covered my face. Why was she crying? This ho was psycho, I thought as her lightning-fast blows came raining down on me. And then all of a sudden, the storm of punches subsided.

"Let me go! Let me go!" I heard her cry and scream.

"I oughta kill you, bitch," Vernon said.

I moved my arms and looked up to see her being lifted off of her feet. Handcuffs were around her neck.

"Scream all you want. There's only one other person who lives in this building, and she's at church. The other units in back of me are being renovated."

How the hell had he got those cuffs in front of him? I wondered as I got to my feet.

"Bitch, you busted my head open. You should've killed me when you had the chance. When I finish with you, you gon' wish you were dead so bad that I got you puttin' the gun to your own fucking head," Vernon said.

By now, I was standing in front of her with my fists balled up. I was just about to take a swing, when her body went limp.

"Fool, you killed her," I said.

Her body fell to the ground.

"Nah, she just lost consciousness. Trust me, she'll be okay. I've done this before. Fuck, my back is broke," he said while stretching. "I thought I'd never get those cuffs under my butt and through my legs."

He used his head and arms to get me to look over at the kitchen counter. "Go look in her purse and see if you can find some keys so I can get out of these damn things."

I just stood there with my hands on my hips, wearing a nigga-I-ain't-yo'-bitch look on my face. My eyes went from his scarred-up bloody head and face to the wet stain between his legs.

"What the fuck you lookin' at?" he asked.

This nigga was takin' pussy. That comment he made hadn't slipped by me. He just said he'd choked another ho uncon-scious before. I couldn't believe this shit.

"What the fuck is wrong with you, woman?" he asked while stutter-stepping toward the kitchen counter where Cheyenne's green purse was.

I took a deep breath and closed my eyes. Juices were dripping down my legs. My pussy was so wet. The way he had her barely hanging on to consciousness was so, soooo hot.

"Vernon, I can't believe you've choked other hoes. You've raped women."

"Hold on—"

"Hold on hell," I interrupted. You ain't never took this pussy," I said while pulling my dress over my head. "And why haven't you ever choked me? You know I like it rough." I put my index finger in my mouth. I could still taste the blood from when she hit me. Uhmm, it tasted so good.

"Take this pussy, Vernon. Choke me!" I snarled. "Fuck me! Fuck me like I'm the one that had the gun to your head. Fuck me like your life depends on it," I said while standing over Cheyenne's unconscious body, dripping wet, with my legs spread.

He was out of the cuffs and the shackles in no time.

"Oh, I'm gon' fuck you. I'm gon' fuck the dog shit out of that pussy all right," he said while grabbing his dick.

"Oh, yeah." I closed my eyes as I stuck four fingers inside myself. "Fuck, keep talkin', Daddy. Tell me how you gon' take this pussy."

"Help me carry this bitch in the bedroom, so we can tie her up." While carrying her and putting her on the bed, he continued. "We gon' beat-rape this bitch too," he said with thunder in his voice and a sparkle in his eyes.

She never knew, but I've always wanted to fuck her.

"She talking 'bout the only way I'd fuck her again was over her dead body. She always said she'd kill herself before she'd sleep with another woman," he said while tying her up with extension cords to the bed's metal frame.

"I'll be right back. I'm going to take a shower. When I get out, we'll wake her up."

I could hardly wait. She needed to see and feel what was about to happen to her. In a few minutes, we'd see who was trash.

Oh, I haven't forgotten. He still doesn't know that I know.

Just then, I came up with the perfect plan. Vernon knew too much. He'd always have something over my head after Bishop was gone. Oh no, he had to go. I had a surprise for Vernon and his lovely wife.

I smiled as I sat beside her on the California king, playing with her long, reddish-brown hair. I was getting hotter by the second.

Murder-suicide. Jealous wife. Cheating husband. Perfect ending.

14

Bishop

The blues. They write them every day in Memphis. I smiled and nodded as I held the woman's hand and listened to yet another sob story.

Hers eyes were glassy. "Bishop, my husband just up and left me. He's been gone two months. Georgia Power cut off the lights last Wednesday. My kids are hot and hungry. He handled all the bills, so it came as a complete surprise to me when I received the letter informing me that our house was going into foreclosure next Tuesday if I didn't come up with $6,372.67."

I knew it was coming, and now the tears were free-flowing. She was all out crying now.

"I don't know what to do."

Cute face, but a little on the chubby side.

"I would've gotten a job. I had no problem working, but . . ."

Isn't there always a but?

"I don't have anyone to keep my five kids."

Same story, different week. I was so bored and tired of these long, drawn-out, sad soap opera stories. I was fed up with my parishioners thinking that I was an ATM. Just because my name was Money didn't mean I was a slot machine.

I wanted to tell this woman to get five empty cans, put one in each of her children's hands, go downtown and beg. She expected me to believe that she had no idea her husband was leaving, or her house note hadn't been paid in months. Yeah, right.

Negroes like her were the main reason I had the church financial aid department come up with the nine-page financial assistance application we used for our tithing members. This way, the church could weed out the scammers and hustlers from the real tithing members with real needs. If they didn't give to God, they shouldn't expect God to give to them.

The church made it as easy as could be. We helped our members tithe. We offered payroll deduction and direct debit to our tithing members. We had a tax department that kept a record of our members' earnings. We kept their W-2s on file to help them keep record and make sure they were giving God his ten percent. We even prepared our members' taxes free of charge. So, there was no excuse for anyone not to be caught up on their tithes. If everything checked out, then the church turned old, sad stories like hers into new fairytale beginnings.

Every Sunday, after the second service, for sixty to ninety minutes I privately greeted members and guests in a small greenhouse-like stained glass room in the west wing of the big church. Each person had three minutes, five minutes tops.

I looked at my watch. It was already 3:30. Her time was up. I pressed the button on my pager to signal the ushers to come and get this woman, who was in my arms, crying hysterically. While escorting her out, I told them to take her to financial aid and cut the line off at the vestibule door leading outside. That meant I still had five more people to listen to. I made a mental note to have the ushers only allow three at a time in the vestibule instead of five from now.

God has yet again shone His light on me, I thought as the next person came through the stained glass French doors.

"Bishop," the young lady grabbed my hand and looked into my eyes, "I just want to tell you that you have touched me deep."

Not nearly as deep as I want to touch you.

"I-I have never felt more love in one place. Here, I feel like I belong." She put her large fingers over her small but firm chest. "I saw girls around me that I feel that I can relate to."

I smiled. I could not praise His Holy name enough for blessing me on this beautiful, sunny Sunday afternoon. I knew I wouldn't be able to find her after service, but He made sure she found me.

I put my hand on her shoulder. "Sistah, this is God's house. Everyone belongs. We are all His children, His sheep. We are all related." I smiled. "I am merely His shepherd."

"Thank you, Bishop. Thanks for being you. Thanks for helping me find a place of worship that I can finally call home."

Her Adam's apple made the choker she wore bob as she spoke. Her skin was so light, you'd think she was white. My rod was rising as we stood there alone, looking into each other's eyes. She was small; not petite, but small. She had the face of a child. She didn't have curvy hips, but she was as pretty as an angel.

I took the little lamb in my arms. I hit the button on my waist ten times, signaling my ushers not to disturb me for ten minutes.

It started with a kiss on the neck. But by the time I started to pull her dress up, my tongue was exploring her mouth. My chest was heaving.

"Wait!" She pulled back.

"Don't be nervous. Nothing's going to happen. I just wanted to see and feel what I had to look forward to later on. Now, how would I look, a bishop defiling God's house?"

"I'm not nervous, but before we go any further, I need to tell you something."

15

Trey

"Vernon is dead." Those words hit me like a tidal wave. What in the hell was going on? Whatever it was, I was about to get to the bottom of it.

It cost me fifty dollars for such short notice, but I had no choice. I needed a babysitter right then, so I convinced the little Hispanic sistah across the street from Cheyenne to watch Ariel for a few hours.

In no time, I was on the freeway doing ninety, racing to get to Buckhead. I knew exactly where Paradise Island was. This was one of Bishop Money's apartment complexes. Why would dummy rent one of Bishop Money's properties? First the card, and now this. I had to save my dumb-as-a-rock brother if there were any way possible. He was a fucked-up-in-the-head individual, but he was still my twin. I loved him, and I couldn't let her do it.

I was still shocked by the finality of her words. I thought I was going to pull up and drop my little princess off at home and go find Vernon to see if the card I received was meant for him. I sure hoped not. But why would Cherry lie? She was a fruitcake when I messed around with her seven, eight years ago. No tellin' if she did what she said. I'd find out soon enough.

The letter I pulled off the front door was a little more urgent than the card, though. If it was true what Cheyenne wrote in the letter, then I could understand why she wanted to kill him. I loved her with all my heart, but Vernon was blood. Now, Cheyenne had my emotions going crazy after reading the letter.

The first paragraph talked about how she'd never stopped loving me and how she was tricked and blackmailed into marrying Vernon. In the next paragraph, she said that she was on her way to the Paradise Island apartment complex. Number 1132 Paradise Island Way was the address she left. She went on to explain that she had his gun, and she was going to kill him. The most confusing part of the letter was the part where she said that if I got there ahead of the cops, to look in her purse, then I'd understand how evil my brother really was.

Oh, shit. I just remembered. Oh Lord, don't let it be too late. Please don't let her shoot that gun at him.

Twenty minutes later, I nearly slammed into the back of a tricked-out white Cadillac truck. I sat on my horn. *Beeeeeeeeeeeeeeeeeeep!* I put my head out the window. "Ayyyyyyy! If these gates close on my damn truck, I'm gon' break your back!" I shouted at some asshole that had stopped right in front of me as I was tailgating him, trying to get through the security gates before they closed.

If I just had a dime—no, a nickel for all the dumb shit my people did, I'd be richer than Rockefeller. What was the point? I didn't understand why someone would try to block me from driving into the apartment complex, and as soon as I rolled down my window and opened my mouth, instead of standing his ground, he takes off like a coward. It was fools like him that made me wanna join the KKK. If I was head of the Klan, the first thing I'd do was form a hit squad targeting ignorant black folk.

I followed the numbers on the buildings until I found Vernon's building. I ran to the door and put my ear to it. I heard voices, but they were faint. And then I heard a shrill scream.

16

Vernon

"Ain't no fun when the dick got the gun, is it, bitch?" I said before slapping her upside the head.

"I bet hitting me makes you feel like a man, huh?" Cheyenne asked.

"Nah, but when I jam my hard dick in your ass—that's right, I said ass—that will make me feel pretty damn manly."

Where was the fear? I had my wife tied up to my bed and was waving my dick and my gun at her, and she wasn't fucking terrified. I looked over at Shemika, who was sitting at the corner of the bed.

"What?"

"Whachu mean, what? Don't fuckin' 'what' me. Help me rip the bitch's clothes off. It's time to get it on," I said.

Has every bitch lost they damn mind?

I hit the play button on my portable CD player. "Yeah, they don't hear you, 50. If a bitch don't like me," I pointed to Cheyenne, "something wrong with the bitch," I said, singing along with 50 Cent.

I put my hand around her neck and ripped her shirt with the other while Shemika undid her pants.

"You don't have to do this, Shemika," Cheyenne said.

"I know. I want to," Shemika said.

Pop! "Bitch, shut your ass up. Damn, that was a good one. I might've slapped the taste out your mouth for real that time."

"Baby, you got Li'l Ricky?" I asked Shemika while admiring the blood trickling down my wife's chin.

"Of course."

Li'l Ricky was our name for the dildo I bought Shemika. "Go and get it while I take the bitch's legs loose." I turned around and crawled over the bitch to get to the extension cords that had her legs. "I don't know why we didn't turn her on her stomach before we tied her up," I said.

"I think you better turn around, Vernon," Cheyenne said.

I was sitting on her right leg, trying to undo the knot I tied in the extension cord.

"Vernon?"

"Bitch, shut the fuck up 'fore I slap the shit out your ass again. I'll turn around when I get good and got-damn ready to rip your asshole apart."

"Nigga, turn your punk ass around!" Shemika shouted.

"Whore, I'm one second away from putting my foot—"

"Putting your foot where? Go on, finish. What did you say a few minutes ago? Ain't no fun when a ho got the gun?"

I was confused. What the hell? I felt my bladder filling up quick. "Why do you have on rubber gloves, and why are you pointing that thing at me?"

"That's what you do before you shoot a muthafucka."

"Huh?" I said.

"You aim at his ass," she pulled the stock back, "put a bullet in the chamber."

"Ho-ho-hold the fuck up, now. What the fuck?"

"Not what the fuck. It's you who is fucked. Your punk ass set me up. I was about to be one rich bitch, but the nigga paid your ho ass to video record me fucking you and that skank ho from the W hotel. You fucked me, now I'm going to fuck you, and nothing personal, Chey, but I can't leave any witnesses. This is the only way I can make sure the disc never gets out after I kill the bishop."

"No. No. No, baby." I put my arms out toward her. "We can work it out. Let me explain."

"You can't explain shit. Only thing I want to know is who's your daddy now?"

The room exploded with gunfire. The funny thing was. . . .

17

Trey

Gunshots! Oh no, I was too late. I used my shoulder to ram the door open.

"Bitch, I'm God. You can't kill me," I heard Vernon say as I ran to the bedroom.

"I-I can't breathe."

"That's the got-damn point, bitch!"

I was standing at the bedroom door in shock. Cheyenne was spread-eagle on a king-sized bed, with her legs and feet tied down, and Vernon was strangling Shemika on the floor next to a bathroom. This couldn't be my brother.

"Let her go. Are you crazy?" I asked while pulling him off of Shemika. "Have you lost your everloving mind?"

"Let me go. I'm gon' kill the crazy bitch. Nigga, she tried to kill me."

I banged my knee on the bed, wrestling with Vernon's naked, dumb ass.

"Let me go, Trey."

Shemika got up, coughing and wheezing.

"Get out of here. Go home. I'll handle him," I shouted right before he elbowed me in the stomach.

Shemika ran past us and out of the room.

"Run," I said, barely holding on to his wild ass. I was trying to catch my breath. "Keep struggling and I'm going to kick your ass, something I should have done a long time ago."

My back was on the carpet, and his back was on my chest as we struggled.

"Let me go, Trey. She's back with a knife!"

I looked around him just in time to see Shemika's arm taking a swing at Vernon with a large butcher knife.

"Nigga, I'm gon' cut it off!" Shemika shouted.

I let him go. He rolled into Shemika, knocking her off balance and making her drop the knife.

"Stop it! Please, stop!" Cheyenne screamed.

I grabbed the knife from the floor before jumping up to my feet.

"Bitch, you cut me. I'll kill your ho ass," Vernon said as he rolled on top of Shemika and started beating his fists into her face.

I didn't know what to do. If I pulled him off of her, she'd attack.

"My purse, look in my purse on the kitchen counter. Go quick, Trey," Cheyenne shouted.

Anger, disappointment, disgust and hate were just some of what made me ball up my fists and hit him in the face as hard as I could before I ran into the kitchen with the knife in my hand.

"Trey, hurry! Hurry!" Cheyenne shouted.

I was back in less than thirty seconds.

BANG!!!!!!!

The sound of gunfire exploded as I shot a hole in the wall with the .38 I got out of Cheyenne's over-sized purse. "Drop it, Shemika, now! And not on him!" I said as Shemika stood over Vernon's limp body with a boom box over her head.

"Over there." I waved the gun in the direction of the bed.

"Shemika, untie Cheyenne, and make it quick." I turned and kicked Vernon in the side. "Get up!"

"Got-damn, nigga, fuck. What happened?" Vernon asked, grabbing his side.

"Trey knocked your bitch ass out with one punch. Pow!" Shemika said while undoing Cheyenne's legs.

"You hit me, man?" Vernon looked at me sideways while getting to one knee.

I was about to apologize until he opened his big mouth.

"Over a bitch. You choose a funky bitch over me, your own brother. Your own flesh and blood?"

No, he would not turn this shit around. This wasn't about blood. It was about right and wrong.

"Damn right. And if you ever lay your hands on another woman in my presence, I will do a lot worse."

"Man, after all I've done for you. After all we've been through, I can not believe you're selling me—"

"You sold him out long—"

"Shut the fuck up, bitch. Ain't nobody said shit to you. I haven't forgotten that it was you who brought that damn gun in here in the first place," Vernon said.

"You," I pointed the gun at Vernon, "shut the fuck up. You will respect the mother of your child when I'm present. And it doesn't matter who brought what where. What matters is that now I'm the one with the loaded gun."

My stare returned to Cheyenne. He didn't deserve her. Why did she marry him? Why did she betray what I thought we had? I know it was only one night, but that night we shared a lifetime of memories past and ones to come.

"Go ahead, baby—ah, I mean Cheyenne. You were saying?"

She seemed very calm considering she was tied up, beaten, and it looked like she was about to be raped before the gunshots were fired. Clad only in a pink bra and matching panties, she sat up on the bed, rubbing her red wrists and ankles.

"Are you okay?" I asked.

"Yeah, I'm fine. Just a little sore from being tied up and hit in the mouth."

I turned toward Vernon. Out of anger, my voice became high-pitched. "You hit her in the mouth?"

He shrugged.

"Psss." I shook my head. "You ain't nothin'." I balled up my fist. "I should fuck you up, but what will that prove? It won't change you. Maybe the card I got in the mail this morning will make you change."

I reached for the card in my back pocket before I heard a loud popping sound.

18

Cheyenne

"If you ever put your hands on me again, as God as my witness, I will kill you," I said to Shemika after I used what little strength I had to slap the fire out of the heffa.

Although she backed up, holding the side of her face, and was now standing a comfortable distance away near the bathroom, she looked like she wanted to strike back. But for some odd reason, she just leaned against the wall and slid down to the floor with her hand still cupped against her face.

I stood up and turned my attention to Trey. "Vernon set you up to take the fall for him. He not only called the police, but he—"

"Bitch, don't even go there. You can't turn my twin against—"

"Shut up, Vernon." Trey turned his attention to his brother.

"I'll be right back," I said as I ran out of the room. A few seconds later, I was back with the mini recorder I had in my purse.

Holding it in the air like I was a preacher with a Bible, I continued. "After you raped and beat me this morning,

there was no doubt in my mind that I was going to kill you.
You took my love and you took my life. I am tired of living in
fear. I'm tired of being scared that you will go to the police
and turn me in."

"Turn you in?" Trey interrupted.

My heart dropped.

"Turn you in for what?" Trey frowned up.

"Murder." I turned to face Trey. "I was addicted to prescription drugs for years. Not that it is any excuse, but I was
high when I evaluated, diagnosed and prescribed medicine
that killed a thirteen-year-old little girl. I made some calls,
shredded old files and created new ones to cover my tracks.

"For two years, guilt had threatened to consume me. I
thought I was going to burst if I didn't tell someone what I'd
done. So, when I called you the day after we met, he answered the phone. He made me think he was you. We met
in—"

"Come on, big dog, I know you ain't going to listen to
her." Vernon held an arm out toward me. "You ain't going to
choose her over your own family."

"I'm not going to tell you again, man. Shut the hell up
and let her finish," Trey said before turning his attention
back to me. He nodded.

"Anyway, we met at Piedmont Park that evening. We sat
under a tree and he was very charming until I bared my soul,
telling him about my past and the demons that haunted me.
"When he asked why I was telling him all this, I told him
love."

Our eyes were locked on each other as I took a step toward Trey. "I knew that you were my soulmate. I was and still
am deeply in love with you. I've never felt anything less than
hate for Vernon." I broke our stare and dropped my head.
"Your twin raped me in the park the night I met him as you.
He blackmailed me, got me pregnant and left me no choice

but to marry him or go to prison for the rest of my life. I should have chosen prison. It had to be a vacation compared to the hell I've lived in for the last five-plus years."

"You are a piece of work, asshole," Shemika said from the spot on the floor where she was sitting.

"Fuck you, ho," Vernon shot back.

She shook her head. "I don't think so."

"Both of you!" Trey waved the gun at them. "So, Cheyenne, if you planned to kill him, why didn't you?"

"I thought about how much you love him. And I love you too much to hurt you. So I decided to load his gun with the box of blanks I bought a few weeks ago when I went and purchased me a gun. I replaced his box of bullets with the blanks, just in case he decided to use his gun on me one day. And if he did, I wanted to be prepared to take him out. So, I brought the guns, the handcuffs, shackles, and tape recorder in hopes of scaring him into telling on himself, which he did. I wanted you to hear what he'd done to me, what he'd done to you. I wanted you to see him for who he was.

"I had the gun loaded with blanks drawn on him, so if I made a mistake and pulled the trigger, it wouldn't be a big deal. But I brought my gun in case of an emergency."

Trey turned to Vernon. "Is this true, Vernon? Please tell me she is mistaken. Tell me!"

"Fuck this shit. I don't have to listen to this shit." Vernon turned.

"Take another step and I will shoot you. I love you, but I will kill you where you stand. You owe me an explanation and I want it now!" Trey said.

He shrugged. "What the fuck you want me to say? Shit, I fucked up. Man, you was getting high. I couldn't do no time. I did what I had to do. I knew you'd soldier that shit. And her," he pointed at me, "I didn't know it was that serious between you and the ho."

"Call her out of her name one more time. Just do it one more time," Trey said.

"Yeah, okay, but I did what I did. It is what it is." He shrugged again. "So, now what? What the fuck you want? You want me to say I'm sorry. Is that what you want to hear?" Vernon's voice broke. Tears were racing down his face.

"I had to live in your shadow all my life. Trey the all-star athlete. Trey the scholar. Trey the pro ball all-star running back. Trey this, Trey that. After Mom and Dad got killed, no one asked me to say a got-damn thing at the double funeral. But you," he pointed a finger at Trey, "you were asked and you gave the eulogy and recited a bullshit poem that even I could have written. Even when you were getting high, you got more respect than I did."

"I got respect because I commanded it. Vern, you were and still are a fuck-up. You don't care about no one but yourself. After today, I'm through with you. You took years away from me, but most importantly, you took my love and raped it and her."

"Okay, if you feel like that, then just go on and shoot me, muthafucka. I'm gone."

"Vernon, catch," I said, throwing the tape recorder to him before he completely turned his back. "Look inside. There is no tape. I forgot to put the tape in."

"Fuck you. Fuck all three of you," he said, turning his back and walking away.

19

Vernon

"Vernon?" Trey shouted as I left the room.

Fuck'em all. I'm a grown-ass man, and I don't have to answer to shit. Trey could call me 'til his hair turned gray. I wasn't saying shit else.

"Cherry has AIDS," Trey said, walking behind me.

I took my hand off the front doorknob.

"Cherry has what?" Shemika shouted as she ran out of the back bedroom.

I pressed my hands to the side of my head. I closed my eyes and tried to shake his words out of my head.

"Vernon?" Trey grabbed me by my shoulders. "Get yourself together, man. Read this." He handed me a multicolored card with the word *surprise* diagonally running down the front of it.

I read the words out loud:

I sold pussy at half the Motel 6's in Atlanta so your ass could get high. Nigga, you said you loved me. I gave up our baby for you. And what did you do? You threw me away like I was sour milk. You fucked me. You fucked me hard. But guess what, baby? Guess what? Are you guessing?

Okay, no more suspense. I want to welcome you to an exclusive club: Club AIDS. I made sure that you got an all-inclusive member-ship to die slowly. Every day, you'll wake up wondering if you are going to get sick, what organisms were eating away at your immune system. You'll spend a quarter of the rest of your short life in hospi-tals, taking medicine, reading new developments, hoping against hope that a cure will be found.

Make out your will, motherfucker, because your days are surely numbered. To make sure you got it, I pricked the inside of your leg with a small needle with a little of my fresh AIDS blood in it. Guess when I pricked you. Are you guessing, huh? Time's up. I pricked you when I was sucking your dick. You are definitely assed out. I was in seventh heaven when you didn't use a condom. Now, wasn't that double dumb? You fucked me, now consider yourself fucked.

Love,
Your used-to-be bitch,
Cherry
P.S. I bet you will never forget who I am again. LOL like a moth-erfucker.

"I swear, Shemika. I swear I have never seen that bitch be-fore that—" I grabbed hold of Trey and looked into his face. "No! No! No!" I said, shaking my head. "You were fucking her. She thought I was you. No!"

"Man, I was getting high out of my mind back then. I'm sorry," Trey said.

"Sorry? Sorry didn't do this shit. Sorry can't save my life."

"Save you? Fuck you. What about me? As much as we've been fucking, I got that shit too," Shemika cried out from be-hind the kitchen counter.

I waved her away. "Bitch, fuck your crabby, trash ass. Don't nobody give a good got-damn about your ass. You ain't noth-ing but a toilet."

"That's enough, Vern. Right now we need to get you both to a doctor."

"Trey!!" Cheyenne screamed.

I jumped and turned in her direction.

"Son of a—"

20

Shemika

I found myself looking into an open kitchen drawer. The blurry image of a human toilet frowned at me through the blade of a larger, shiny stainless steel steak knife. My eyes widened as I realized that it was my reflection that stared back at me. The reflection of the ho, bitch, piece of shit that Vernon said I was. Cheyenne was right. I was nothing but trash. But I was on my way to being a respectable woman until Vernon killed me, my future and all my dreams. With all the money I was about to inherit, I could buy all the respect I wanted. But now that shit was out the window. Everyone was laughing at me. Even the steak knife ridiculed me with its smiling serrated edges. The walls, the doors, the furniture, Chey, Trey and asshole.

Bitch up, I said to myself as a tear streaked down my face. *Same thing that'll make you laugh will make you muthafuckin' cry.*

I nodded and took the smiling knife out of the drawer.

I want all you bitches to laugh at me in a few minutes.

As long as I had my clothes on and my legs closed, I was invisible. Like now, for instance, no one saw me walking toward them until I was in his face.

Trey turned and slipped after Chey screamed. Vernon

ducked his head when he turned and saw the blade. He tried to get away, but I followed his every move.

"Die!" I shouted while lunging for his chest and missing, plunging the steak knife into his neck.

Out of his mouth came a lot of garbled words. All I could make out were the words *sorry*, *love* and *Treyvon* as blood flowed from his neck. I pulled the knife out and was about to take another swing when he grabbed my neck in a vice-like chokehold.

"Die!" I screamed as my arm came down and stuck the knife in his face.

His grip loosened. I coughed. He started to fall.

"Die!" I stabbed him in the ear.

Blood was everywhere.

And then the room exploded.

21

Bishop

I was breathing in the day's air when she walked up to the table.

"What's up, Bish?"

No matter how nice a figure she had, once she opened her mouth, she just turned me off.

"How was the fun'ral?" she asked.

What in God's name is a fune role?

We were at the Starbucks café not too far from the graveyard. It was the most beautiful dreary overcast day that I'd ever seen.

I looked up and smiled. "The funeral was absolutely beautiful. I never imagined that things would work out so perfectly."

Cherry took a seat on the other side of the table.

I couldn't help but look down through the glass table. Her legs were wide open.

Yep, I knew it. I knew it. She didn't have panties on under her skirt.

It was starting to drizzle, but I could care less. We were under the umbrella outside on the patio.

"I know. Coming up wit' the whole AIDS thang and shit,

and putting the card in his mailbox was smart as fu—" She put her hand over her mouth. "My bad, Bish."

If she calls me Bish one more time . . .

"No problem," I said, giving her a fake smile.

"I ain't never expected her to go crazy and cut Vernon's throat neither," she said, using her hands to make a slashing motion across her own neck.

I wish she would've done that with a knife on that cancer, Treyvon.

"Too bad she only cut Treyvon on his cheek and ear. I will never forget how he played me. But on da real, dough, he gon' probably blame himself for his brother's death, so I guess I really done got my revenge. Wha'chu think, Bish? Too bad, right?"

"No, it's not. If it weren't for Shemika trying to kill Treyvon, Cheyenne probably never would have picked up the gun and shot Shemika in the head." I put my hand in my inside suit jacket pocket and came out with a large, bulky envelope. Sliding it across the round glass table, I said, "And if it weren't for Cheyenne, you wouldn't be a thousand dollars richer."

"A thousand? You was s'pposed to give me two hundred."

"I know, but you did good, so I'm giving you a bonus. Is that okay with you?"

"Hell yessirree-bob, junior. Thanks, Bish. You all right wit' me. I might have to give you some. I ain't never did it with no preacher."

And I won't be your first.

"Now, what is too bad is Vernon telling me about you and giving me your phone number. You could say he caused his own demise."

"True dat, but still, though, don't you think it was ironic that Trey checked his mail on a Sunday, when I put that card in his box on that Wednesday evening? And I mean, just the whole thing. I expected him to fall for the AIDS thing, but I still don't understand how the whole AIDS scam would help you get out of your marriage."

I pushed my chair back and got up. "I would like to stay and chat with you, Ms. Cherry, but I have to run. Maybe another time we can sit down and I'll explain everything to you." I put on my raincoat and turned back to her. "Oh, and by the way, there are no accidents, only purposes. Purposes in which God's divine influence causes everything to happen."

What was I going to do now? It was only a matter of time. Oh well, I just had to face the music when that time arrived.

22

Two years later

I gently slid the onyx ring on her finger. "Dr. Cheyenne Amerie Gant," I held her hand and looked deep into her auburn eyes, "I promise that I will love, take care of, and respect you, my queen, forever and the day after."

I wiped the tears from her face before she put the onyx band on my finger. "Treyvon Octavious Gant, I promise I will love, honor, and respect you, my king, forever and the day after."

"By the power vested in me, I now pronounce you husband and wife. You may now kiss the queen," Reverend Barashango said.

On the white sandy beaches of Grand Cayman, I had to pinch myself. I could hardly believe this was happening. Was it worth it? Would I go through it all again to get where I am now? Hell yes.

I missed Vernon, but what can I say? I lost a brother, but I gained a queen, a princess and I don't know what else she had brewing in her stomach. I hoped it was a boy, but I'd love whatever God decided to bring forth from her womb.

I never got re-instated to the NFL, but I could have played overseas. However, I decided to stay home with my family. In the fall, Cheyenne and I were cutting the ribbon to the new holistic healing health club and clinic we were opening. I was a little against it. No, I was all the way against it, but Cheyenne convinced me to allow Bishop Money to be one of our clients. It was the craziest thing.

I couldn't tell her the real reason I didn't want the bishop as a member. I know it was low down, but I figured Bishop swung both ways. A long time ago, on three different occasions, I was questioned about coming out of an apartment with him—the same apartment my brother lost his life in.

I didn't want to think it, or believe it, but I had to know if my brother and the bishop had something going on, so I paid a very attractive-looking transvestite prostitute to try to set the bishop up. As a matter of fact, they met the same Sunday my brother passed.

Even after Shannon told the bishop he was HIV positive, which, at the time, I didn't even know, the bishop still had relations with the man.

Although now I wish I did, I had nothing to do with nor did I even know Shannon was writing a book. And now, two years after he and the bishop met, Shannon was on virtually every talk show and on the cover of every major magazine it seemed. His book, *Preaching on the Down Low* was an instant hit. Bishop—I mean the former Bishop T.J. Money has to be the most hated man in America, even moreso than Osama Bin Laden.

Like He says, gluttony is a sin. Gluttony as far as sex, money, anything. God said it is easier for a camel to go through the eye of a needle than for a rich man to enter the kingdom of God.

Last Chapter

Bishop

I took off my glasses and looked at my watch. It read 12:30 P.M. There was no way I could make it through customs and out of the airport by 1:00.

"Sir, can you push my wheelchair faster?" I asked.

"No Ingles, Señor," he replied.

I had to laugh. Now the Mexicans were even taking the jobs from the Chinese.

It was 1:30 before I was pushed outside into the hot Asian summer sun.

For the last time, I took off my bifocals and put them on the side of the chair before I got up and jogged over to the dark-tinted black limousine.

For six months, I wore makeup to make myself look sick, and I let myself be pushed around in a damn wheelchair. I threw my arms in the air, stretched, and took in a deep breath. It felt good to be in public and not have to worry about the media.

"It's about time," Shannon said as I got into the limo.

"I got out here as fast as I could. As much money as I've made you, you shouldn't complain," I said.

"You mean *we* made each other," he said.

"Hey," I pointed at him, "don't forget I'm the one who paid for phony lab results. The whole down-low homosexual preacher angle was my idea. I'm the one who's been ridiculed and embarrassed."

"That was your idea, remember. I wrote the book. Or did you forget? I'm the one traveling all around the U.S. doing TV and radio."

I interrupted. "And you're getting half of all the royalties from the book, TV, the movie deal, and whatever else."

Too bad he'd never live to spend another dime. *Just wait until I leave Thailand in a few months and emerge back on the church scene in the States a cured man.* The few million I made so far from *Preaching on the Down Low* was peanuts compared to what I would make after I left Thailand and went back to the States in excellent shape and health, with no trace of the AIDS virus.

I'll tell the world that God laid His hands on me and pulled the virus out. I'll tell them that He spoke to me and told me to go back and teach His Word and through me, He will show that through Him all things are possible.

If I had the whole world believing that I was a gay bishop with AIDS, then surely I can trick them into believing this.

IN STORES NOW

a street saga by
roy glenn

1-893196-37-2

COLE RILEY

1-893196-41-0

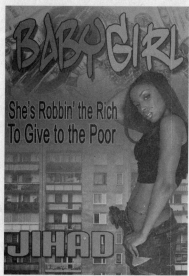

She's Robbin' the Rich
To Give to the Poor

1-893196-23-2

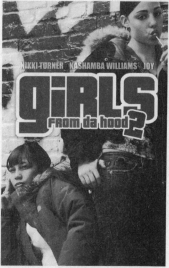

NIKKI TURNER · KASHAMBA WILLIAMS · JOY

1-893196-28-3

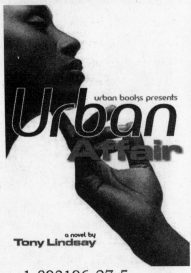

shoulda, woulda, coulda

La Jill Hunt

1-893196-25-9

MARRIED To The GAME

CHONICHI

0-9747025-9-5

urban books presents

Urban Affair

a novel by
Tony Lindsay

1-893196-27-5

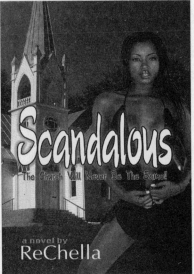

Scandalous
The Church Will Never Be The Same!

a novel by
ReChella

1893196-30-5

OTHER URBAN BOOKS TITLES

Title	Author	Quantity	Cost
Drama Queen	LaJill Hunt		$14.95
No More Drama	LaJill Hunt		$14.95
Shoulda Woulda Coulda	LaJill Hunt		$14.95
Is It A Crime	Roy Glenn		$14.95
MOB	Roy Glenn		$14.95
Drug Related	Roy Glenn		$14.95
Lovin' You Is Wrong	Alisha Yvonne		$14.95
Bulletproof Soul	Michelle Buckley		$14.95
You Wrong For That	Toschia		$14.95
A Gangster's girl	Chunichi		$14.95
Married To The Game	Chunichi		$14.95
Sex In The Hood	White Chocalate		$14.95
Little Black Girl Lost	Keith Lee Johnson		$14.95
Sister Girls	Angel M. Hunter		$14.95
Driven	KaShamba Williams		$14.95
Street Life	Jihad		$14.95
Baby Girl	Jihad		$14.95
A Thug's Life	Thomas Long		$14.95
Cash Rules	Thomas Long		$14.95
The Womanizers	Dwayne S. Joseph		$14.95
Never Say Never	Dwayne S. Joseph		$14.95
She's Got Issues	Stephanie Johnson		$14.95
Rockin' Robin	Stephanie Johnson		$14.95
Sins Of The Father	Felicia Madlock		$14.95
Back On The Block	Felicia Madlock		$14.95
Chasin' It	Tony Lindsey		$14.95
Street Possession	Tony Lindsey		$14.95
Around The Way Girls	LaJill Hunt		$14.95
Around The Way Girls 2	LaJill Hunt		$14.95
Girls From Da Hood	Nikki Turner		$14.95

Girls from Da Hood 2	Nikki Turner		$14.95
Dirty Money	Ashley JaQuavis		$14.95
Mixed Messages	LaTonya Y. Williams		$14.95
Don't Hate The Player	Brandie		$14.95
Payback	Roy Glenn		$14.95
Scandalous	ReChella		$14.95
Urban Affair	Tony Lindsey		$14.95
Harlem Confidential	Cole Riley		$14.95

Urban Books
74 Andrews Ave.
Wheatley Heights, NY 11798
Subtotal: _____
Postage:_____ Calculate postage and handling as follows: Add
$2.50 for the first item and $1.25 for each additional item
Total: _____
Name: _____
Address:_____
City: _____ State: _____ Zip: _____
Telephone: (   ) _____
Type of Payment (Check: ___   Money Order: ____)
All orders must be prepaid by check or money order drawn on an American
bank.
Books may sometimes be out of stock. In that instance, please select your
alternate choices below.

Alternate Choices:

1._____

2._____

PLEASE ALLOW 4-6 WEEKS FOR SHIPPING